YOU'RE NOT ALONE

G.M. LAWRENCE

INKUBATOR
BOOKS

Published by Inkubator Books
www.inkubatorbooks.com

ISBN (eBook): 978-1-83756-097-4
ISBN (Paperback): 978-1-83756-098-1
ISBN (Hardback): 978-1-83756-099-8

Previously published by the author as See You Fall.

1

The heat from the man's stare, this stranger, radiated towards Chloe as he watched from the bar. She felt it, of course, because the sense of being watched was so much more than catching something, or someone, in the corner of one's eye. It was a sixth sense; a residual instinct carried forward from more primitive times. An awareness designed to protect. And now, as she felt it penetrate every part of her, inhabiting her, she didn't need the confirmation, but a quick glance his way indeed revealed his attentive eyes in the lights of the club as he followed her movements.

She wasn't surprised. Places like this were prime hunting grounds for men like him. She didn't need to consider what his intentions were because they were obvious – he wore them on his sleeve and, although she understood his motives, an ever-present feeling haunted her mind that this was both the beginning and the end for her somehow. Of what, she wasn't quite sure, but she shrugged it off, knowing that tonight it didn't matter. Nothing did, except keeping her focus on the task of getting her life back on track. A life that had collapsed over the last few months since David had abandoned her. Everything had blurred since he'd gone.

She needed respite. After enjoying a meal in the restaurant upstairs with her friends, washed down with plenty of prosecco, they had come to the basement club for a dance. The sunken blue and pink LED ceiling lights cast a purple hue across the room, illuminating the white padded seats of the booths dotted around the edge of the dance floor so they glowed in ultraviolet. It was oppressively hot in this subterranean vault, tomb-like, the minimal ventilation trapping the air within until it became a cloying mix of sweat, perfume, and dry ice. The music pumped through her body, and the crowds bustled around her. If she took another jab of an elbow to her ribs, she would make a scene.

'I'm going to get a drink,' she shouted over the music to Laura, who was lost in the beat.

Laura didn't hear, so Chloe tapped her arm. 'I said, I'm getting a drink. Do you want one?'

'No,' Laura bellowed back, clutching Chloe's arm. 'Stay, I love this song,' she cried, as she raised her hands to the ceiling.

'Wish I could,' Chloe replied. 'But I need a break and a drink.'

'Ah, okay,' Laura called. 'Well, I'll be over in a second.'

Chloe smiled at her friend's delight in the music, and knowing that Laura would be staying put for the foreseeable meant Chloe was now on her own.

She fought her way through the heaving dance floor, pushing her way past barely clothed, gyrating bodies towards the glitter-fronted bar where crowds of people congregated. The air was no cooler here, so she grabbed an abandoned serviette on the bar and fanned herself as she waited to be served. A group of girls further along were busy with their phones, posing and taking Instagram-worthy shots of themselves with the club's signature candyfloss and rainbow cocktails. It made Chloe a little sad that they chose to do that rather than just enjoy themselves and make memories they could reminisce over in years to come. Something about a photo saved to a social media site felt cold to Chloe.

Considering the possibility she might be getting old, she turned away to glance elsewhere and caught the eye of the man who had been watching her all night, still standing at the end of the bar. Why would he stop now? Ignoring the claustrophobic air that had descended around her from his scrutiny, she tossed her clutch bag onto the bar, grabbed a menu and focused her attention on whether she'd have the espresso martini or the pink gin fizz. If she could get the butterflies in her stomach to settle, of course.

Laura hadn't taken no for an answer when Chloe had muttered something about devouring a box set instead of going out. Ignoring Chloe's lack of enthusiasm, Laura had waited tight-lipped as Chloe took an age to find a suitable outfit for the evening. She had critiqued each one until she was satisfied that the little black dress and strappy shoes exuded an equal mix of sexy and classy before dragging her out for the evening. The only stipulation Chloe made was that she got to choose the club.

But Chloe appreciated the effort Laura took to get her back out into the world. She'd looked after Chloe in the months following the collapse of her marriage and all the devastation that ensued in its wake, and Chloe appreciated her support in a way she could never fully convey. And, despite everything, she found she still enjoyed these nights out when they came around. Time with friends, anyway. Time to let her hair down and forget about all her woes, just like everyone else. Laura had insisted it was okay to like a little drink and a little dance every now and then, and what, she would say to anyone who cared to criticise, was wrong with that?

Next in the queue, she raised her hand, holding a twenty upright in her fingers, just as a man bumped her arm, cutting in and leaning over the bar as much as his round belly would allow, and barked out his order. Tutting loudly, she let out a frustrated sigh and continued to wait, pushing herself against the bar. She hoped to be more visible next to this man whose chubby features glistened with sweat, pasting his hair to his forehead.

The man's shirtsleeve, also damp with sweat, brushed against her. The feeling was unpleasant enough that she felt the need to take a small step to the side to create some distance between them. On top of that, she noticed the stranger at the end of the bar was now making his move, walking towards her, drink in hand. She couldn't contain the groan that sounded in the back of her throat, but she knew it would be swallowed by the heavy thump of the music anyway.

'Having trouble?' he asked with a smile as he stood adjacent to the man at the bar.

'Yeah, the place is full of gents tonight,' she said with a sideways glance at the sweaty man. 'But I've got it covered, thanks.'

'I'm sure you have,' he said. 'But let me help.' He reached out to tap the sweaty man on the shoulder and leaned in to speak to him. The man snapped his head around and shot him a hostile glare, but it soon faded as the stranger continued to speak, and Chloe watched as it slowly morphed into an expression of alarm. Eventually, the sweaty man nodded and conceded as he sidled further along the bar, away from them both. The stranger moved into the space and turned to face Chloe, a calm smile tipping the corner of his mouth as he leaned against the bar.

'Thank you, but you really didn't have to do that,' Chloe said calmly, hoping it would hide the unease she felt at what he might have said to the sweaty man to make his expression change in the way it had.

'It was my pleasure,' he replied. 'Someone like him has no business being next to someone like you.'

'Like me?'

'Yes, someone beautiful. You stand out in this crowd, believe me.'

'I see,' she said with an uncontrollable eye roll. 'So we have a charmer here, do we?'

'Just saying it as I see it,' he replied.

There were many beautiful people here, peacocks desperate to be admired, but he clearly had an agenda. She turned her focus from him, back towards the bartender and the white, backlit cubby holes behind the bar, stocked with multitudes of bottles and cocktail-making equipment. When the bartender finally made eye contact with her, she waved her twenty and he strode her way. She gave her order, wondering if the guy lingering next to her would move along. But he remained, watching.

He was smartly dressed, and not too bad in the looks department if she was being honest. Not that she cared. Relationships were something she avoided these days. He had sharp eyes and angular features, with a hint of stubble over his cheeks and dark hair the colour of which she struggled to make out in the artificial light of the club. Just another guy in a place jammed full of people who just wanted to drink, dance, and perhaps hook up. Someone to join him for a single night, to forget their troubles together, beneath the sheets. And by the look on his face, that person was her.

With a drink in her hand at last, she spoke. 'Well, I guess I should go back to my friend,' she said, ready to leave this man to his hunting.

'So soon?'

'What were you expecting?' she asked, through pursed lips. 'This place is hardly best suited for long conversations over loud music.'

'Maybe not, but I'd hazard a guess that you're not enjoying this place as much as your friend,' he said as he glanced over to Laura, who was still lost in the crowd on the dance floor.

Chloe followed his gaze towards the revellers, all of them throwing bizarre, laughable shapes with their arms, seemingly part of a strange new cult as they danced to a beat that connected them all. 'Regardless, I don't need any company, so I thank you for your help with that man, but you are free to move along.'

'Ah.' He paused, seeming to enjoy the moment. 'I like it just fine here by the bar, so I think I'll stay. You're welcome to join me, though.'

'Why would I do that?'

'Question is, why would you not?'

He was determined; she'd give him that. 'Because I don't know you.'

'Well, my name is Danny,' he said, then pointed to the dance floor, 'and I'm here celebrating a friend's birthday.'

She followed his gesture and spotted a group of guys milling around a particularly animated man, who looked to be very drunk, with his tie around his head, white shirt open to the navel, and a large badge pinned to his sleeve with glittery digits to signify his thirtieth birthday. She fought the smile threatening to form and looked at Danny.

'I know,' he said, grimacing. 'So now you know why I'm at the bar.'

She took a sip of her drink and relaxed her shoulders a little. 'Okay, Danny, whatever. I guess we are both dance avoiders, however much we've had to drink.'

'I guess we are.' He touched his glass to hers. 'Cheers.'

A silence followed. Chloe was not about to fill it with aimless conversation. She watched the dancers instead, knowing she'd regret the espresso martini she'd just ordered. That, on top of the prosecco she'd polished off earlier, would leave her dehydrated and hungover tomorrow.

'So, do you come here often?'

Chloe's eyes widened. 'Oh dear, did you really just say that?'

Wincing, Danny glanced at the floor, and nodded. 'Yes. Yes, I did.'

Chloe was about to give an appropriate retort when the impact of someone stumbling into her launched her drink out of the glass and over the floor. She turned and saw Birthday Boy staggering next to her, struggling to keep himself upright. He wrapped his arms around her, using her for support, and she groaned as more sweat covered her skin.

'Danny boy!' he slurred. 'Come and join us.' He turned his attention to Chloe and smiled, his glazed eyes seeing but unseeing. 'Hey, lovely lady. How are you? Sorry about this,' he said, glancing down at his hands gripping her waist. 'I can't stand by myself now.'

'Well, be that as it may,' she said as she took hold of his hands and placed them on the bar. 'Let's keep it like this, shall we?'

He was no threat really, but she still preferred him to keep his hands somewhere other than on her body.

The action prompted Danny to react, too, as he motioned to his friend to take a step back, as if marking out his territory. She didn't like it. She wasn't anyone's to mark, especially not these two.

'Sorry, sweetie,' Birthday Boy sang, pulling his phone from his pocket. 'Come on, Danny boy, a photo.' He gestured, and Danny moved closer to them both. He held up the phone and snapped a selfie of the three of them before Chloe had time to react. 'Perfect,' he said as he tucked it away. 'If you're not gonna join us on the dance floor, get the drinks in, mate,' he said in a throwaway comment to Danny. 'I'm going for a piss. Bye...er, sorry, what's your name?'

'Doesn't matter,' Chloe said. 'You won't remember any of this tomorrow, least of all my name.'

'Holding on to a beaut like you,' he slurred. 'Of course I'll remember.'

He threw her a wink and turned, staggering off towards the toilets, bumping into the crowd of people that hung around the bar – the peacocks, holding themselves perfectly, wanting to see and be seen. Or people like her, who did not want to dance.

'Seeing as I have my orders, can I get you another drink?' Danny asked. 'Most of it is on the floor. It's the least I can do to make up for *him*.'

Normally, she wouldn't allow anyone to buy her a drink, but she was in control of this situation and knew she was in for a wait before Laura had got whatever it was out of her system. So, just for tonight, she decided to break her rule, but only because she had full visibility of it being prepared. She could bear this moment with this stranger a little while longer, too. 'Okay, thanks. Another espresso martini would be great.'

Danny nodded and raised his hand for the bartender, and it left Chloe stunned as to how quickly he was served. Typical.

With a fresh drink in hand, she perched on the barstool next to her.

'So, what brings you here, then?' he asked. 'I'm on birthday celebration duties. What's your excuse?'

She shrugged. 'Night out with friends. Just because.' Then she glanced around for Gabby and realised she hadn't seen her for ages. She'd come out with her other half, Rob, and whenever they came out together, they would get themselves hyped up and loved up. They'd probably left long ago. It was always herself and Laura who were the last standing at these events. 'Although one of them has obviously had a better offer.'

'Is that right?' He kept his eyes on hers while taking a drink.

She sipped her own. 'I'm sensing you disapprove?'

'No, not at all. We've all been there.'

'Yes, I suppose we have.'

His smile changed. She'd probably offended him, not that she cared.

'Although I'm over the instantly-gratifying-but-emotionally-hollow one-night stands.'

She raised her brows. 'Oh, that's surprising, especially since that little group of girls haven't been able to take their eyes off you the whole time we've been talking,' she said, gesturing behind him with a nod.

'Ah, that's flattering,' he said, not bothering to see for himself but instead choosing to keep his focus on her. 'But I'm not interested in girls. I'm more interested in women. Intelligent women. Women who know their own minds.'

He had become the hunter again, the man with the intense stare, and although he was here as part of a birthday celebration, Chloe knew it was just a front. He'd always be looking for his next conquest; there was no doubting that.

'I'd certainly want more than one night, too,' he continued, leaning forward onto his elbows, closer to her. 'I'd want something deeper, to understand what makes someone tick, what they enjoy and what drives them mad. That sweet spot that you simply can't learn in one night.' His smile was genuine, his body language relaxed, but there was something behind it that sent a small chill of fear down her back. 'It takes devotion and commitment to get to that stage. To really *know* someone.'

She needed to get out of here. The air had been sucked from the room, and beneath his impenetrable gaze she fought the urge to run.

'You're very sure of yourself,' she said, her muscles tense and posture rigid.

'I am,' he replied, tilting his head. 'Years of practice.'

She spotted Laura leaving the dance floor and heading in her direction. It wasn't a moment too soon. He noticed her, too, and waited for Chloe's response.

'I think it's time for me to go,' she said hurriedly. 'My friend is done, by the looks of it.'

He nodded. 'Well, it was very nice to meet you,' he said, leaning back and taking on a much less intimidating demeanour.

'Thank you for the drink,' was all she could manage in return. With Laura in her sights, she hopped off the stool and walked towards her friend, only turning back when she had linked arms and felt there was a suitable distance between them.

He smiled and raised his glass to her, seemingly unbothered by her swift removal from their chat.

She looked at Laura, seeing the alcoholic glaze in her friend's eyes. It reminded her of the birthday boy earlier. 'Let's go. There's nothing to stay for. The others have already gone. Are you ready?'

Laura nodded clumsily and let Chloe help her to the exit.

As they waited to collect their coats, Chloe tapped her finger against the counter, once again sensing the weight of someone's stare. She turned to look, but there was no one there. She kept her arm linked through Laura's, safety in numbers, and had to slow her breathing as she grappled with their coats once they were served. They were close to the exit when two men, intent on fighting, nudged against them both, their drunken posturing laughable if she'd had the humour for it. But she kept moving, forcing her way through the crowd of tired clubbers, all too ready to leave this place and move on to the next, or find food.

And that's when she realised something was missing.

'Damn it.'

'What's up, babe?' Laura slurred.

'Left my bag in there.'

Laura wobbled a finger in the direction of the club's dance floor. 'In there?'

Chloe sighed, 'Yes, in there,' she said, mildly irritated.

'But that was your favourite, wasn't it?'

'One of them.'

'We have to go back then,' Laura said resolutely.

'It'll be long gone by now.'

Laura glanced around the room.

'What are you doing?' Chloe asked.

'Looking for security.'

They both spotted the man standing by the door, who was clearly the heavyweight bouncer. His military-style, closely-cropped hair made it hard to dispute.

Laura grabbed Chloe's hand and proceeded to drag her across the room.

She rolled her eyes. This really wasn't necessary, but Laura would not take no for an answer, and she supposed she should at least try and look for the bag.

As they approached, the bouncer appraised them both with indifference. 'What can I do for you, ladies?' he said, without an ounce of interest.

'It's fine, honestly,' Chloe said, pulling at Laura's arm. 'Come on.'

'No,' Laura said. 'That was one of your favourites. We've got to go back in.'

'What's this all about?'

'I've left my bag by the bar,' Chloe replied. 'But it's probably long gone.'

'We just need to go in,' Laura said. 'It might still be there.'

The man shook his head. 'You'll have to pay entry again.'

'Oh, come on,' Laura whined. 'You've just watched us come out.'

He shrugged. 'Not my problem.'

They lingered together, unspeaking, until his expression changed and he sighed. Their silence must have nudged at his conscience, or more likely it was her friend, who swayed on the spot and looked like she might bring up the contents of her stomach as she leaned and stumbled.

'You have two minutes, and then I need you out of here. Understand?'

Leaving Laura with the oh-so-helpful security guard, she strode towards the bar. This was a pointless exercise, walking from one end to the other, checking the bar and floor below, dodging clubbers waiting to be served. This was more to appease Laura. When she'd checked the area as much as she could, sure enough, the bag was gone. Great.

Despite the loss of a handbag she'd grown sentimental over – something that had been with her throughout her singleton years, her married life, and back to where she was now – it wasn't the end of the world. A seasoned pro at losing things, she always took the necessary steps to minimise any real damage on nights like these. She'd left her phone at home and utilised her watch for payments. She could live without the lip gloss and had carried very little cash for the evening, and most of it was now spent.

When the bouncer found her again, he had to bellow over the music. 'Hey, lady! You've had your two minutes. You and your mate need to leave. She doesn't look good, and I'm not going to be responsible for her decorating the lobby with whatever's in her stomach.'

She nodded and walked quickly towards Laura, not stopping her pace as she grabbed her friend's arm and escorted her from the club.

'Did you find it?' Laura slurred as she stumbled beside her.

'No, but let's go,' Chloe muttered. 'I want to get out of here before I get myself into any more trouble tonight.'

2

The thumping in her head, loud and echoing in the caverns of her mind, woke Chloe, pulling her from the cocoon of bedsheets. She flipped the duvet down, poked her head free, and reached for her phone on the bedside table. When she realised what day it was, she groaned – Valentine's.

She lay there for a moment and allowed herself to drift back into her past, something she'd given up trying to avoid, despite her counsellor's attempts to instil more positive behaviours. She returned to a time when she and David were happily married and would have done their usual on this day of love – a nice dinner at Café Rouge, a walk along the river, then home to a night of comfortable, marital sex. But those memories of her life with David inevitably collided with those of Melissa, too, who'd come along and ruined everything.

Mornings like these used to involve tea and painkillers, brought to her by David. He always understood her need to soothe the hangover that would engulf her if she did nothing to stave it off.

'Hey, my little club-bunny,' he would say cheerfully, if a little too loud for her liking. *'Get that cuppa down and those painkillers. Then you can return to the land of the living.'*

Two lives combined, and a simple desire to care for one another. That's what they had. Togetherness; for richer or poorer, and in sickness and in health. They'd had an agreement they would always look after whoever had the heavy night out, and she'd always returned the favour after one of his benders. Though the frequency of his nights out awakened her suspicions towards the end.

She should have fought more when he chose to leave; should have tried to save what they had rather than let him walk away from his marriage to be with Melissa. But she countered the feelings of despair by reminding herself she had tried. She had tried so hard to keep him but finally understood that love could not be forced, and once his had faded, there was nothing she could do to rekindle the flame. He was out of her life, and there was no going back. The wound in her heart was still raw, and her feelings remained, yet through the hurt and anguish she hoped that, wherever he was now, he was happy.

She flung her arm across her face and placed the crook of her elbow over her eyes, moaning quietly with the effort. 'Fuck it,' she mumbled.

Part of her wanted to hold onto the idea that it was solely Melissa who was the cause of her pain. It was certainly much easier to blame her, the other woman, just as every betrayed wife had done before her. But she knew it wasn't the whole truth. They were both to blame. Sneaking around as they had, making plans for their future, while Chloe had remained blissfully unaware.

Their marriage had not been the grand success she'd wanted it to be. She had set out to prove to her family, and his, that they weren't rushing ahead too quickly. That six months was enough time to really know someone enough to marry them. Their relationship had been what her mother called a 'whirlwind'. But that was David, rushing in where angels feared to tread, and she refused to wallow in it. And she refused to let the tears threatening her eyes to flow. She hadn't let that happen since the twentieth of August last year.

The headache bomb lodged in her brain was about to explode, hovering on the peripherals, ready to detonate. All she needed was tea and painkillers, but she remained where she was, not ready to join the fully functioning world just yet. In the grey wintry light of her bedroom, she imagined David standing in the corner in front of the wardrobe. The doors would be pushed wide as he selected clothes – the bearded hipster, adorned with tattoos that covered most of his body, and dressed in a uniform of tight-fitting shirts and waistcoats. A complete look. Then he would close the doors, pull a suit jacket over his shoulders, and check himself over in the full-length mirror: a ritual he had done every day since she'd known him.

Life had been exciting then, so full of promise. All because of David: a man totally different to anyone she'd dated before. He took her by surprise the day she met him, and she couldn't help but be drawn into his charmed, if not reckless, life. They worked and saved to buy the little flat they shared, and while Chloe planned and budgeted, David, a gifted salesman, had found work wherever he chose. Somehow, he had the Midas touch, always landing on his feet. She'd never met anybody who'd managed to refuse him anything.

They skipped down the aisle of Marylebone registry office, feeling the nostalgia and love of the many couples who had married there before. A place where musicians and celebrities of the past had made their vows – for better or worse – and sealed the deal in ten minutes. Hip, edgy, and cool, wearing a Boho-style white-lace maxi dress, Chloe had arranged her honey-blonde hair into small sections, tied back from her face and secured with clips and sprigs of daisies and lavender, the rest hanging in loose curls at her shoulders. She tried her best to fulfil David's idealised view of hipster girl-friend to hipster wife, and from the smile that radiated across his face when he first saw her, she knew she'd nailed it. It was a perfect day. Not what she'd envisioned for her wedding, but she still rode the wave, as anyone in love does.

Family on both sides rushed to the beat of David's drum, too, without hesitation, driven by his contagious and addictive enthusiasm. But it was not sustainable. And after the heady rush of their impromptu nuptials subsided, the cracks began to show. The little moments of intolerance towards each other where once there would have been humour. Irritation over the small things: the bin not put out, dirty clothes left next to the laundry basket rather than in it, wet towels left on the bed. But even during this time, she knew she loved him. She had always loved his obsessive little rituals: the way he got dressed every morning, how he maintained his precious beard with oils and trimming. It was an intimate part of a person's life, something she hadn't paid enough regard to until it was no longer there.

'Well, I guess today is going to be a nightmare for you,' she imagined him saying. 'Do you feel like death yet, or are you still floating on the alcohol?'

'You guessed right,' she said to the empty room, as she threw the duvet back and swung her legs out of bed. 'I just want it to be six o'clock right now.'

'Well, it soon will be,' his imagined voice replied, and she remembered the feeling of his lips swiping her cheek with a brief kiss before leaving the room.

No use dwelling on the past, she told herself with a sigh, and staggered to the bathroom. That six-month 'whirlwind' had become three years of marriage, and she was thankful for that, if nothing else.

Hoping that freshening up would give her the much-needed energy to get through the day, she cleaned her teeth and showered, applying a little make-up to hide the fact she looked like death as much as she felt it.

She needed to impress today. She needed her report to shine so her boss, Jeff, would be assured she was ready to move to the next grade. After finishing her economics degree and a gap year travelling through Asia, she'd racked up five years in one of the largest corporations of global banking in London. She'd worked hard within the risk management team, working with a portfolio of clients to identify and assess data to help control threats to their capital and earnings. She'd progressed through the ranks – from a project lead for new tech designed to help combat financial crime and cyber threats – to a risk control supervisor for a team of five.

Now, after years of commitment to the company's 'work hard, play hard' ethos, she was waiting for the much-coveted promotion to Associate. It would open up a whole new set of doors for her and provide a bump in salary that would not go unappreciated, now she was the sole provider. With little else to fill her life, her career was the constant she needed.

She shifted her thoughts to dissecting the evening before. Well, not so much dissecting as overthinking it – something Laura said she could win a gold medal at, if it ever became an Olympic sport. She mulled it over in her mind. She'd encountered men like that on nights out before, but the experience as a once-again singleton made it surreal, and one that she hadn't expected at this point in her life.

She dressed in a cream blouse and smart black trouser suit, and styled her hair before heading to the kitchen. The only thing that mattered now was a huge mug of tea and a

selection of tablets to numb the pain inside her head. And
the stone in her stomach she'd been carrying for longer than
she cared to remember. She might even force down some
toast. She grabbed a glass, filled it with water from the tap,
and downed the painkillers. Then she flipped the switch for
the kettle, dunked a tea bag into a mug, and popped a slice of
bread into the toaster.

Settled at the small pine table, an old hand-me-down
she'd never replaced and a perfect fit for the corner of the
kitchen, she fired up her laptop. There was just enough time
to log on to check her emails and glance over her social
media before she left for work. Although she could have
easily passed on the socials, especially Facebook. She'd had
enough surprises there. Learning of David's infidelity by an
anonymous message had been enough to cause her world to
implode. Now she couldn't help but to associate the site with
adultery and bitterness.

A couple of notifications popped up and, intrigued, she
clicked. A friend request from Danny. Strange, especially as
she had no recollection of giving him her name. She hit
confirm, just to lurk in his timeline to satisfy her curiosity.
She would have a little peruse, like everyone else on this site,
and then unfollow. No harm done.

She scrolled through his posts and photos of outdoor
activities – climbing, hiking – and nights out, arms around
friends, drunken smiles. The usual. She sipped her tea and
continued to scroll, noticing how his posts began to change at
the beginning of last year. He'd seemingly found love, with
quotes and memes about finding a soulmate, finding 'the
one', and as many positive affirmation posts you could poke a
stick at.

She went back and checked his status: single.

Whatever he had going on seemed to have come to an
abrupt end by the summer and his status had reverted. His

posts had become mundane, almost melancholy. He obviously hadn't felt the need to curate his account anymore and was keeping his timeline as a portfolio of his life for anyone to see.

David had never shared anything like that about her on his socials. No outward declarations of love. No posts about finding a soulmate. She didn't let it bother her – he hadn't done it with Melissa, either. He simply did not use social media, always saying he was too busy living his life to waste time sharing it with people he didn't know. Chloe also considered he might be more cautious about sharing the details of his relationship with Melissa anyway, given the circumstances. Many of his friends had offered their opinions about the mistake he was making. He even lost a few because of it, but he went anyway, determined to be with Melissa. How he'd behaved once their marriage broke apart had forced her decision to delete the posts and photos she'd shared of their life together. Something she now regretted. She knew she had done it out of anger and, as time passed, she came to regret what she'd lost. Something she wouldn't be able to recreate.

Dread fluttered in her stomach as she remembered the day she saw the message, showing details of his liaisons with Melissa. There were times and dates they were together, a grainy photo of them sitting in the window of a café, his hand over hers. Four weeks later, she'd noticed a real change in him. A distance that went further than casual disregard. He had become a stranger. After she'd received the messages, she knew there was no choice but to confront him, and he'd surprised her by confessing straight away. At least he'd had the decency to do that. There had been no denial or accusations of overreacting, nothing like that. Just a straightforward admission of guilt. She thought it was because he wanted to work things out but, in reality, it was because he'd always struggled to lie. That's when he declared their marriage was over and he wanted to be with Melissa.

He'd thrown all the clichés at her when she'd confronted him: it was a mistake, he felt tied down, marriage wasn't for him. All things that would have been helpful to share *before* their wedding – before she settled into a life she thought was forever. But the little voice of reason asked her how they could ever know these things after six months. They'd rushed everything, even their feelings. Chloe had been completely unaware of his intention to propose to her during a trip to Paris. After an evening spent visiting the Eiffel Tower, he'd dropped to his knees and produced a ring. All him. He couldn't have made it any more obvious he was ready to settle down with her. Not only had her life imploded, but she also knew that learning to trust again would be the hardest part.

Chloe brushed it off, closing the laptop. She finished her breakfast before placing the mug and plate in the dishwasher and prepared to leave for work. She hoped to check in with Laura on the way, wanting to hear how she was doing after she'd staggered out of the taxi last night.

———

CHLOE SHUFFLED through the revolving doors to her office and into the large, glass-fronted atrium, the February sun flooding the room and spreading a gentle warmth over the reception desk on the furthest side of the room. It instantly improved her mood. She reached to her right and swiped her card through the turnstile entry before heading to the elevator and selecting floor seven.

The office was alive with the buzz of planned Valentine's events for the evening and casual chats about what people had given and received – a competitive one-upmanship being the general tone, as it always was. Flowers were already proudly displayed on desks, and Chloe caught Penny and Stella standing by the water cooler, their eyes glued to their phones. They were no doubt embroiled in their own dramatic love lives, a joy of being in their early twenties. The excitement of this universally recognised day of romance would have once meant something to Chloe, too, and she would have delighted in gossiping with her colleagues about it. But the last six months had managed to leave her usually sunny disposition clouded with cynicism.

At her desk, she pulled her laptop from its case. She glanced through her emails, wishing to distract herself from her surroundings, needing to focus. Her hangover meant the motivation and ability to be productive would be in short supply today, and she knew she needed to prioritise before her output dwindled to scrolling the internet aimlessly. She persevered and managed to knock out replies to all of her enquiries – and, as an added bonus, finish the KPI report Jeff had thrown her way.

She collated the printout just as Penny, a recently employed graduate to her team, sidled up to her desk with a couple of files balanced in the crook of her arm.

'So, how did it go?' she asked, wanting all the gossip from last night. 'Hangover from hell?'

Chloe smiled. 'No, actually,' she lied. 'Although I didn't sleep a wink.'

Penny held out her hand. 'Woah, I don't want those kinds of details,' she said. Then looked over her shoulder as she edged closer. 'Actually, I do,' she whispered enthusiastically, tucking her hair behind her ear. 'Did you get yourself a little liaison?'

'Of course not,' Chloe said, as she tucked the report into a plastic file. 'And someone your age should not be interested in the love life of someone my age. What's going on with yours?'

'Hm, nice little deflection, madam, but you don't get off that easily. Spill.'

'Believe me, nothing to share. I am more than happy with how things are at the moment. I like the peace, and I don't need any further complications in my life.'

'Men aren't always complications.'

'But if they are, a twenty-year-old beauty like yourself has the luxury of kicking them to the kerb.'

'Oh, stop,' Penny exclaimed. 'You're gorgeous, and not that much older than me.'

'Try seven years.'

'That's nothing. I just think you deserve some fun. It's okay to begin your life again.'

'It's lovely that you care, but if you *really* want to save me, please take pity on my complete lack of coffee,' Chloe said, gesturing at her desk. She smiled and swallowed away the pain that caught in her throat – the precursor to tears – adept at deflecting comments made about her life and how she should move on.

'Need the caffeine?'

'Like you wouldn't believe.'

'I knew it!' Penny chimed, thrilled. 'The lady *can* drink!'

Chloe softened. 'She certainly can. Enough to lose her bag last night, too.'

'Oh,' Penny said, abandoning her excitement. 'Shit.'

'Yes, so you can understand my lack of coffee situation is a dangerous one. Also, please appreciate my lack of something sweet, too – something with a ton of sugar on it, actually.' Chloe ran her hand through her hair. 'Once I have these things in front of me, I'll have the stomach to receive your sermon.'

'Leave it with me, boss,' Penny said, with an understanding nod. 'I'll drop my stuff and go downstairs. They have some divine pastries today.'

Chloe leaned back in her chair. 'You are an angel from above.'

'I know. It's an affliction,' she said with a cheeky wink. 'I should warn you that Jeff is on the warpath. He's waiting for your report, and it doesn't look like he's had his coffee yet, either. Are you ready?'

Chloe sighed. 'Yes, I have it here. Europe and the Middle East. All ready. I am really not in the mood for him today. I care even less for this report.'

'Do you want me to drop it off to him?'

'Would you? That would be great. I just want to hide behind my desk this morning.'

'No problem,' she said, taking the report from Chloe. 'I'm meeting Stella later for lunch. Do you want to join us?'

'Tempting,' she said, 'but not today, I'm afraid. I have to catch up with the admin I've missed while getting this damn report ready. Have a drink on me, though, and I'll be there next time.'

Penny smiled and went to her desk, seemingly happy with the adequate amount of intel on the night out to share with the others.

It hadn't taken long for Penny to establish herself as a moderate alpha female amongst her peers, and while Chloe didn't like to stereotype, Penny certainly fit the mould. From a family of high achievers herself, Chloe read between the lines enough to understand the expectation to follow a corporate path. Not that Penny seemed to mind – she enjoyed her status and the money she earned – her designer outfits stylish and meticulously put together. Chloe liked her, and she enjoyed mentoring someone so keen to learn and progress. She often had to rein her in whenever she tried to jump too far ahead before she was truly ready, but Chloe knew that, with time, Penny would learn to adapt.

Alone now, Chloe pulled out her phone and called up Laura's number.

'Hello,' a voice croaked from the other end.

'Jesus, you sound worse than me,' Chloe said, facing her laptop in an effort to look busy. 'Maybe we're getting too old for this.'

'No way,' Laura replied as she cleared her throat. 'Listen, how long have we been friends?'

'Since forever,' Chloe said with a smile.

'And do you remember our motto?'

'Of course. We'll sleep when we're dead.'

'That's right. Okay, a little dramatic, but hey, that's who we are. But a better motto would probably be "We're only as old as we feel."'

'I feel ninety.'

'Oh, stop,' Laura replied lightly. 'Remember Ibiza?'

'Yup,' Chloe said, mindlessly flipping a pen between her fingers. 'When you said you were only as old as the bar owner you were feeling.'

'Hey, he wasn't complaining.'

'I know,' Chloe said, laughing, with a quick glance over her shoulder. 'I was in the next room and subjected to the sound of him "not complaining" all night.'

'Ah, yes, good times,' Laura reminisced. 'They'll carry us out in boxes before we stop.'

'You, maybe.'

'Lady, if I'm going down, I'm taking you with me,' Laura chuckled.

'Okay, okay.'

'So anyway, how are you doing?' Laura asked. 'Did you sort anything out with your bag?'

'No. Not the best end to the night, but I didn't have anything in there of any real value, so there's no loss, really. I've had it forever, though, so that was disappointing.'

'That's a shame. And what about that guy last night?'

'Who?'

'The one at the bar? Listen, I may have downed enough prosecco to floor an elephant, but I notice men, and good-looking ones at that. Even more so when you're talking to one of them.'

'Oh, nothing going on with him,' Chloe said dismissively. 'I got caught up in his friend's birthday celebration, that's all.'

'Well, that's disappointing. I thought you'd have his number at least.'

'Sorry to disappoint, but no. Although I did get a friend request on Facebook.'

'Well, that's a start, I suppose. But you've got to get back out there, Chloe. You're entitled to have a little fun every now and then.'

'I know, I know,' Chloe replied. 'I've already had the lecture from Penny. Perhaps I should take a leaf out of your book.'

'Not anymore. Sam is my main man, now.' Muffled voices echoed in the background. 'Chloe, sorry, I've got to go. My ten a.m. has arrived early. Catch you later?'

'Perfect.'

Chloe stood and wandered over to the small kitchen area tucked into the corner of the office. Essentially a glass box, it was filled with brightly coloured swivel chairs and white melamine tables that were impossible to move; she knew because she'd tried. It was a nice breakout area for the department if staff didn't feel like trudging to the café downstairs for their break. She knew Penny would soon be back with her order, but she still grabbed a couple of biscuits from the stash in the cupboard and filled a cup with water from the cooler. Anything to soothe the unsettled feeling in her stomach.

Too bloody old for this, she thought, as she demolished the biscuits.

'Hi, Chloe.'

She turned to see Tom stroll in, looking more alert and ready for the day than she felt.

'Hey, Tom.'

'Can I get you one?' he asked as he grabbed a mug from the cupboard, spooned in some coffee and filled it with hot water from the tap.

'No, thanks. Penny is grabbing me one from downstairs. A large one.'

He smiled as he stirred, rinsed the spoon and put it on the dish rack by the sink. 'Sounds like a hangover cure to me. Heavy night?'

'Yes, I feel like death,' she said as she took a sip. 'Not that I'd admit to it to anyone else.'

'I'm guessing Laura was involved?'

'Again, yes. Another heavy night with Laura.'

'Ah, I see,' he said. 'Explains everything.'

Tall and lean but powerfully built, he had the striking features of his Scandinavian heritage, and his sandy blonde hair was seemingly untouched by the blustery elements of this cold February morning. She cast her eyes over his tailored suit, brown leather shoes, and blue-checked tie. She also caught the fresh scent of his cologne.

'You're looking very dapper this morning.'

He smiled and gave her a sideways glance. 'Always look my best for you, Chloe.'

The warmth in his eyes did not go unnoticed – or the mischief. She'd known Tom since she'd worked here, and they'd clicked immediately. He was a good friend, and she relied on him at work. It was his opinion that she would seek out if she ever needed advice. 'Well, it's not gone unappreciated today. A sight for very sore eyes.'

'I'm glad I could be of assistance then,' he said, as he reached into the cupboard and helped himself to a biscuit, too. 'So, what was last night then? Celebrations?'

'No, Laura wouldn't take no for an answer.'

'Ah, I see. Good time?'

'Yeah, not bad, except for the hunters out for a bit of flesh.'

'Bet you needed that.'

'Yup, like a hole in the head.'

He smiled. 'There will always be the predatory kind in places like that, guaranteed. Low lights, alcohol flowing, and they know they'll get lucky. No one cares at that point that they have nothing going for them.'

'So you're not going to tell me I should get out there and have a little fun?'

'Nope. Not my style. That's your choice.'

'I appreciate it. Everyone else has an opinion on the car crash of my life. I'm well aware it's been water-cooler gossip for the last couple of months.'

'I never pay attention to the office chatter. I make up my own mind about people.'

He glanced at her with a smile that caused heat to flush in her cheeks. He'd always been respectful on that front and never delved too deeply unless she wanted to talk. She appreciated his almost telepathic ability to read her emotions. It was as though he could tailor his mood to match hers, knowing when she wanted to discuss something or when it was best to leave her alone.

He did this with everyone else, too; he was well known within the company for his warm and approachable nature. But in recent months she'd begun to believe that, with her, he was different. Kinder, more thoughtful maybe. Not that it mattered. She wouldn't allow herself to fall down that particular rabbit hole. She had to remind her inner voice she was done with deep emotional connections. She had her friends and her family, and that was enough.

Penny appeared, coffee and pastry in hand, and Chloe immediately noticed her giddiness, eyes gleaming with excitement. It was like watching an impatient child on Christmas morning.

'Chloe, there's someone in reception for you.'

'What? Who?' Chloe said, placing her water cup on the side as she took the food from Penny. Priorities.

'I don't know, but it's a *man*.' Penny grinned. 'You need to go and see, and then update us.'

'Calm down, Pen,' Chloe said as she sipped at her coffee. 'Probably just a delivery. You can stand down.'

'Probably,' Penny said, a glint in her eye as she glanced at Tom.

'Thanks for the breakfast,' she said, taking a bite of the pastry. 'I owe you.'

3

C hloe crammed the rest of the pastry into her mouth in a few large bites as she hurried down to reception, hoping her stomach would accept the offering and stop grumbling. Walking into the large atrium, she saw Danny leaning against the reception desk, dressed in a smart business suit, chatting easily with the receptionist. Chloe paused, immediately recognising the bag in his hand – her handbag from last night – as he tossed it around loosely in conversation. He'd found her bag, and in doing so had somehow discovered her place of work. Taking a calming breath, she crossed the room towards him.

Dressed a little more formally than last night, his dark suit and tie indicated business attire that gave a very professional air to a man who seemed to suppress a darkness within. An intensity that could become a threat in a moment. Of course, to those who didn't see it or simply chose to ignore it, he was still a very appealing prospect to someone who would be interested. But not Chloe. She'd ensured her walls were high. The receptionist was certainly charmed, though, and enthusiastically engaged in their conversation. All she needed was the cute giggle and hair flip and she'd be good to go.

As if sensing her presence, Danny turned to face Chloe and pointed at her, the reason for his visit, and thanked the receptionist as he left the desk and strode towards her. 'Hello again,' he said, a broad smile on his lips.

Seeing him again, only this time in the daylight and no longer under the neon glow of the club, she noticed the eyes that had followed her every movement were hazel-coloured and his olive skin was clean-shaven this morning. His hair was as she remembered, tousled on top and cropped short at the sides, but today she could make out its ebony shades.

'I hope you don't mind me bothering you at work,' he said, and held out her bag. 'I thought I should return this to you as soon as possible.'

She took it from him, delighted. 'You found it.'

'I noticed you left it behind on the bar, but when I tried to find you, you were already lost in the crowd. There was not much in there apart from some loose change and a pass card with this company logo tucked away in the side pocket. I thought I'd pop along just in case you were still working here.'

'I see,' she said, realising that's how he'd found her on Facebook and today, at the office. An old card she'd left in the bag.

'Your colleague said she'd come and find you. I hope you don't mind?'

'No, not at all.' She looked down at the bag, sifting through the scant contents inside.

'It's all there,' he said, watching closely.

Her face flushed. 'Of course it is,' she said quickly, glancing at him. 'Thank you for returning it to me. I'm very grateful.'

He smiled, a look of genuine happiness that he'd been able to help. But he also wasn't making any move to leave.

She caught the receptionist watching their conversation. After an awkward pause, she smiled and pointed to the doors behind her. 'Well, I guess I really ought to get back to work.'

'Yes, of course you must.'

'But thank you again, Danny. I'm glad I have it back.'

'Hey, it's my pleasure. At least it fell into my hands. It would be gone forever if someone with less honourable intentions got hold of it. Tossed in a bin somewhere.'

She nodded, thinking of Jeff and the mountain of paperwork waiting for her upstairs. 'Well, I'm very pleased it's not lost forever.'

He hesitated and ran his hand through his hair.

'Is there something else?' she asked.

'No. Well, perhaps just one thing. I wondered if you might like to meet for a drink sometime? Or dinner? I mean, if you're free.'

'Oh,' she said. 'Well, I don't know...'

'Just think of it as a thank you.'

'But you don't have anything to thank me for.'

'Well then, perhaps this is my clumsy way of saying I'd like to see you again.' His smile was a mix of humour and embarrassment. 'And an opportunity to give the bag another outing.'

Laura's voice filled her head, telling her to go for it, but she chose to ignore it. 'Ah, maybe, I don't know. I'm a little out of the game.'

'No pressure,' he said, although his eyes seemed to demand something else. 'I'm sure we'll bump into each other again.'

She looked towards the turnstiles. 'I really should go, or my boss will be on the warpath. Thanks for this,' she said as she raised the bag a little.

'Absolutely.'

She swiped her card at the turnstiles, about to disappear into the corridor leading back to the elevator, when she dared to glance behind to see him watching her walk away. He held his hand up in a wave and she could still feel the weight of his stare burning into her skin even after he was long out of sight.

Back at her desk, she tucked the clutch bag into her larger leather tote by her chair and sat down. Fleeting panic caused her breath to catch in her throat, but she calmed herself with practised breathing techniques her counsellor had shown her in the aftermath of David's betrayal.

She leaned back in her chair and considered taking a moment to hide in the toilets, if only to get her composure back, but the sight of Penny walking towards her ended that plan.

'Penny.' She sighed. 'Everything okay?'

'Could ask you the same thing,' Penny replied with a smile. 'Have you checked your Facebook yet?'

Apprehension filled her. 'No, why?'

She pulled out her phone and opened the app. Scrolling through her feed, she saw Danny had tagged her in the photo with him and the birthday boy from last night. They were all smiling, and Danny was a lot closer to her than she had realised at the time, with his arm outstretched and disappearing behind her. The pose created a far more intimate scene than the reality. From the way he was standing, it was hard to know if his hand was on her back rather than resting on the bar as it had been. A clever tactic to create ambiguity.

'Great.'

Penny batted it away. 'What are you talking about, Chloe? He's gorgeous, and you are too. You're glowing. I mean, the other guy is out of his head, clearly, but you two? It's cute.'

'It's not cute. It's weird. He's created something out of nothing.'

'So?'

'So my private life is *private,* and I have people here, at work, who will see this.'

Penny snorted a laugh. 'Then why the hell are you on Facebook?'

'Good point,' Chloe mumbled.

'Relax, Chloe, it's nothing. This is Facebook.' Penny shrugged. 'Most of the people in this office have much more questionable photos running through their timeline.'

'I just don't want anything to jeopardise my promotion.'

'No way. In this party-hard environment, you've probably done yourself a favour. And, anyway, we've all got evidence of nights out we'd rather forget. Yours is completely tame by comparison.' Penny continued to scrutinise the picture. 'I mean, it's not like his tongue is down your throat, or he's snorting a line of coke off your boobs,' she said, transferring her scrutiny to Chloe's face instead. 'I mean, there's nothing like that, is there?'

'No,' Chloe said forcefully, and raised a brow at Penny's deflated expression. 'I left with Laura shortly after that. Went home.'

'Well, then, I think it's going to be fine. Let it go.'

THE COLD FEBRUARY night air nipped her skin, stinging her ears and nose. Grateful for the soft sky-blue scarf wound around her neck, gifted to her by her mother a couple of Christmases ago, she pulled her coat a little tighter around herself as she made her way to the station. She had been careful to leave work on time, deciding there would be no overtime tonight, even though it would mean a heavy commute. All she wanted was to be at home, cook herself a meal, and binge on episodes of *Friends*. Anything to get this night over with.

She walked with the crowds, and at first she didn't pay much attention to the group of lads behind her, but as they drew closer she realised their lewd little conversations were about her. Soon enough, the hairs on the back of her neck prickled with discomfort. Amongst the people all trying to make their way home, a sense of vulnerability crept over her. It was too early in the evening to be feeling so at risk, but life always managed to keep her on her toes.

She glanced over her shoulder. Three of them.

Not so bad, she thought. *They're just blokes out for some fun, making the best of an evening reserved for couples.*

Ignore, don't engage – a mantra that's been ingrained in the female psyche for decades – even though she wanted nothing more than to turn around and shout her own obscenities to these poor excuses for men.

It's not a problem, just keep walking, she repeated over and over in her mind, but as one of them caught her looking, he shouted something at her. *Damn it.*

She kept her eyes ahead and her pace swift. She was in the crowd of commuters, but acutely aware that it didn't mean a thing.

'Hey, beautiful,' came another voice from behind. 'Wanna be my valentine?'

Laughter filled the evening air. She kept her pace.

'Oi, lady. I'm talking to you.'

She wrapped her hand around the strap of her bag and hurried, looking out to the road to see if she could dodge the light traffic and cross over to remove herself from the situation. Another tactic to avoid their catcalling and keep herself safe, together with keys between fingers, personal alarms, and, if necessary, the knowledge she'd retained from the self-defence classes she and Laura had attended. They were chanting at her now, and she felt heat rise in her face. Panic began to swirl her insides. She wanted to cross, but that would have meant slowing to wait for the cars to clear, and she felt it better, safer, to keep moving.

Someone called her name, causing more confusion in her mind. This voice was different; a man, not a childish lad out for kicks. She turned and saw Danny threading through the traffic and jogging towards her, his winter coat open and flapping in the wind.

'Chloe, hi, everything okay here?' he said as he approached.

The lads repeated his words, parrot-fashion, like kids in the playground. But whatever they were thinking, they seemed to get the message and kept going, with shrieks of laughter as they went. She paused and waited for her heart rate to level out, confused by the gratitude she suddenly felt to see him.

'Everything's fine,' she said as her heart thumped in her chest. She watched the group of lads saunter up the road. 'I'm sure they meant no harm, but I was worried for a moment.'

'I don't know how they think that's acceptable,' he said, as he glanced down the road to them. 'Are you okay?' Close now, he reached out and rubbed his hand up and down her arm. 'You're shaking.'

'I'm just cold,' she said, an obvious lie. 'And I should get going, or I'll miss my train.'

He looked up the street at the pub on the corner, a place near her office she'd visited many times for a boozy lunch. 'Look, let me buy you a drink in there. Think of it as medicinal. Something to warm you up and soothe your nerves.'

She checked her watch. She could handle one drink, and it would be good to get some distance from those lads because, knowing her luck, she'd bump into them again on the train. She knew the pub well – it would be busy with regulars not yet ready to go home. She could always catch a later train.

'Okay, that sounds good. Just one drink, and then I should get home.'

He smiled again and tilted his head. 'Got someone waiting for you?'

Her eyes darted at the crowd navigating their way past them as she adjusted her bag on her shoulder, and then she turned and fixed them on his. 'People will know where I am,' she replied.

'You don't need to run that line with me,' he said calmly. 'You're safe enough. But someone as lovely as you should definitely have someone waiting. To be cherished.'

'Maybe that's not what I want,' she replied. 'And you really need to brush up on your chat-up lines.'

A smile tipped his lip. 'Maybe you can help me with that, and I can try to persuade you that two is always better than one?'

They lingered this way for far too long before he spoke. 'One drink at that pub and then I'll let you go. What do you say?'

She glanced up the road. This was more about not being rude. 'All right. I know it well. It's a cute little place, if you don't mind being watched over by monks.'

He stared blankly at her.

'You'll understand once we're there.'

She noticed how his eyes lit up at her agreement to join him. He turned and took her hand, wrapping it through his arms as they strode together, making the three-minute walk towards the pub wedged between an intersection of roads and Blackfriars station just behind. The perfect place to get a drink in this dockside location, it was a historic gem loved by locals and commuters alike whilst they waited for a train home. Walking under the large clock and a statue of a rotund monk hovering above the door, they shuffled through groups of people chatting loudly as they clutched their drinks, towards the people congregated at the bar.

'It's called Blackfriars for a reason,' she said as she moved in familiar surroundings, pointing to the fresco of monks high above them. 'Or at least humorously imagined versions of their medieval counterparts.'

These stout friars circled most of the room just below the wood-panelled ceiling, depicting day-to-day activities of fishing, singing, and eating. Lower down, large bronze statues of devout friars stood proud in alcoves carved deep into the marble walls. A huge arched recess to the left of them housed a fireplace that tonight was home to roaring embers, again overlooked by a metal fresco of singing friars.

He studied them, fascination on his face. 'Ah, now I see.' He moved his gaze from the wooden carvings to her. 'What better place to be than under an ecclesiastical eye? You'll feel safe here, at least.'

4

They found a table near the fire, and Chloe hung her coat on the back of her chair as Danny checked out the bar. She was uneasy, despite the fact that the intensity in him from the previous night seemed to have disappeared.

She willed herself to calm as her cheeks flushed from the change of cold night air to the warmth of the pub.

Danny smiled. 'Wine, beer, or fizz?'

The notion of what she was doing created an internal whirlwind, picking up speed in a heartbeat. Fighting her emotions and filled with doubt, she considered the situation and as she did her smile faded. Within this very normal, everyday setting, everything to Chloe felt weird. Wrong. Was this a mistake? Would she be better off calling it quits now? She wanted to leave, but to struggle out through the crowds would only draw attention to the fact she had no idea what she was doing.

Danny noticed the change in her expression. 'Chloe, everything okay?'

'I'm not sure this was a good idea,' she blurted out, and began reaching for her coat.

He quickly reached over the table and placed a hand on her forearm. 'Wait, Chloe. Please.'

She paused, looked down at his hand and twisted in her chair to face him again.

He relaxed his brow. 'Look, I don't know what's going through your mind, but it's okay. It's just a drink, that's all. You're here. I'm here. Would it kill us to spend a couple of hours in each other's company? Give me ten minutes, and if you still feel the same, then you can go.'

The storm inside her subsided. She found a level base on which to gain control. 'Well,' she said, her voice shaking, 'when you put it like that, how can I refuse?'

Satisfied, he smiled. 'It's always best not to.'

He removed his hand, and she tucked her hair behind her ears, a nervous gesture.

He stood and pulled out his wallet. 'So, what would you like?'

'No, please. Let me get these,' she said as she lifted her bag onto her lap. 'As a thank you.'

'No,' he said. 'I suggested we go for a drink, and the one who makes the invite always buys the drinks. It's the law.'

She conceded. 'Well, the last thing I want to do is break the law. If you're sure, wine would be great.'

Alcohol probably wasn't the best idea as she hadn't eaten much, but she needed the courage.

He nodded and walked over to the bar and ordered. With a wine bottle, two glasses and a couple of bags of crisps, he strode back towards their table. He placed everything down and took the seat opposite.

Here, she did feel safer. The crowds, the laughter – they all provided a barrier from being totally alone with Danny.

That, and the friars looking down on her protectively, was comforting.

'Cracking little pub this,' he said as logs crackled and spat in the fire. 'Feels like a real local.'

'It's divinely absurd, and grade two listed, thanks to John Betjeman.'

'You know it well?'

'Of course. It's the perfect place for an office celebration or lunch.' Her eyes scanned the unopened bottle and clean glasses. Untouched.

'Yeah, it's safe. I haven't tampered with it or anything,' he said. 'You can relax.'

Embarrassed that he'd read her so easily, she stammered, 'No, I didn't think that at all.'

'Of course you did,' he replied, 'and so you should. Not all of us are good guys, Chloe. I'm glad you think of these things. You need to keep yourself safe.'

From people like you?

'Years of looking out for myself,' she said. 'It's something we learn as women, sadly. To protect ourselves. We all look out for each other, too, keep each other safe.'

'Sounds admirable.'

She shrugged. 'It is, and the only way to stop the bastards out there from ruining our lives.'

'Good for you,' he said, handing her the bottle.

She checked the label and felt the click of the bottle top as she twisted it open. 'Very nice,' she said lightly, wanting to move on.

'I thought you'd like it. You seem like a Cabernet Sauvignon kind of woman.'

'Who doesn't like Cabernet?' she said as she poured.

He took his glass and held it up. 'Cheers, Chloe. Thank you for coming here with me tonight.'

She clinked her glass against his and took a sip, the sweet

hint of vanilla and cherries bursting on her tongue, and then noticed him watching her.

'What?' she asked, confused.

He gazed. 'I just like watching you.' He held his hands up. 'Sorry, too much.' He let out a small, uncomfortable laugh. 'I guess it's been a while since I've been in the game, too.'

She thought back to his Facebook timeline. It had been a while, but no longer than any other singleton out there.

'Well, alcohol is a great healer,' she said, taking another sip. She needed to keep her head and not drink too quickly, but the wine was delicious. Her empty stomach would be her downfall if she wasn't careful. This was just a moment, time to pass, but it definitely seemed to mean more to him than it did to her.

His fascination with her was obvious.

'You're still uncomfortable here,' he said, breaking the silence.

He was also perceptive.

'I hardly know you.'

'But it's more than that. There's something about you...' He studied her. 'A sadness.'

She shifted in her chair. 'We all have our sad stories.'

He nodded empathetically. 'We do, I suppose.' He drank his wine and placed the glass down.

'So what about you?' she asked, opening a bag of crisps from the selection he'd brought back. 'What does life look like to Danny...ah, I don't know your surname.'

'It's Harris.' He smiled, pushing his drink away and resting his arms on the table. 'I can tell you that I'm a photographer. I've lived in London for about seven years, and red wine is not my favourite drink.'

'And where were you before you came to the big smoke?'

'Here and there, but mainly down south.'

She'd noticed the hint of a southern accent when they'd

talked earlier, and now that he was relaxing, there were hints of a London intonation too.

She nodded. 'And family?'

'Is this all about me, or are you going to share?'

'Maybe, in a minute.'

'Well, the answer is no, I'm afraid. I have no family.'

'No one?'

'Nope, no one. Grew up in care. I never knew my parents, but it was a pretty significant case of neglect. I was only a baby, so I don't remember the details, but I was handed over to the authorities.'

She saw in his eyes that she'd lost him for a moment. 'So do you have a foster family?'

'I went to a couple of foster homes, especially as a young kid. I mean, who doesn't love babies and toddlers? But after that, fostering never really panned out for me.'

'And what about your biological parents? Did you ever reconcile?'

'No, never. Their love for drugs meant that there was no room for me. It killed them in the end. I believe they were found in their dirty little flat by their neighbours, who stole anything of value lying around before alerting the authorities. So that was the end of that,' he said with a shrug.

'Oh,' she said. 'I'm sorry.'

He smiled. 'Don't be. What doesn't kill you and all that. The homes I stayed in were pretty steady. Well, when you compare what some kids have to put up with. It made me the person I am today. I've got my work, my friends, a nice place. Life's okay.'

She smiled. 'And is there a significant other?'

'I'm not the kind of guy to be out with a woman if I have someone at home. I commit, you see. Completely. One hundred per cent.' He glanced down. 'But that leaves you exposed, and I would be lying if I said I hadn't been hurt in the past. But no more than anyone else, I suppose.'

His gaze moved from the drinks, his eyes settling on hers. 'But that's all in the past, and I've met you now.'

'Even though I'm married,' she said.

He nodded, his face expressionless. 'I see.'

Now, for a more truthful statement. 'Well, I was.'

Still silent, he studied her for what felt like an age. Summing her up? Deciding what to believe? She didn't know. His expression remained neutral, but she could almost hear his mind working.

'Well,' he said. 'Maybe now it's your turn to share.'

———

THE CROWD in the pub that had soothed her began to disperse. Some of them off to find a club, others for food, maybe both, but she considered on this night of the year that perhaps all of them had the expectation of other, more lascivious delights. Perhaps Danny expected it, too, even if the only thing she was sure of was that she would be returning to an empty home, alone.

The evening hadn't been a disaster, and she'd been careful to share only those snippets of her life that she was comfortable with. She checked her watch. Ten-thirty.

'Well, I guess that's us,' she said as she stood and pulled her coat around her shoulders. She was clumsy about it, the wine making her mind hazy and unable to concentrate. She shouldn't have agreed to the second bottle.

He stood and helped her with the coat arm she couldn't find, his body close and hands lingering on her shoulders.

She turned to face him, an uneasy feeling prickling her skin as his eyes explored hers. 'Thanks.'

He smiled as he looked down at her. 'You're welcome, Chloe. My pleasure.'

He pulled on his coat and then placed a hand on her back, guiding her out of the pub. She increased her stride to avoid it.

The outside air shocked her and she clutched her arms around herself. 'Well, goodnight, Danny,' she said as she looked at her watch. 'I could catch the ten-forty-five if I hurry.'

He nodded as he reached into his jacket and pulled out a packet of cigarettes and a silver Zippo lighter. 'Unless, of course...?'

'What?'

He held out the pack to her and grabbed one for himself when she refused. Holding it between his lips, he flipped the wheel of the lighter to spark a long flame, which he cupped with his hand as he held it to the tip. The flame was bright, as was the soft haze of light that surrounded it. Chloe was hypnotised for a moment, both fearful and beguiled. Fire frightened her, and the devastation it could wreak on people's lives. She hated it and everything associated with it, and jumped when he snapped the lid of the lighter shut.

'Well, what do you say about sharing a taxi?' he asked, tipping his head back slightly to blow out a plume of smoke. 'I can make sure you're home safely and we can split the fare.'

She hesitated. 'How do you know we're not going in different directions?'

He edged towards her and took the liberty of lifting a hand to her face to brush aside the wayward hairs that had blown over her cheek. 'Maybe we are, but it's really important to me that you get home safely. I couldn't live with myself if a night out with me ended badly. It's late. Should you be travelling alone on a train at this time of night?'

His words were spoken as if he had a right to tell her how to live her life.

'I look after myself well enough, thank you, and I always catch the train with no problem at all.'

'Of course you do,' he chuckled. 'I'm just looking out for you, that's all.'

She sighed, tired and a little drunk. 'I apologise. I get a little defensive sometimes.'

He looked out to the street and raised his arm to hail the taxi approaching him. It pulled over, and he walked out into the road and tugged on the door, flipping his cigarette into the gutter. He turned to her. 'Taxi's here now. Might as well travel in relative comfort.'

It was probably the wine that influenced her next decision. At least she told herself it was as she stepped forward and dipped her head to get into the car. He followed and shut the door.

'Where to?' the driver asked.

Danny gestured for her to go ahead first.

'Westbourne Green, please. Shrewsbury Road will be fine, and I'll take it from there.'

It wasn't necessary for him to know exactly where she lived. The night was crisp and the short walk would help clear her mind.

The journey was quieter than she expected. Perhaps they were all out of things to say, but Danny seemed content just to be in her company. As they approached Shrewsbury Road, she pulled open her bag and grabbed her purse.

'No, it's fine,' Danny said, shaking his head.

She opened her purse. 'No, really. I'd like to pay. You bought the drinks.'

'This was my suggestion, so I'll cover it,' he said. 'Besides, I've had an awesome evening in your company. That's payment enough.'

She wanted to persist, but staring at her purse empty of cash, she struggled to argue her case.

He noticed and smiled. 'I tell you what, why don't we share numbers and then perhaps we could meet up for another drink sometime, and I'll let you shout the drinks and the fare home?'

'Oh, well, perhaps,' she muttered, flustered by his suggestion. 'I don't know.'

'Look, it's not the end of the world, just a thought,' he replied.

Feeling her cheeks flush, she nodded.

The driver pulled up at the side of the road, and she pulled the strap of her bag onto her shoulder.

'So...?' he asked with an enquiring look.

She shook her head, a little confused.

'Your number, then,' he said, amused. 'I'm probably going to need that.'

She smiled. 'Of course.'

'Perfect,' he said, his eyes glinting with satisfaction. He reached into the inside pocket of his jacket, pulled out his phone and handed it to her. 'Phone your number, and then I'll have a record of it.'

She took his phone as steadily as she could, her fingers trembling as she tapped in the numbers. This was so far outside her comfort zone it felt like more of an out-of-body experience than simply entering contact details into a phone. She masked her feelings as best she could, though. She wouldn't want him to see how she really felt. The muffled ringtone from inside her bag confirmed the connection and she hung up, handing his phone back to him.

'Thank you, Chloe. I'll call you.'

She pushed away the weird feeling that seemed to permeate through her body and nodded her agreement. 'Well, thanks for returning my bag, seeing me home safely, and for the drink.' She also thanked the driver and pushed open the door. 'Goodnight, Danny.'

'Goodnight, Chloe.'

As she got out of the car, she caught Danny speaking to the driver, but she couldn't decipher his words. The car slowly pulled away and she waited for a moment until it was further along the road before pulling her keys from her bag and setting off for home.

Muzzy-headed from the wine, she breathed in the night air, keen to get back to the warmth of her flat. She turned into St. Stephen's Gardens, and in the silence that surrounded her she caught the faint crunch of footfall on frozen ground. It was intermittent enough for her to question if it was indeed footsteps or her imagination playing tricks, but it was enough that she quickened her pace and, with every stride, the intuitive feeling of another person nearby heightened her awareness.

She wasn't alone.

Clutching her bag close to her body she strode purposefully, her heartbeat thumping in her throat. The footsteps were unmistakable now. She checked over her shoulder but was unable to see any movement in the darkness that hovered just out of reach of the pools of light from the streetlamps above. She continued down the road, breathing heavily as she marched past the terraced townhouses to her left and the gardens to her right until she reached her flat. A basement residence that benefited from its own front door, she grabbed the railing, ready to hurry down the steps.

'Chloe, wait!'

Startled, she turned and squinted to see who was there, poised and ready to dart to her door if needed. The dark silhouette moved closer to the streetlamp nearest her flat and she stared as the light slowly illuminated the shadowy figure. Danny's features emerged as he jogged towards her.

'What are you doing?' she cried, her heart pumping in her chest.

'I didn't mean to scare you,' he said. 'It just didn't feel right to leave you alone.'

'So you thought you'd follow me home?' she asked, irritation clipping her words.

'I'm sorry, I didn't mean to offend,' he said, glancing towards her flat, which was shrouded in darkness and so obviously empty.

Her muscles tightened. The combination of wine and the sudden spike of adrenaline made her head spin. In one glance, he'd established that she lived alone, no partner or flatmate waiting for her return. No competition. 'Well, now you know I'm home, I think it would be a good idea if we actually call it a night now. I have work tomorrow, as I'm sure you do too.'

He turned his attention back to her. 'You're right, of course.'

'Okay, Danny,' she said with a sigh, impatient for this 'date' to be over. 'Goodnight.'

'Goodnight, Chloe,' he said with a strange smile. 'Until next time.'

She lingered at the top of the steps as he turned to walk away, wanting to be sure he would really leave this time. When Danny eventually disappeared from sight, she ran down to her front door and the two Mediterranean blue plant pots with their triangular-shaped conifers on either side. She pushed the key into the lock and shut the door firmly behind her.

5

Strange energy filled the office. A subdued, post-celebration mood that hinted at hangovers and fatigue. Eyes moved to her as she weaved her way through the sea of desks, murmuring her good mornings as she went. Her desk was clear – just as she had left it, except for a single yellow Post-it note placed in the centre. As she drew near, she dropped her bag onto the seat of her chair and scanned the office for anyone nearby who might have left it there, but as none of her colleagues reacted, she ascertained it was nothing to do with them. She picked it up, and her heart jumped when she read the words.

Hi, Chloe,

Danny dropped by this morning. He wanted to check you were okay.
Please can you call him on the number below?

Thanks,
Jim, Security Office

The number was written in one long stream of digits. She furrowed her brow. She already had it in her phone. He'd made sure of that. And now this, the morning after the night before, he could have texted her but chose to visit her office instead, requesting a message be left on her desk. She walked to the window and scanned the street below, busy with a steady crowd of commuters wrapped up against the elements in coats and scarves of varying colours, all making their way to work. She gazed up at the frozen blue-pink sky and felt the hairs prickle on the back of her neck, aware of the unmistakable feeling that she was being watched.

'Chloe, are you okay?'

Chloe turned to see Penny walking towards her. 'Hi, Pen,' she said, moving away from the window and back to her desk. 'Yes, I'm fine.'

'What's that?' Penny asked, pointing to the note in Chloe's hand.

'Oh, nothing. Just a message from the guy who returned my bag yesterday.'

Penny nodded and then, without warning, snatched it from her hand.

'Hey!'

'Oh, Danny,' Penny said, her face lighting up. 'We're on first-name terms now, are we?'

Chloe reached out to playfully swipe the note from her fingers, but Penny held it high in the air. 'I want all the details, boss. Why does he want to check you're okay after last night? What did you do?'

Chloe snatched it back. 'Nothing. And none of your business, lady.'

'I'm not gonna leave until you share,' Penny sang.

Chloe groaned and held up her hands. 'Okay, okay. We went for a drink last night. That's all.'

Penny reacted like any self-respecting schoolchild would.

'Oh my God, Chloe. Where? What was he like?' She paused, breathless, and fanned her face with her hands. 'Jesus, I have so many questions.'

'Take a chill pill, Pen.' Chloe laughed. 'It was just a drink. This is just him getting a little over-enthusiastic about where he thinks this "friendship" is going, but there really is nothing to it.'

Penny smiled mischievously and shook her head. 'Methinks she protests too much.'

Chloe sighed, but couldn't help but smile at Penny's high spirits. 'No, she doesn't. Now go and collect the compliance report I'm just about to print, if you want to be useful.'

She clicked the print icon on her screen and then watched Penny bounce off, her long ponytail swinging as she walked, and was glad of the peace. A woman like Penny, barely twenty, and with a naïve joy for life, would find this little intrigue thrilling and totally acceptable, whereas Chloe knew life was more complicated than that. Still, she needed to decide what to do about this situation with Danny. She sat down, tapping her fingers against the desk.

Tom strode into the office, his laptop bag slung over one shoulder, his phone pressed to his ear. She imagined the conversation he'd be having and who he might be talking to as he spoke animatedly. He exuded confidence, but none of the arrogance that usually accompanied it. The jacket of his suit had hitched up under his bag slightly, exposing his white shirt and taut midsection. Whatever he was discussing made him laugh, and the sight and sound of it made Chloe's lips form into an involuntary smile. It was light and carefree, something she had felt so little of in recent months. He glanced at her, caught her watching, and winked without missing a beat of his conversation.

Found out, she looked away and glanced around the office, quickly scanning the room. She didn't have time for more office gossip about her, and as she looked down at the note in her hand she felt her stomach sink.

Still with some time on her hands, she decided to go down to reception to find Jim and discover exactly what was going on. Danny had overstepped by coming here again, and she needed to know the details.

The security office was locked, which meant she'd have to speak to the reception team. They were a tricky bunch. They felt responsible for what came into the building and what went out. They had a log for everything, and all of them seemed to have a handle on every bit of gossip that circulated the building. They were also very protective of their reputation within the company hierarchy and, as such, patrolled their space with a level of suspicion towards other members of staff that likened them to a pack of wolves.

As Chloe approached, she fixed her smile. 'Good morning, ladies,' she said cheerfully.

'Good morning,' one of the ladies murmured, a clipboard in hand. 'How can we help you?'

'The security office is closed, but I just wanted to speak to Jim about this message he left on my desk.'

'Was it left with the wrong person?' the lady asked, glancing at the note. 'Are you not Chloe Stark?'

'Yes, that's me. It came to the right person. No problem there. I just wondered if I could speak to Jim?'

'We are the reception team, not a concierge for security. I would suggest you either call and ask to speak to Jim, or email him. Security opens officially at nine-thirty today, as they have their team meeting.' Far too busy and important to devote any more time to this conversation, Little Miss Snarky moved along the desk to greet another poor unsuspecting victim.

'Thank you so much,' Chloe said with a tight smile as she turned to walk away.

'Did I hear someone say my name?'

Chloe turned to see Jim walking towards her – a bald-headed man dressed in the standard uniform of a white shirt and black trousers – looking every inch of a burly nightclub bouncer. But he had a friendly smile, and Chloe was glad to be speaking with him rather than the stuffy reception team.

'Ah, Jim, hello.'

'Hello there. What can we do for you?'

'Well, it's about this note you left on my desk.'

'Of course,' he said. 'Everything all right?'

'Yeah, fine, but the man who left this message for me ... did he say anything else or do anything odd?'

'No, not really,' he said. 'Very nice chap. Wanting to come in as soon as I unlocked the doors. Actually, I think he might have been waiting outside when I arrived, but I can't be sure. Said he wanted to leave this for you because he was looking forward to seeing you again. He was very charming.'

Her face flushed.

'He just left his number and asked me to pass it to you. There's not a problem, is there?'

'No, not at all. Well, nothing you've done, anyway. It's odd because there's no need for him to come by to give this to me, so I wasn't expecting him to show up. I just wanted to discuss the circumstances, and I appreciate you passing the message on.'

'You're welcome.'

She smiled. 'Perhaps you could let me know if he ever visits here again? Is that okay?'

The man smiled. 'Yes, of course. Although, if you want my opinion, he seemed very keen. Very keen indeed. Reckon he looked rather smitten, if you ask me.'

She nodded. The last thing she wanted was his opinion, but she said nothing. She didn't want to risk being rude. Danny's actions were not Jim's responsibility. No need to shoot the messenger. She tapped her fingers against the note. 'Right, well, I'd better get back to it. Thanks for your help.'

As she crossed the floor, she glanced at the entrance, scanning the area, sure to see Danny's face waiting for her. But she saw only passers-by, hurrying to wherever they needed to be.

Back at her department, she walked out of the lift and turned the corner too quickly, stopping moments before she collided with Tom.

'Whoa, Chloe,' he said as he placed his hands on her arms, a steadying action she didn't need. 'What's the emergency?'

'None,' she said hurriedly. 'Just don't want to be late.'

He held her still and studied her. 'Wait, I know that face,' he said gently as he looked down at her, his pale grey eyes kind and sincere. 'Something's rattled you.'

'Really, I'm fine,' she said, a little too forcefully.

'Come on, we're going for coffee. You need to talk.'

'What about the office?'

'There's still time before the bell rings,' he said light-heartedly. 'I've left the kids in charge. They'll be fine.'

She calmed, and a faint smile tipped her lips at the reference. Being around the same age as Tom and working with younger teams had a kid-versus-parent vibe to it. Tom actively encouraged it and seemed to like having that link with Chloe. She liked it too.

———

'Look, if you feel like that, you've obviously got to call him and tell him you're not looking for anything serious. Sounds like he's getting a little too keen and needs to back off,' Tom said, as they sat at the corner table at the back of the company's restaurant. The room was large, decorated in neutral white except for the intermittent feature wall with bursts of colour, matching the array of dining tables and chairs. It was a known fact that people who took this particular spot wanted privacy and were not to be disturbed. 'You had one date with the guy and now you're done. No problem.'

'It wasn't even that,' she replied, as she caught the cooking aromas coming from the busy kitchen in readiness for the lunchtime rush. 'It was nothing more than a drink to say thanks for returning my bag and getting rid of some kids.'

'Kids?' he asked.

'I was being heckled by a group of lads. It was nothing, but he showed up and intervened. Once they saw us talking, they soon scurried off.'

'Really? That's interesting,' he said. 'Convenient, don't you think?'

'Okay, well, now he's just gone up a couple of notches on the weirdness scale,' she said. 'So thanks for that.'

'He obviously thinks there's more,' he said as he leaned back in his chair. 'But if you don't like it, then just tell security to block him and forget about it.'

She placed her elbow on the table and rested her head on her hand. 'If only it were that simple. I stupidly agreed to give him my number.'

'Ah,' Tom said, pulling a face. 'That's awkward.'

'I know, I know. What was I thinking?'

'We've all been there, don't worry. Did you not think of giving a fake one?'

'No, he handed me his phone to call my number. It would have been odd if my phone didn't ring.'

'Could have been on silent.'

'You're not helping.' She sighed with a wry smile. 'I'd had wine.'

Tom chuckled. 'Look, you've done nothing wrong. He's keen. He knew he was lucky to have you for the evening, and whilst he could have messaged you, I'm guessing this little tactic was to let you know he is *very* interested.'

'Lucky to have me?'

'Are you kidding me?' he said quickly. 'My God, Chloe, you're funny and smart, and your looks aren't too shabby either. Who wouldn't feel lucky?'

Her face flushed.

'I mean, don't get ahead of yourself,' he snapped back with a grin. 'It's just a compliment. I'm a nice guy.'

She rolled her eyes and groaned.

'And if you don't stare too hard, you'd never see your squint or gammy leg.'

'Thanks a lot, loser.' She smiled and prodded his arm playfully. 'It's the squint that gets them every time.'

'Seriously, though,' he said, leaning in to make his point. 'It's how you deal with him now that matters.'

'I know,' she said with a sigh.

'And I know you don't want to discuss your past,' he continued, 'and I've no right to tell you what to do, but I know how hard you've struggled. You've lived through a nightmare, and I admire your strength. And now you have everyone telling you to move on, have a little fun, but it's difficult, isn't it?'

'It is,' she said, fiddling with her coffee cup.

'And it's bullshit. This is *your* life, so you have to do it at your own pace and only when you're ready.'

'But I do want to move on. Desperately.'

'I know, and I see you, every day, trying to get on with your life and nobody deserves happiness more than you, Chloe. Nobody. But be careful. You're a friend and I care about you. Guys like that are persistent, and they often don't like being told no. Cut him off before he gets any ideas. Block him or change your number if you have to.'

'I know. I fully understand the situation, but it may be a little late for that.'

'Why?'

'I got the taxi to drop me off on the road next to mine so he wouldn't know my address, you know, the usual, but he followed me right up to my door.'

'Jesus, Chloe.'

'I know. Not great.'

'You see? Persistent, and tipping into crazy-man-land. Do you need me to accompany you home?'

'You want to be my bodyguard?' she asked with a raised brow, hoping to lighten the mood.

'If you need one.'

'Good to know. But I'm fine. I'll deal with it,' she said as confidently as she could.

'You know I'm here if you ever need a chat.'

'I do, and I appreciate it, but right now I'll have Jeff to deal with, too, if we don't get back up there to our desks.'

He smiled, checking his watch as they both rose to stand. 'Absolutely. But I'm glad we had this chat. You've got more colour in your cheeks now.'

'Thanks, Tom. I needed it, actually.'

'Everyone needs my counsel from time to time,' he said smugly. 'You're no different.'

She laughed. 'I was referring to the coffee.'

He linked his arm through hers. 'Of course you were, sweetie. Of course you were.'

Her chat with Tom told her nothing she didn't already know, but just being in his company and having someone listen helped to clear the fog in her mind. And, as an added bonus, she regained her focus. She found she was able to run her reports, catch up on emails and prepare for a meeting the next day. Then her phone buzzed on her desk. Laura. She grabbed it.

'Hey, hon. What's up?'

'Are you free later? Fancy a drinkie and a catch-up?' Laura asked.

'Ah, I don't—'

'No, no,' Laura interrupted. 'I think the answer you're searching for is *Yes, Laura, that sounds like fun, and I need to have fun, so I will be there.* Yes?'

Chloe laughed. 'All right, you win,' she replied, glancing around, aware of her surroundings. 'Sounds good. Where?'

'You know I always win. I'm thinking of coming over to you, but I can't talk now, got to go. One of my regulars – a sixty-five-year-old lady who's never had a wax in her life – has requested her first Hollywood.'

'What the hell?'

'I know. It's what I like to call New Boyfriend Syndrome. Thirty years of marriage, hubby finds himself a newer model and then, not to be outdone, she's out there finding herself a toy boy. I don't know what she thinks she's getting here today, but it's either going to go really smoothly, if you'll pardon the pun, or really, really badly. There will be no in-between.'

'I don't know how you do it. You need a medal.'

'Well, a new salon with a crippling mortgage is going to have to do. Can we say seven-thirty at The Westbourne?'

'I'll be there.'

'Perfect. I'll call Gabby, too.'

'Great. See you then.'

6

Chloe shuffled past tables and mismatched wooden chairs, soon to be full with people wanting to escape the cold February night. Only smokers braved the arctic temperatures out on the terrace, huddled in groups, where they chatted and drank. The unproblematic journey home meant she'd had time to shower, refresh her hair and make-up, and throw on her favourite jeans and a soft pale grey jumper that had a wide neck skimming her shoulders. She also grabbed a bite to eat before making the ten-minute walk to the pub, not because the food there was bad – it was delicious – but this was a liquid dinner date, and she didn't want to go out hungry.

She found Laura already sitting at a round table with a bottle of fizz in a cooler and three glasses. Her friend's loyalty to the bottle was admirable, and it reminded Chloe of their early days in London: a carefree time before their significant others came onto the scene.

Friends since school, they had both left their parents and their sleepy Dorset hometown, nestled on the south coast, and embarked on a life in London. Laura started her technician training and Chloe studied for her economics degree. Both followed their dreams and partied hard – here, and on holidays abroad, when they could scrape enough money together. Gabby came onto the scene not long after Chloe's arrival, when they worked together in a bar, and they'd all been friends ever since. At a petite but gorgeously curvaceous five-foot-two, with a pretty face with freckles dotted across her nose and cheeks, and mocha-coloured spiral curls, Gabby was the bar's pocket rocket. She ran an orderly shift, never afraid to get the rowdy troublemakers ejected from the establishment by the bouncers, if necessary. There would be no trouble on her watch, and everyone loved her for it.

'Hey, you,' Laura said, pulling Chloe into a hug. 'I've got the bottle on ice, and Gabby's on her way.' Dressed in a black turtleneck, perfectly paired with a gold satin pleated skirt and black suede boots, she was effortlessly styled, as usual.

'Perfect.'

They sat, and Laura grabbed the bottle from the ice bucket just as the familiar shrieks of Gabby sounded from behind, notifying them of her arrival.

'Ladies,' she squealed, as she pulled them into an embrace. 'I swear to God that tube is getting worse. I was sandwiched between two men. Thought I'd lose them when I got to Oxford Circus, but the bastards jumped onto the Central line with me. For fifteen minutes of the journey, they used the crowded space as an excuse for a quick feel.'

'Bet they regretted it,' Chloe remarked.

'Too right. A quick thump with my bag into the groin of the most pervy guy soon took his breath away, let me tell you.'

'Ha, thought so.'

'They got the message, no doubt about it. But I was glad to get out of there.' Gabby removed her coat and adjusted her corduroy pinafore dress. 'Love this place and its quaint front-room style,' she said, pointing at objects around the room. 'All these pictures on the walls, the fireplace, the cool vibe.'

'It's great, isn't it?' Chloe said. 'It's a nice little local just down the road from my place, even though the prices here are skyrocketing. I couldn't afford it if I were starting over. Me and David worked hard to get that little flat.'

'I know you did, and I bet you're glad you bought David out when you did,' Gabby said, as she made herself comfortable.

'Certainly am. I dread to think of the position I'd be in if I'd put it on hold, like he suggested, even if the mortgage is astronomical. I wasn't about to lose my home just because he decided to leave.'

Laura reached out to Chloe, understanding the sensitivity of this subject. 'Damn right. But we're not going to think about that now.'

Chloe agreed. 'Let's raise our glasses to something. Anything.'

Gabby rubbed her hands together in anticipation, as Laura poured the fizz into each glass. Chloe relaxed in the company of her friends, needing this normality after such a difficult night the day before.

'Got yourself some spectacular talons there,' Chloe said to Gabby, as she took her glass from Laura.

Gabby shrugged. 'I'm glad you noticed. The longer, the better.' She wiggled the fingers of her free hand. 'Thought I'd have a little treat before Rob whisks me to La France in a couple of weeks.'

'They look like opals,' Chloe said. 'Or Mother of Pearl. They're gorgeous.'

'That's exactly the brief,' Laura said, handing a glass to Chloe. 'I had my best technician on those.'

'How do you get the iridescent look?'

'Top secret,' Laura said.

'Well, they're lovely, but I wouldn't be able to do anything with those things,' Chloe said.

'Ah, come on, Chloe. You're telling me you don't want these beauties on the ends of your fingers?' She raised a brow. 'Work wonders, too, when you scratch them down the spine of a gorgeous male.'

'And who would that be?' Chloe said with a smirk.

'Rob, of course,' Gabby replied indignantly.

'So you're exclusive now?'

'Have been for a couple of months. I tried to resist, but you have to let them in some time.'

Laura sighed. 'You do.'

'I think it's great,' Chloe said. 'Rob is one of the good ones, and he's very keen on you.'

Gabby patted her hair, jokingly, as if preening herself. 'And why not? He's only human. A mere mortal.'

'Let me know if the mini breaks are going to tail off,' Laura said. 'Rob's trips and your prep for them are propping up my business right now.'

'That reminds me,' Chloe said. 'How did the wax go this afternoon?'

'I've never seen a woman jump up from the bed as quickly as she did when she realised what was involved, poor thing. She said, like it or not, natural was the only way for her; hot wax had no business being anywhere near those parts.'

'Thought as much,' Chloe said. 'I didn't think she'd go through with it, not at that bloody age.'

'Couldn't charge her for any of it either, she was that shocked. Lost the appointment completely.'

'That's a shame. Talons aside, I'm probably due a mani-cure and a wax or something.'

Chloe understood all the sacrifices Laura had made to get where she was today. A hotshot beautician, she'd spent the last couple of years winning all the local competitions, and the subsequent social media coverage meant she soon outgrew her premises. Despite the heavy mortgage, her new salon was larger, more central and modern, tucked in the row of shops on Lisson Grove in Marylebone. Nicely decorated, too: white marble floors, flower walls, and soft, silver velvet furnishings. Chloe noted to book an appointment when she got home so she could enjoy a little pampering of her own, but she'd pass on the talons – leave those for the 'ladies who lunch'.

'So come on then, ladies, spill,' Laura said, drink in hand. 'I only want the juiciest gossip. I don't come out on a school night for the boring stuff. I've got an empire to build, a new salon and a swanky new place in Gloucester Place. The mortgages on both are crippling. Time is money.'

'Well,' Gabby said, 'I think Chloe should go first.'

'Why me?'

'Because Rob saw you last night in Blackfriars with a man. Care to share?'

'Rob is too nosey for his own good,' Chloe mumbled.

'He likes to call it attentive.'

'Well, he would, wouldn't he?'

'So, it's true, then.' Gabby raised her eyebrows. 'Rob's such a wind-up, I wasn't sure I believed him.'

Chloe sipped on her prosecco. 'It was nothing. A quick thank-you drink with the man who returned my bag. Okay, Mum?'

Gabby clapped her hands together and squealed again. 'More details, lady. Right now.'

'Wait a second,' Laura said. 'This is the guy from the club, right?'

'Correct. Danny just wanted to—'

'Ooh, Danny,' they both chimed, giggling.

'Oh, stop.'

'Sorry,' Laura said. 'Continue.'

'Well, I would, but there's nothing more to say.'

'Nothing?' Gabby probed.

'No, nothing. We shared a taxi, and that's it.'

'Oh,' Gabby whined. 'The first date since David, and that's it?'

'I'm not going to throw myself to the first man who shows an interest in me.'

'Why not?' Laura asked.

'Because I'm not like you.'

'She's right,' Gabby agreed. 'You're like a dog on heat most days.'

'That's not true!' Laura argued, but then considered it. 'Okay, maybe a little, but why not? I don't see Sam complaining. I'll jump his bones any day of the week.'

'Ah, young love,' Chloe joked.

'So, are you going to see him again?' Laura asked.

'Well, it wasn't in my plans, but he came to the office again today. Left me a message. Wanted to check I was all right.'

'Nice.'

'Not really. It's a little intense, actually.'

'Ooh, I like intense,' Gabby said.

'Not that kind of intense.'

'Well, I'm just glad you found a connection with someone after that little shit, David,' Laura replied.

'Laura,' Chloe warned, 'we're not going there tonight, all right?'

'Okay, I'm sorry. I didn't mean that. But picking up a hot guy? Good on you.'

'I'm not interested in any way.'

Gabby and Laura exchanged glances.

Laura drained the bottle of fizz into the glasses. 'Well, I

think you need a one-nighter. A little palate cleanser. That'll get you back on track.'

'So eloquently put,' Chloe replied.

'Exactly,' Gabby said. 'A little distraction is just what you need right now. Get a little spice in your life with no strings.'

'I will get out there, when I'm ready, but definitely not with Danny.' She placed her glass on the table. 'But there's one thing that's never in doubt,' she said as she watched their confused expressions. 'We can get through the bubbles. I'll just pop to the ladies and then the bar. Same again?'

'Absolutely,' they both agreed in unison.

After negotiating the pub toilets, which involved a queue for two working cubicles out of five – both less-than-appealing, and in stark contrast to the rest of the pub – she went to the bar and nestled herself between the crowd, waiting to be served.

'Hi, gorgeous.'

She turned on her heels, face to face with Danny, who looked down at her with a mischievous grin and quickly dropped a kiss on her cheek.

'Danny,' she said, startled. 'What are you doing here?'

'I was in the area. Supposed to be meeting a friend but they've just cancelled on me, so I thought I'd have a quick drink here before I made my way home.' He reached out and touched her arm with what she guessed was supposed to be affection. 'What are the chances, eh? I'm so glad I bumped into you. Can't stop thinking about you.'

She calmly moved his hand away. 'Now is not a good time. I'm here with my friends.'

'Great,' he said as he beckoned the bartender over. 'What do you want to drink?'

'It's fine. I can get it.'

Danny looked over at Chloe's table and turned to the

bartender. 'Bottle of prosecco, please, mate,' he called, pulling out his wallet. 'And an extra glass.'

'No, Danny, you don't need to—'

'Hey, it's fine,' Danny said, as he handed the bartender a couple of notes. 'It's my pleasure to do this for your friends, especially if I'm going to meet them. It'll be a nice introduction.'

'You want to come over?' she stammered.

'Of course I do, Chloe,' he said with a smile. 'I want to meet all the important people in your life and your friends are the best place to start.' He glanced down at her. 'This is great. What a coincidence I should bump into you when you're here with your friends. Perfect timing, really.'

'But—'

He gathered up the bottle in the ice bucket and the glass. 'Come on, then. Let's go.'

'Wait,' she called out, grabbing his arm.

He turned to face her, his expression now serious. 'What's the matter? Do I embarrass you?'

'No, but this isn't appropriate. I mean, it was just a drink last night. That's all. We're not a couple or anything.'

His gaze was fixed on her. 'Oh, Chloe, it was much more than that, and you know it. You can fight it, but it'll end up the same. Now, let's not keep your friends waiting. They'll think you've upped and left them.'

He strode towards Laura and Gabby, threading his way through the busy tables as she trailed behind. As they approached, she watched her friends' jaws drop as he neared them.

'Hi, ladies,' he said with too much confidence, as he placed the drinks down. 'Sorry to gate crash, but I just met Chloe at the bar and thought I'd come over.'

Laura eyed him and then Chloe. 'Er, hi,' she said, as she gave her best 'Is this him?' expression to Chloe.

Chloe nodded her agreement. 'This is Danny.'

Gabby straightened and smiled, looking like she might explode with excitement. 'Hi, Danny. I'm Gabby.'

'Lovely to meet you both,' he said, as he placed himself down on the stool opposite and patted the one next to him for Chloe to sit.

Her body tight with nervous tension, she sat next to him in silence and watched as he commanded everyone's attention.

'So, to what do we owe the pleasure?' Laura asked Danny.

He popped the cork and poured the fizz into each glass. 'Happy coincidence. A friend bailed on me. I saw Chloe at the bar and thought, perfect.'

He placed an arm affectionately around Chloe's shoulders, but she subtly managed to detach herself from his hold as he continued to chat, even though she was unsure how he'd react. She thought it might anger him, and she almost wanted it. She wanted her defiance to be seen, but he appeared to ignore it.

After thirty minutes of social but banal conversation – Chloe knew exactly how much time had passed, having constantly checked her watch – she wondered how much longer he would prolong this agony.

As though he had read her mind, he said, 'Back in a minute, nature calls.'

He walked off in the direction of the toilets as Gabby squealed.

'Oh my God, Chloe,' Laura said as soon as he was out of earshot. 'He's pretty gorgeous. I'd have my coat and be out of here, if I was you.'

'I think Sam must have his work cut out keeping you in check,' Gabby said.

Laura raised a brow and then nodded thoughtfully. 'Yeah, he does have it hard, bless him. But I keep him in check, too, you know. He's no angel. He loves it and wouldn't keep coming back if he didn't.'

'Well, don't go getting any ideas of setting me up or abandoning me,' Chloe said. 'I can't wait to be rid of the guy, but he's not taking the hint.'

'He is totally smitten,' Laura said to Gabby.

'Absolutely,' Gabby said, then held her hand to her ear. 'And, wait, is that church bells I can hear?'

'Okay, ladies, that's never going to happen,' Chloe corrected. 'And I need your help to get rid of him. He'll be back in a second. What are we going to do?'

'We're going to ride it out with style and class,' Laura said assertively. 'Gabby, tell him you've got the shits or something and we have to leave.'

Gabby slapped Laura on the arm. 'I will not!'

'I'm glad this is so amusing to you two,' Chloe chided.

Laura held up her hands. 'Sorry, honey. We do know. It's simple. We'll go back to mine. Girl stuff. He can't follow there uninvited.'

Chloe glanced over her shoulder and saw him approach. Her heart pumped.

'It was lovely to meet you,' Laura said, as soon as Danny sat down. 'But I'm afraid we're going to have to call it a night.' She stood and swung her leather jacket over her shoulders and grabbed her long blonde hair, always on the chic side of messy, from inside her collar and tossed it over her shoulder. 'I've got some stuff to sort out with these two at home. Do you mind if I steal Chloe for the rest of the evening?'

The implication that Chloe was Danny's date and needed to be excused seemed to delight him. The idea that they were an item was heavy in the air, and Chloe considered it may have made things worse, but she couldn't worry about that now. She just wanted to leave.

'Of course,' he said as he stood, too. 'I'll call you later,' he said, and pecked her cheek.

She flinched and pulled away. This was getting out of hand. 'I don't think so, Danny.'

'Tomorrow, then.'

She sighed. 'Maybe.'

7

Chloe's day had not started well. She'd managed to burn her favourite blouse with the iron, drop her morning mug of tea, and had received numerous calls from Danny, all of which she had ignored. She rushed out the door and up the steps to the pavement, straight into the path of her new neighbours, John and Louise, a middle-aged couple who had just purchased the top flat of the building.

John was tall and silver-haired, memorable to Chloe only for his ability to combine multiple tones of beige in one outfit, and Louise, a bottle-blonde, who seemed to want to counteract his insipidness by opting for bright blocks of colour mixed with equally lurid floral patterns. Chloe almost heard the clock ticking as they shared, in great detail, the renovations that would be starting soon and apologised for any noise in advance. She'd tried to be attentive, nodding and maintaining eye contact, but she zoned out when John began the protracted story of how they came to purchase the property. Somehow, at a point when he paused the chit-chat enough to draw breath, she'd managed to excuse herself with an appeasing smile, muttering about needing to leave for work.

She rushed to her morning meeting, late, and knew she'd have to face being the last to arrive. Pulling open the large door to the glass office, she was met with a sea of faces glancing up from their phones or laptops with low hums of chatter. She murmured her apologies and found a seat at the farthest end of the table – which was, thankfully, next to Tom.

'Hey,' she said to Tom and sat, grabbing her laptop from her bag.

'Hey, you,' Tom whispered, as the hum of voices grew louder. 'What's going on? You're never late to these.'

'You don't want to know,' Chloe whispered back as she opened her laptop.

'Well, good morning, everyone,' Jeff began, as others in the room hushed those still talking. 'Now that we're all here, perhaps we can begin?' he said, with a sideways glance at Chloe.

Chloe looked at the blank screen before her.

'You got the side-eye,' Tom murmured. 'Must be bad.'

'Something you'd like to share?' Jeff asked.

Tom raised his hands. 'No, not at all. Just making sure Chloe is all right.'

'Well, quite,' Jeff said, having the decency to soften his expression. 'Is everything okay, Chloe?'

With heat flushing her cheeks, Chloe wanted the ground to swallow her whole. 'Yes, everything is fine. Sorry for being so late.'

Jeff nodded and wasted no more time launching into his company update, and Chloe knew this meeting was going to be a long one. She tried to set her expression to 'interested and engaged'. Her phone buzzed in her bag, and her mood instantly dropped. She knew who it would be. The answerphone would have to continue to take it today. Another buzz and then another. Her palms became clammy, and the air within the room was suddenly oppressive. The phone buzzed again, and Chloe reached into her bag to switch it off. She couldn't risk Jeff's displeasure if she disrupted the meeting any further.

She breathed, focusing on long, calming inhalations, in and out through her nose, as she listened to Jeff discuss in length the key risk and performance indicators and the monthly compliance report.

She had just managed to pull her focus back to the meeting when, through the glass walls of the office, she saw Penny approach, her notepad in hand. The quiet *tap, tap, tap* against the door halted Jeff, to which he did little to hide his eye-rolling frustration.

'Come in.'

Penny poked her head into the room. 'Sorry, everyone, I don't mean to interrupt. I have a situation that needs attention. I just need to borrow Chloe for a moment.'

Chloe stood, leaving the room and closing the door behind her.

'Penny, I'm having a nightmare. Jeff will be wanting my blood in a minute. What's up?'

'Well, things might get a little harder. Danny has just spammed the reception phone lines because you're not picking up your mobile. They're getting pissed off and have asked me to come and let you know. Sorry.'

Chloe held her hand to her forehead. 'Great. He's not getting the message.'

'I guess not, but I think you're going to need to deal with it before the big chiefs are informed.'

Chloe nodded. 'Yeah, I suppose I will. Unless you want to do it for me?'

Penny scrunched up her nose. 'No, I think I might leave

this one to you. He's certainly a persistent little fucker, so maybe I'll keep out of it.'

'Fair point,' Chloe agreed. 'Can't blame you for that.'

Telling Penny to wait, she turned the handle of the door and walked back into the meeting as quietly and unobtrusively as possible, mouthing her apologies to the people in the room.

Tom never took his eyes off her, his concern evident.

She sat and tried to catch Jeff's attention, as she closed her laptop and tucked it into her bag.

'Okay?' Tom mouthed.

She hadn't managed any more than a nod when Jeff turned to her.

'Is there a problem, Chloe?'

'Sorry,' she said. 'I have a situation I'm going to have to deal with.'

'Will it not wait?'

She shook her head. 'No, sorry, it won't.'

'Right, then,' Jeff said, with an irritated sigh. 'This is probably a good place to end this today. Thanks, everyone.'

Chloe stood as the others began to pack up their laptops, then she shuffled her way out to rejoin Penny.

'Chloe,' Tom called from the corridor, as the others piled out behind him and made their way back to their desks.

She turned. 'I can't talk now, Tom. I'll come and find you in a bit.'

'Do you need my help?'

'No, this delight is for me, I'm afraid. But I appreciate the offer.'

Penny rushed alongside Chloe as she hurried towards the lift bank. Wherever he was, it would take longer than ten minutes to get to the office, so he shouldn't show up just yet. Unless he was already outside. Waiting. The thought sickened her.

'Why do I have the feeling you're about to tell me something else I don't want to hear?' Chloe said when she spotted the apprehension on Penny's face.

'You may be right,' Penny said. She swiped at her phone and held it for Chloe to see.

A grainy, low-light picture came up on the screen of what looked to be a couple in bed. Chloe squinted to get a closer look. Danny laid bare-chested on his back, exposing his heavily tattooed torso, the bedsheet covering his lower half. But worse – so much worse – was someone who looked just like her next to him, tucked under his arm and covered with the same sheets, likely naked underneath, from the tone of the shot. Fast asleep, her head resting on his chest, her hand on his stomach. Her face was obscured – her hair tumbling over most of her features, but the colour and length were a good match to Chloe's. He wore a sleepy, satisfied smile as he held the phone up to snap the picture.

She recoiled, horrified at exactly how this looked.

Penny hit the button for the lift and directed her gaze back to Chloe. 'So, who's been a naughty girl, then?'

Chloe pointed at the phone. 'But that's not me.'

'Sure, of course it isn't,' Penny said sarcastically. 'Come on, Chloe, it doesn't matter. But I understand why he's keen. Probably wants more.'

'How did you get this?'

'Danny tagged us in.' Penny scrunched her face when she saw Chloe's pained expression, suddenly understanding the photo had not had the intended reaction. 'Don't get mad. Just hear me out.'

'Start talking,' Chloe ordered, as they both stepped into the lift.

'Well, what with all the drama with you and Danny, we couldn't decide if this was some dead-end thing, or if you two would suddenly become enemies-to-lovers. So...we stalked him and kind of friend-requested him.'

Chloe slowly and deliberately folded her arms as though she were a mother admonishing her child. 'Who's "we"?'

Uncomfortable now, Penny twisted the phone in her hands. 'A few of us in the department.'

'What?' Chloe blurted out. 'So everyone here has seen this?'

'I didn't think it was a big deal. I thought it might be the start of something for you and wanted to be part of it.'

'Really?' Chloe said forcefully. 'I've been telling you there's nothing going on. You should have left it at that.'

'I'm sorry, I didn't think. It was just a bit of harmless fun. I didn't think he'd be the type to go and spam the office.'

The doors to the lift opened, and they walked towards the reception area.

'Penny, do you even realise why he's doing it?'

'Because he's keen?'

'No! Because this is punishment for not taking his calls, for ignoring him. He wanted to get my attention somehow.'

'No,' Penny said in disbelief. 'No one would act like that, surely.'

'I just need this to go away before Jeff gets wind of it.'

Penny smiled. 'Honey, even with my social media clout, I'm not sure I can influence what people look at here.'

Chloe stood at the turnstiles. 'Do your best. I'm going to deal with this and then hide at my desk for the rest of the day. Please, please, please don't let this escalate.'

'On it, boss,' Penny said. 'I'll catch you later?'

Penny strode away, leaving Chloe to deal with this mess alone. She went to the desk and made all the apologies she could, and listened patiently while the team offloaded their frustration and anger at having to deal with Danny's bombardment of their precious phone system.

When she had made all the apologies she could, plus baseless guarantees it wouldn't happen again, she made her way back to her office. Deciding on the stairwell over the lift, she pulled her phone out of her pocket and listened to the multitude of voicemails he'd left her. The first few were happy enquiries, the next having a tone of concern at being ignored. The rest were angry, threatening calls, demanding to be heard and for Chloe to call him back immediately or there would be consequences. Working her way up the snaking stairwell and with a sigh, she hit the number and waited for the ring tone.

When Danny picked up, there was an audible huff of relief. 'Chloe! Finally.'

'What the hell are you doing, calling my office like that?'

'I was simply trying to get through to you. I don't know what you're playing at, but you seemed intent on ignoring me. I don't like that; I really don't. You should know that about me.'

'What are you talking about?'

'If we're going to be together, then I have certain expectations. I don't think that's unreasonable.'

'We're not together!'

'Chloe, we both know that's not true. I don't know why you keep insisting on denying what's going on here.'

'I'm not denying anything,' she snapped, through gritted teeth. 'I don't want to see you again and I want you to take the post down. Today.'

A low chuckle rumbled down the phone. 'Oh, so you found out about that. Your work colleagues are too curious, and you care too much about what people think. You're going to need to work on that.'

'Take it down,' she repeated. 'Unfriend all my colleagues and stop bothering me at work.'

'Chloe, I can tell you're angry, so I'll let you have this little outburst, but you need to remember who you're talking to.'

'Oh, I know exactly who I'm talking to and I want it to stop.'

He sighed. 'Well, that's not going to happen. What we have is too special.'

'Don't make me tell you again.'

'And you're special, too, but you're fragile, alone. You need protecting.'

'From what exactly?'

'The world,' he said. 'It's a dangerous place. You need someone to take care of you. Take the other night, for example. How lucky was it that I was there when those louts decided to heckle you?'

The atmosphere changed, a new mood, dark and claustrophobic. She felt the need to inhale, to get air into her lungs. 'That's ridiculous.'

'Is it, Chloe? I think it's fate that's brought us together. I know I can take care of you.'

'I'm quite capable of taking care of myself. I don't need anyone to look out for me. Least of all you. Do you want me to prove it?'

'You think you don't need anyone, my love, but you deserve someone. You need to be loved,' he replied calmly. 'Not how you were treated before. I'd never let you slip through my fingers.'

'What the hell are you talking about?' she spat, as she burst through the doors that would take her into the corridor adjacent to her office.

'It was written all over your face the other night. You've been hurt badly, and you're all alone now. It doesn't take a genius to see why.'

'That's enough!' she snapped, her voice high. Remembering where she was, she glanced around, aware of how inappropriate it was to be having this conversation at work. She lowered her head and her voice. 'You know nothing about my life and what's happened to me.'

'Then we need to take the time to get to know each other.'

She sighed. 'Danny—'

'Look, how about I call you later and we can discuss this properly. You're just nervous.'

'No, Danny, I just want—'

'You can't deny our chemistry is off the charts.'

She could deny it. There was no chemistry for her, none at all, just a silent loathing. Yes, she felt that, deeply. 'Danny, do not contact me any more, and don't post questionable pictures on Facebook that aren't true. I don't want to get heavy about you intentionally damaging my reputation, but I will go to the police. Are we clear?' she demanded.

He didn't reply, but unmoved, she hung up.

Back within the noise of her office, Chloe strode to her desk, eyes down, avoiding the looks from everyone as her cheeks burned.

As she drew near, the sight of Jeff waiting at her desk caused a nauseating swell of anxiety she tried hard to quash. *What now?*

'Hi, Chloe,' Jeff said with a tight smile as she approached. 'My office, now?'

'Yes, of course,' she said, and followed him.

They both remained silent as they crossed the office. Chloe ran through all the scenarios in her mind to help absolve her of her earlier actions.

Jeff opened the door to his office and held it for her. 'I wanted a quick chat,' he said, gesturing for her to sit on the chair in front of his desk.

His office was a modern space, the walls in muted neutral colours but sparse of any personal touches. A white melamine desk sat in its centre with his laptop, a couple of pens, and a photo of himself, his wife, and his two teenage sons in a sunny holiday location. Jeff was one of the lucky few who managed to flip his hours between the office and home, so everything he needed to do his job was portable, carried in the brown leather laptop bag that lay on the carpeted floor against a leg of the desk.

Chloe couldn't help but gaze at the snapshot into his personal life, at the family looking relaxed and happy in the photo – his sons, tall, with dark hair and brown eyes – mini versions of himself, before the receding hairline had kicked in, wrinkles had lined his face, and years of food and drink had created a significant paunch. It was a nice photo. His wife's kind eyes smiled at the camera and her hands rested over her boys' shoulders. Quality family time, the potential for which Chloe felt sure had been erased from her future. She tore her eyes away and opened her notebook.

'This morning was a surprise,' Jeff said. 'You're never late to our meetings, and I've just spoken to the reception supervisor. They've had to field several personal calls to you. From a chap named Danny, was it?'

She thought she'd done enough damage limitation that the incident would not find its way up here. 'I'm so sorry,' she said, glancing down to hide the heat still burning her cheeks. 'I thought I'd dealt with it. I hadn't realised you knew.'

'Who is he?'

'Nobody, really. I met him the other night.'

'So, you're seeing him?'

'No, not at all,' she replied without hesitation, mortified that she had to have this conversation with her boss. 'I had no idea he'd do what he did. I'm so embarrassed, obviously.'

'Well, it's none of my business, but they can't be expected to have to deal with the phone lines being jammed by one person.'

She nodded. 'Again, I'm so sorry.'

He leaned forward against the desk. 'But everything is okay?'

She shrugged. 'It's got out of hand very quickly. He is a little enthusiastic. Well, after this morning's episode, more like demanding.'

'Chloe, if you're in trouble—'

'No, no, I'm fine,' she replied, with a tight smile. 'Honestly. It's tricky, but I've got a handle on it.'

'Are you sure?'

'Absolutely.'

He pulled out a file from his drawer and a notebook of his own. 'Good, because I'm happy to see you're on track with your Associate training. I think the next round of promotions will see success for you, if there are no distractions.'

Chloe nodded. 'I understand. And really, there is nothing to be concerned about. I've worked hard for this. I would be mad to allow anything to jeopardise it.'

He tapped his pencil on the table. 'You just need to keep your focus. I've noticed that slip recently, too. I realise the recent months have been hard for you. You've been under a lot of pressure. I understand that.'

The implication plunged ice into her heart. Another reminder that David was no longer part of her life. She swallowed back the pain. 'I'm fine. I'll admit that life has been an adjustment recently, but I'm getting there. My job is keeping me grounded.'

'Yes, I can't imagine how difficult it's been. I'm glad we've been a support for you.'

She looked at his family photo again. Of course he couldn't imagine it. He had the perfect little family set-up there. How could he possibly know?

'But let's not lose focus now,' he continued. 'To derail from your goal would be a mistake I wouldn't want to see.'

Worry nudged her conscience. Had he caught the office

gossip? The Facebook post? Was she going to have to have words with Penny? 'Absolutely not. I am completely focused. I'm ready.'

'Good. And my door's always open, Chloe. If you need anything, I'm always here.' He laughed a little. 'Well, I can be. The office is only an hour's drive, if I'm ever at home.'

'Thank you. I appreciate that.' She kept her voice level and steady, hiding all the turmoil she felt inside. *Keep it hidden,* a voice in her mind spoke. *You're doing the right thing.*

She left his office with a ten-point plan for her upcoming assessment, together with another report she needed to complete and submit.

8

Looking out of her window at the darkening sky, tinged with orange from the streetlamps below, Chloe decided this disaster of a day was done with and packed up her desk. The muscles in her shoulders were now pulled so tight she ached from the tension. Tied to her desk all afternoon, it seemed everyone had wanted the gossip, and she had started to lose her sense of humour when people began to congregate by her workstation.

When she had finally been left alone, she had managed to plough through the endless emails, figure checking and report setting, on top of fielding the unrelenting calls from Danny on her mobile. She diligently listened to each message to check his mood, so she could intervene if necessary to prevent him from spamming the office again. Or worse still, appearing in person instead. But there had been no threat to speak of in the calls, only declarations of affection.

She pushed open the heavy glass door, nodding to passing colleagues and returning a wave from Jim, standing outside his security office. Walking out into the street, she felt the grasp of a hand on her arm and plunged into a sudden panic. She snapped her head around, dreading the sight of Danny's face. But instead, a woman stood there, petite and slim, the hood of her black padded coat pulled over her head.

'Chloe Stark?'

'Who wants to know?' Chloe stammered, her heart beginning to race.

'It doesn't matter who I am,' the woman said, as the breeze pulled wisps of dark hair from underneath her hood. 'But that man you're seeing, you need to stay away from him, do you understand?'

Chloe swallowed. Who was this woman with heavy-lidded eyes and gaunt, pallid cheeks? How did she know about Danny? The thoughts circling Chloe's mind increased the pace of her heart. 'I don't know what you're talking about.'

'I think you do,' the woman replied.

She looked exhausted, broken somehow. And was it fear Chloe saw in her eyes, or fury?

'Look, I don't know what you think you're doing, but I don't want any trouble. Please take your hand off my arm.'

'I mean it,' the woman continued, her fingers digging into Chloe's coat. 'Stay away from him.'

Although initially caught off guard by this strange woman, Chloe soon felt the snap of irritation. 'Don't threaten me.'

Another employee walked out of the building, briefly distracting the hooded woman as he glanced over at their altercation. 'Everything okay?' he asked, as he slowed his stride.

The woman checked over her shoulder before quickly returning her gaze to Chloe. 'Just do as I say.' The stranger released her grip and hurried away, disappearing from sight as she rounded the side of the building.

'Everything is fine, thanks,' Chloe said to the man with a smile.

He smiled too, nodded, and went on his way.

Flustered, but more than a little curious, Chloe hurried to pursue the woman and followed in her direction. She rounded the corner, but the woman was already gone. Chloe walked the length of the building and back again, lingering for a moment and doing a full 360 to see if she could spot her, but it was quiet. Not a soul around. 'What the hell,' she murmured, running a hand through her hair. After a moment, she abandoned the plan and rerouted towards the station.

The train journey home was crowded and unpleasant. The heating had been ramped up to the max and, combined with bodies jammed together in thick winter coats, it made the air unnaturally hot, even for a cold February night. Struggling to breathe, she had to concentrate hard on calming the panic forming within her as people packed in tighter to allow for new passengers to board at each stop. When the train finally arrived at her station, she abandoned all manners and shoved her way to the door, grateful for the cold air. She drew in large, restorative breaths as she joined the wave of commuters leaving the station, and her mind returned to the earlier incident.

Who was that woman, and what could she possibly gain by accosting her like that? Chloe struggled to comprehend. Maybe she was a jealous ex, wanting Danny for herself. Yes, that's what it could be: someone infatuated with him. Although Chloe couldn't see why. Well, she could have him, for all she cared.

The walk home was needed. The clear night was lit by the ice-white glow of a full moon in the black sky above, soothing her spirit.

She walked down the steps to her front door and fumbled for her keys. Something was off: the air was too quiet, and it set the hairs on the back of her neck on end. With a greater sense of urgency, she pushed the key into the lock, about to open the door when she felt a hand on her shoulder. She turned quickly, the moment she had dreaded the most – a sudden reality, as she came face to face with Danny, standing close.

'Hi, Chloe,' he said, bending slightly to kiss her on the cheek.

'Don't,' she said, backing away, an action that wiped the smile from his face.

'Come on, surely you knew I'd want to see you after our little argument earlier?'

'You shouldn't be here,' she said, waiting for the opportunity to nudge her foot over the threshold.

'I just want to talk, Chloe,' he pleaded. 'I realise things got a little heated, but we can sort it out.'

'There's nothing to say.'

'You don't mean that,' he said.

'I do, and if you don't leave I'll have no choice but to call the police.'

'That would be a mistake.' He moved closer, the white mist of his breath curling in the night air.

'You know you're crossing a line, don't you?' she asked defiantly, looking up at him. 'You know this is wrong.'

'I know what I want, Chloe. Simple as that.'

She felt his hand grasp her arm and then move down to capture her wrist. She resisted, tried to free herself from his grasp. 'Danny, stop.'

He tugged her close, his lips pulled tight as his anger dissipated into a chilling calm. 'Chloe, Chloe, Chloe. You need to understand there's no fighting this. Fate made us cross paths. We're meant to be together.' With his grip still firm on her wrist, his gaze drilled into hers. 'Now, are you going to let me inside, or are you going to make me wait?'

The intonation of his voice ensured she picked up the

double meaning instantly. She tried to inch out of his grasp. 'Danny, let me go.'

He didn't. Instead, he lowered his lips to hers, his kiss firm. Territorial.

Anger and disgust jolted her into action, pushing him away. 'Leave me alone!'

She used the space between them to jump through the door and slam it firm in his face.

'It's okay, Chloe, I know you're nervous,' he called from the other side. 'Especially with what you've been through. I can wait. I can be as patient as you need me to be. Don't you see? I will always be here for you. Always.'

She glanced through the obscured glass to see Danny's form standing there, unmoving.

Backing away, the silence ringing in her ears, it was only when his silhouette faded from the doorway that she began to breathe again.

In the darkness, she peeked through the living room curtain and watched him walk away. She hurried to close every blind and curtain, and fill each room with light. But it wasn't enough. She needed further security. She locked herself in the bathroom and sat on the floor, pulling her knees up to her chest as she listened to the silence for any hint of noise that might indicate his return.

After twenty minutes of sitting against the hardwood floor, her back beginning to ache, Chloe unlocked the door. If he had returned, he would have made his presence known by now. She went into her bedroom. Her heart rate had settled, but the confrontation had left her drained. She changed out of her work clothes and into her pyjamas, hoping it would help her relax. It didn't. Still listening for anything out of the ordinary, she went to the kitchen and checked the back door again, wanting to be sure it was locked. She had to calm her mind. She focused on dinner and stared at the contents of the fridge, but every sound outside, a car or passer-by, the faintest creak in the flat, put her on edge.

Unable to decide, she grabbed a yoghurt and some strawberries and took a granary roll from the bread bin. She sat at the kitchen table and picked at the food as she pulled up her mum's number on her phone. No answer. She considered calling Laura instead, but it was her night with Sam; she didn't want to interrupt.

Then her phone beeped, making her flinch and causing the bread roll to slip from her grasp. She swiped at the screen.

I'm sorry. D x

Discarding her phone, and him, she let out a shrill cry when the dull crack of a toppled terracotta plant pot outside sprung her from her seat. She edged to her living-room window that backed onto the garden and moved the curtain just enough to peep outside. There was nothing to see, just the garden table and chairs still stacked up for the winter, and wilted plants in a collection of pots on the small patio outside her front door.

She let the curtain fall back into place and stood listening for any other sound, and when there was nothing, she went back into the kitchen and grabbed her phone, clutching it tight, ready to call the police if needed.

Needing noise to drown out the silence, she switched on the TV and selected the early evening news. She just needed the noise – white noise – and she considered the way people drift off to sleep to the sound of a hoover running or a spinning washing machine, or some other mechanical appliance. Something to listen to; something to drown out the loneliness amidst the quiet. There were even apps to download solely for that purpose. Maybe that's what she needed – something to help drown out the fear.

She filled a large glass with water and headed to the bedroom, deciding that, tonight, she'd leave all the lights on. It was somehow more reassuring to banish any shadows or any places to hide.

She switched on the TV in the bedroom, too. A mindless gameshow played and she focused on the questions in a bid to distract herself. She settled on the bed, but couldn't bring herself to get under the covers. She didn't feel safe enough to relax that much. Instead, she arranged her pillows against the headboard and rested against them, staring aimlessly at the TV until she could no longer battle the heaviness in her eyelids

Stomach empty after being denied a proper meal, and mentally exhausted, she slipped away into sleep.

BRIGHT MORNING LIGHT shone through the curtains in Chloe's room, pulling her from sleep. She knew immediately she'd overslept because her current weekday morning routine was usually shrouded in winter darkness. The sound of a drill overhead marked the beginning of the renovations her friendly neighbour had warned her about. With an eye-roll and a groan, she pulled back the duvet. She'd fallen asleep on top of the covers rather than underneath them, but she supposed there was nothing strange about that. She could have easily moved into a more comfortable position in her sleep, and she'd certainly been so exhausted and her brain so fried she could have done anything and not fully remembered it.

She climbed out of bed, almost treading on her phone, which lay on the floor, and wandered to the bathroom, aching, her shoulders still tight. She rolled her shoulders and stretched out her arms to loosen them as best she could before stepping into the shower.

Trying to muster up some motivation for the day ahead, she made tea and chucked some cereal in a bowl, listening to the music from the builders' radio blaring from upstairs, mingled with banging footsteps and the muffled sounds of laughter. She wanted to find it soothing, especially with Danny prone to lurking nearby, but she found it irritating that they were spoiling the only peace she was likely to have today. Only managing a few mouthfuls of her breakfast, she discarded her mug and bowl in the sink and checked her phone. No more messages from Danny allowed her the hope she would need to be okay to leave the safety of her home.

Pulling on her coat, she noticed the collection of letters lying on the doormat. She hadn't seen them yesterday when she was trying to rid herself of Danny, but the outline of her footprints blotted over the top layer of envelopes confirmed what she'd done. She flicked through the junk mailouts, ready to chuck them, when she spotted the postcard poking out from in between. The photo of white buildings against azure blue skies and clear seas was unmistakeably Grecian. She flipped it and read. Greetings from her in-laws, sharing details of their holiday and asking if she was well. Another reminder of David's absence from her life. She tossed it down on the table by the front door, not wanting it but knowing she would be unable to throw it away.

Not that she had anything against her mother and father-in-law. They had always been kind to her and had welcomed her into the family as if she was one of their own. And that was not to be taken for granted. Chloe knew from experience how mothers of boys could be tricky to handle, and sometimes their unreasonably high expectations of what a girlfriend should be to their dear little princes could be difficult to navigate, to say the least. Damned if you do and damned if you don't. But it hadn't been like that with David's parents.

It had been a lovely summer evening barbecue when she'd met everyone; a family event, everyone from aunts, uncles, and cousins to David's friends. It could have been a baptism of fire, but it wasn't. It had been perfect. From the colourful array of summer flowers housed in beds and pots that swayed in the pleasant warm breeze, to the hazy evening sun that cast shades of orange and red over everything it touched. The clinking of glasses, the popping of corks, laughter, food sizzling on the barbecue. She'd laughed at funny teen anecdotes, listened to the obligatory baby stories, was ushered away by David and his friends for some questionable university stories and drunken mishaps shared out of earshot of the family. And all the while, David was at her side, attentive, an arm slung around her shoulder and the other clutching a beer. From the moment she had arrived, she felt welcomed. The fact she and David had no siblings was another connection. An understanding only present due to their shared experiences growing up as only children.

But their close relationship soon waned when David left. Of course it would. She understood, and never blamed them. It was just too difficult for them to reconcile what had happened, feeling caught in the middle. Chloe also considered perhaps she, too, was a reminder of what could have been. Because it was like that for her, too. Seeing them and knowing what could never be ... it was painful.

So it had come to this; written correspondence in the form of holiday postcards, birthday wishes, and Christmas cards, so as not to lose contact completely. But they would never have to face any awkward meetings in person where everyone struggled to fill the silence with facile conversation.

It was for the best. For all of them.

9

The sight of Jeff waiting at her desk when she arrived in the office pulled a sigh from her mouth, and she shook off her coat, not in the mood for one of their chats, or for him to query why she was late. He'd taken it upon himself to monitor her in the aftermath of her marriage breakdown, and now it seemed he was doing the same after the incident with Danny. It was exhausting, as though he were on some sort of box-ticking exercise rather than actually caring.

She kept her tone light. 'Morning, Jeff. Everything okay?'

'Morning, Chloe. Was the train running late?' he said, glancing at his watch.

'A little,' she said. 'I'll make it up by taking a shorter lunch.'

'That would be appreciated,' he said. 'And I assume there's been no more incidents with that man?'

'No, nothing.'

It wouldn't help for him to know the truth, not if she was going to get the promotion.

'I'm glad to hear it.'

'I'm just going to grab a coffee and then I'll get stuck in. Is there anything I can help you with?' She tossed her coat over the back of the chair.

'Yes, unfortunately, there's just one thing,' he said. 'The report you gave me was not up to your usual level of accuracy. I know you've been under a lot of stress, Chloe, but...'

She couldn't help but blink back her surprise and, at the same time, notice Tom looking in her direction. 'What was wrong with the report? I checked it and checked again. It should be fine.'

'You're missing the whole Europe division, Chloe. It affects everything.'

Her stomach sank, and heat flushed her cheeks at her mistake. This had only happened once before, in the early days when she was still learning the ropes. 'I'm sorry,' she stammered. 'I thought I'd checked it thoroughly.'

Jeff's expression softened. 'It's okay, Chloe. There's time to crunch the numbers again, but only because I looked it over before handing it to the senior management team. If they'd got wind of it, you know they would not be impressed. They hold very high standards, and rightly so.'

'Yes, absolutely,' she said, now mortified. 'I'm so sorry. I don't know how I missed it.' Realising he'd been holding the report by his side, she reached out her hand to take it.

'It was a surprise, that's all,' he said, handing it to her. 'You're normally the one I count on for accuracy.'

She sighed. 'It won't happen again.'

Just then, Tom strode over, catching Jeff's eye. 'Jeff, I couldn't help overhearing, but I might have to take the bullet with this one. I was late giving Chloe the numbers. My bad.'

Jeff looked at her. 'Is this right, Chloe?'

Temporarily dumbfounded, she struggled to form the words in her mouth. Tom had done no such thing.

'She didn't want to land me in trouble,' he continued.

Jeff was silent, likely assessing if this little show of fiction was to be believed, and Chloe was suddenly a child again, hiding some trivial playground incident from her teachers.

'Well, okay,' he murmured. 'But I'm going to have to ask you both to make sure this report is done by the end of today.'

'You'll have it in your inbox by five o'clock,' Tom confirmed.

Satisfied, Jeff nodded and walked away, shutting himself in his office.

Re-running this report would eat into her already busy day. It would be a long one. At least she didn't have the burden of having to call a significant other to explain that she'd be late home. But the thought still made her sad.

She looked at Tom. 'Why did you do that?'

'I just saw how mortified you were. I know you're under pressure at the moment, and I wanted to help.'

She conceded a smile. 'That's really sweet of you, but I don't need saving.'

'I just wanted to help you out, Miss Independent,' he said, nudging her arm with his. 'I know you're up for promotion and a mistake like this could make a difference.'

He leaned against her desk and she suddenly felt drawn to him for a moment, her mind toying with the possibility that perhaps he could be the one to take all the pain away. As quickly as it came, she discarded the thought. No one could do that, only herself. She needed to focus and remain on track.

She smiled at him again. 'You're a good friend, and I'm grateful that you're looking out for me. But whether I get this promotion or not, it'll be my doing, okay?'

He nodded, silent for a moment. 'Friend, eh? Well, I'll take that.' He smiled. 'I'm going to grab my stuff and some breakfast – you look like you need something to eat – and then I'll join you to tackle this report. Two heads are always better than one on these things. Anything you fancy?' He raised a brow in a way that made her lip curl with amusement.

'So much I could say,' she replied, tossing the report onto the desk. 'But I guess as far as food is concerned, I need something healthy. My diet has resembled that of a university student in recent weeks.'

'No problem,' he said.

'And in the absence of vodka, I could really use a coffee.'

'All right. I'll be fifteen, max.'

His expression was warm, sincere, and she thought about how she would prefer to have an afternoon to just sit and talk with him, figure out all her problems together. Instead, she would have to settle for a collaboration at work.

She sat and reached for her phone. A string of calls had gone unnoticed after she'd switched it to silent when she first arrived. Seventeen missed calls and ten texts. Feeling a deep sense of dread, she opened the first text.

> Chloe, I understand you don't want to talk to me this morning and I'll let it pass, even though I hate it when we fight. I wanted to be there when you arrived at work today, but security wouldn't let me in. Unacceptable, really. I'll be in touch. All my love, (I love saying that to you). D x

The other messages were much the same. She hit the screen and began to punch out a text.

> Danny, I don't want to talk, and you can't come here. Please leave me alone.

Hitting send, she took a breath. A text pinged back immediately.

> No, Chloe, that's simply not possible. You're tired and stressed. You need me to help you with that.

And then another immediately followed:

> Please understand that I know you better than you know yourself. Our connection is deep. I'll never leave you. Not now that I've met you. We belong together.

She tossed the phone across her desk and held her head in her hands. 'What the hell have I done?'

'Cinnamon Twist was all I could get,' came Tom's voice, bringing Chloe back.

She looked up to see him walking towards her with two snacks wrapped in white paper and a cardboard tray holding two corporate branded coffee cups.

'Fine by me,' she murmured, as she cleared some space on her desk. 'Who eats healthily for breakfast anyway?'

'You need to tell me what's up, too. No bullshit either, okay?' he said as he pulled up a seat from the empty desk behind hers and sat.

'I'm fine.'

'I saw you hunched over your phone just now, and I'm going to take a guess as to why. So give me the details.' He handed her a pastry and laid his own on the desk, pulling a cup from the tray.

'Things are getting tricky with this guy,' she said, helping herself to the other coffee cup. 'But it's under control.'

'Is it?' he asked, unconvinced. 'You sure about that?'

Her phone screen lit up in the silence that followed. Another couple of messages only confirmed just how serious this was.

'Is that him?'

She checked her phone and nodded.

'Fuck's sake, Chloe. This is so far from normal and healthy.'

She nodded and let out a long sigh. 'Yes, I know,' she said. His opinion of her mattered, even though she was strangely embarrassed at having to share this with Tom. Or was it shame?

'So what are your options?' he asked, before taking a bite of his twist.

'Not sure right now.'

'If you don't mind me saying, I think it might be time to consider the police.'

'Yeah, thanks, Sherlock,' she said with a smile. 'I came to that conclusion myself.'

He laughed and held up his hand. 'Okay, okay. Stating the bleeding obvious. My bad.'

'But it seems a bit extreme,' she said. 'I mean, is it really necessary? Feels like I'd be wasting their time. I got myself into this mess, after all, I should get myself out of it. Besides, I know nothing about him except that he lives here in London, and he's a photographer.'

'Then leave that to the police. They'll find him. After everything you've been through, you don't have to deal with a loser like him, too. You need him out of your life. Take screen-shots of the texts he sends. Give them to the police and let them deal with it. Someone spineless like him, who likes to threaten women, will back right off after a visit from the boys in blue.'

'Yeah, I think you're right. Spineless,' she agreed. 'But I don't think he'll give up that easily.'

'You've got good security at home, haven't you?'

'Well, just what anyone else would have: keychain, dead-bolts. The usual. I never really bothered before, but I've started using them.'

'Glad to hear it.' He used his finger to mop up the crumbs of the cinnamon twist that had flaked and fallen onto the wrapping. 'You need to keep yourself safe.'

'I am safe.'

'Then you need to tell yourself that, too, because you sound like you believe it as much as I do.' He reached across the table and placed his hand on her arm. 'Chloe, you're funny, strong, independent, and totally lovely, but you need to take care of yourself because someone like him is a real threat. He's dangerous.'

'Lovely, eh?' she said, touched.

'Yeah, lovely,' he said without hesitation. 'And because of that, I worry about you. You need to make sure you don't put yourself in a dangerous situation. With him, or anyone else for that matter.'

She smiled. 'We are way past that point. But I understand what you mean.'

'You still don't see it, do you?'

'See what?'

'Your blasé attitude. It'll get you in trouble, and you act like it doesn't matter.'

She shrugged her shoulders dismissively.

He placed his hand over hers. 'But it matters a lot, Chloe. To your parents, your friends. To me.'

She glanced into his intense eyes and felt her guard come tumbling down. In that instant, she wanted to share everything with him – how alone she felt, the hurt, the emptiness. 'No one has spoken to me like that for a long time.'

'Like what?' he asked.

'Like they care. I mean, really care. My friends are amazing, of course. My parents, too. But it's not the same.'

'Well, it seems I do care. A lot,' he said. 'I always thought David was a fool. He let the best thing that ever happened to him slip through his fingers.'

His gaze lingered, and she lowered hers. 'I thought he'd come back to me. Get it out of his system and return. But there's no chance of that now.'

'Would you really have wanted that?' he asked. 'After how he hurt you?'

'No, I don't think so, but I feel so lost now. Adrift. I knew what my life was before, and now everything has changed.'

'You're doing an amazing job of getting your life back together.'

She snorted a laugh. 'Hardly.'

'You are,' he replied. 'It may not feel like it now, but the police will help.'

She shook her head. 'No, it's not just that,' she said, not wanting to look him in the eye but ready to confess. 'I may have got myself into a bit of trouble.'

He moved closer, concerned. 'What is it? From the look on your face right now, you look like you've got the weight of the world on those shoulders.'

She hesitated, not sure where to begin.

He smiled. 'You know you can trust me, right?'

She nodded. 'Well, it's just—'

'This looks nice and cosy,' Penny interrupted, as she approached the desk.

Startled, Chloe spun her head around. She'd not heard or noticed Penny's arrival. Perhaps that was her aim.

Chloe sat back and cleared her throat, as Tom retracted his hand from hers. 'What's up, Pen?'

'This is nice,' Penny said, watching the pair of them. 'This looks good.'

'Okay, Pen. Chill out,' Chloe said. 'We're just having a chat, that's all.'

'Right,' Penny said disbelievingly.

Chloe smiled. 'But we've got a report to finish, so unless there's nothing you need we'd better crack on with it.'

Penny's smile was knowing. 'Of course,' she said. 'I'll leave you two to finish your "chat" and get to it. The report, I mean.' With a raised eyebrow, Penny departed as quickly as she'd arrived.

'We'll be office gossip for the next couple of weeks, guaranteed,' Chloe said as they both laughed.

'Couldn't wish to be gossiped about with anyone but you, Chlo,' he replied.

'Charmer.'

'What were you going to say?' he asked, taking them back to their conversation.

'Oh, that. No, it's nothing. I'm just a bit stressed.'

'You sure?'

She nodded. 'Yes, absolutely.'

'Well, you can call on me anytime if you need anything.'

She looked at him and smiled gratefully. 'I know, but I'm sure you don't want to get involved in all my drama.'

'Of course I do, Chloe. I meant what I said earlier.' He drank his coffee, but his eyes remained on hers over the rim of the cup.

Her face flushed.

There was no doubting their friendship, but the way he spoke to her, the words he used, confirmed what she'd always felt – there was something more between them, a spark, an unspoken attraction that went beyond the boundaries of friendship. But her marriage to David, plus Tom's periodic relationships, meant it had always remained unsaid. He had a confident, easy charm that made him likeable and fun to be around. That, in turn, made him very popular. He was very pleasant in the looks department, too. In another world, they might have been a match, but even as a friend she relied on him and valued his opinion more than anyone else she worked with. She needed all the friends she could get right now, that was what mattered, and if he was offering his support, she'd take it. She'd grab any offer of help, like a branch held out to a drowning man.

He watched, smiled. 'Seriously, Chloe. Anytime.'

She glanced over at the clock. 'I'll investigate my options later, but I'd better get to work if I'm going to fix this report.'

He wiped his hands with a serviette. 'I'm here for you. I cleared my diary to help, so let's get on with it.'

The rest of her day was tied up with correcting the report, fending off her clients, and working with Tom. When she felt like she'd taken up enough of his time, she released him from his self-imposed obligation, which he reluctantly accepted and returned to his desk. With the amended report pinged over to Jeff, she thought of home and the scant food supplies in her cupboards. She should organise a delivery later. Restock. She was no Nigella, David always the cook, and right now she longed for one of his lasagnes or curries. The way the fragranced spices permeated each room of the flat with the aromas of the feast to come. When she could no longer bear the memories of her past, she focused on her work, desperate to be finished for the day.

Once she was done with the last of her tasks, she looked around and realised she was alone, save for one or two other stragglers. Probably in the same boat as herself – no one waiting for them either. She packed up her desk, her eyes sore and tired from staring at the screen for most of the day.

She called out her 'goodnights' as she made her way out of the office, to the bank of lifts, through the atrium, and finally outside.

10

'Hey, Chloe,' Nina said from the sleek chrome and glass-topped reception desk. Dressed in workout gear, her dark hair tied up in a ponytail and with exquisitely applied make-up, Nina was a picture-perfect advertisement for the gym. 'Long time no see.'

It had been a while since Chloe had worked out, and her body and mind were calling out for it. The prospect of going home to an empty flat and another potential confrontation with Danny was unappealing, so, with a kit always kept in her desk drawer for impromptu moments, she'd strode the fifteen-minute walk from the office to the nearby fitness studio.

She'd always kept herself in shape. Even in the early days of her heartbreak, it had been her lifeline. A reason to get up in the morning. Focus on the burn – let the sweat wash away the hurt and despair. It was addictive, too, and the gym soon became a haven where she could forget herself within the repetition of exercise. And it had paid off, her body toned and firm.

Chloe smiled. 'I know, I know. But to be fair, Nina, it's only been a couple of weeks.'

Nina rolled her eyes playfully. 'A couple of weeks is all it takes.'

'Okay, boss. I'll get in there.'

Nina chuckled. 'I'm kidding. You look great, if a little tired.'

'You're not wrong there. I'm exhausted, but a good workout should help me sleep a little better than I have been.'

'Sorry to hear that,' Nina replied. 'Everything all right?'

Chloe sighed. 'Well, that's a question I can only answer if you have a good few hours to spare. But I'm okay, I think. Maybe I should just get in there and get to it.'

'Yep, that'll help. Exercise whatever is bothering you out of your system. Works wonders.'

'On it,' Chloe said, and made her way over to the double doors leading to the workout area. 'See you later.'

She swiped her card into the reader and entered, and was immediately met with the familiar mix of disinfectant, air freshener and sweat hanging in the air. The modern black and grey equipment lined the edges of the large warehouse-style room. Large black floor mats covered the centre for body workouts, stretching, and yoga sessions. Dance music floated from above, playing to an empty room that had accommodated the earlier daytime gym users but was yet to welcome the evening crew. Chloe wasn't sure how she felt about this; usually, when the room was busy with others working out, a group energy somehow manifested to keep her going. She crossed the floor to the changing rooms, hung her work clothes in the locker, and pulled on her leggings and top, strapping the keychain over her wrist.

She should take advantage of an empty gym and do a cardio circuit of burpees, push-ups, crunches, and squats, but it felt just a little too complex for her mood. So instead, she jumped on the treadmill and set it into action. She built the pace slowly, beginning with a walk that increased to a jog. It felt good to pound the floor, feel the sweat on her back and clear her mind of chaotic thoughts. She increased her speed and focused on her rhythm and posture. She'd left her air pods at home, but that was okay; she appreciated the peace and the space to just be. No one asking anything of her. No expectations. Free to do as she pleased. The sense of balance in her mind and the diminishing anxiety felt good.

After a quick warm-down, she headed for the lockers and showers, telling herself she'd done enough for today. She'd chosen to do something positive rather than focus on the negative, which meant she could go home content, if nothing else.

Pushing open the heavy door into reception and running food options through her mind, she noticed him immediately. Danny leaned against the counter, his back to her and his posture loose and casual, and Chloe watched him happily engaging in what looked to be a pleasant conversation. But then, he was the kind of man who could charm the birds out of the trees, if he put his mind to it. It was only the unlucky ones – the women who caught his eye for more than just friendship – who saw the real man behind the smile.

She stood for a moment and considered slinking back through the door she'd just pushed through, but it would make too much noise and would disturb them enough to expose her attempt at escape. And even if it didn't, the emergency exit in the next room would set off a series of alarms that would land her with a tidy fine. There was no other way out than to pass by Danny directly. He turned his body purposefully to face her, as if he'd known she was there all along. But, of course, he would know that, because he chose to follow her here and wait, making small talk until she appeared.

'Chloe,' he said calmly, confidently. 'What a surprise. You use this gym?'

She inhaled deeply. 'You know I do. Why else would you be here?'

Nina glanced between the pair of them, the smile fading from her lips.

'Thought I'd join up,' he said with a smile, clicking his fingers. 'Hey, we can train together. Wouldn't that be great?'

The room felt small, with her imprisoned in its four walls and trapped with him. 'I really don't want anything to do with you,' she murmured, breathing hard, as if the air had thinned. 'I don't know how much clearer I can make it.'

'Is everything okay, Chloe?' Nina asked, stepping back from Danny and the cosy little chat they'd been having over the counter.

'No, not really, but he's going to leave now, aren't you, Danny?'

His face changed, the jovial smile wiped away, replaced with a sinister mask. 'No, I'm not going anywhere, Chloe. I want to use this gym, so I'll use it.'

'Well—' Nina interrupted.

He snapped his head her way, his smile back in place, but an expression that screamed defiance. 'Now, Nina, have I broken any rules here?' he asked, his palms upturned. 'Or is Chloe part of the team and able to refuse memberships?'

'No, but—'

'Well then, I'm sure you wouldn't discriminate against me. I'm sure your seniors wouldn't take kindly to a complaint of that nature. Especially on your watch.'

'Please don't threaten me,' Nina said.

'No threat. Chloe doesn't like me for reasons unknown, but that shouldn't reflect what I can do here.'

'Are you kidding me?' Chloe exclaimed. 'You endlessly contact me, follow me to my home, to my place of work, and now here. You are harassing me.'

Nina glanced at him. 'Is that true?'

'Not at all. Chloe has a very low tolerance on this matter, but it's not harassment. Not when it's a relationship.'

'You know that's not true, Danny.' Chloe pulled her phone out of her bag. 'I will have to call the police. This cannot continue.'

Nina picked up the phone and quietly asked for security.

'Okay, there's no need for that,' Danny snapped. 'I'll leave.' He directed his gaze and all of his silent anger towards Chloe. 'Seems like you've won this one, my love. For now.'

Chloe waited for twenty minutes after Danny had left the gym before she would do the same. The night air had somehow become even colder as she trudged to the supermarket on her way home. She should have returned to the relative safety of her flat immediately but she needed groceries, otherwise she wouldn't eat tonight. The streets were quiet now, except for the odd office worker making a quick dash, just as she was, or a runner out to make those last goals of the day count. But plenty of people were milling around the supermarket, and that meant she felt reasonably safe under the bright lights above the aisles of produce.

She pushed her trolley aimlessly, tossing in supplies as needed – toiletries, pasta, bread, milk, a stack of fruit and vegetables, and far too many ready-made meals. These, together with the supply of chocolate that had found its way into the trolley, were her treats, and she happily lied to herself that the exercise she'd done would offset the calories well enough.

Rounding the corner at the end of the aisle, she noticed a figure moving swiftly from view. Suspicious, Chloe shoved her trolley forwards and marched in their direction, just losing them as they rounded another aisle. This figure was not a man, or tall enough to be Danny. It was a woman. As Chloe continued her chase into the next aisle, she caught a flash of the woman's features as she scurried away. Her small frame wrapped in a padded coat confirmed what Chloe had suspected. It was the woman who had threatened her outside her office the day before.

'Hey!' Chloe shouted, as she strode towards the woman, who turned and ran. 'Stop!'

Weaving through the aisles, Chloe lost sight of her and let out a frustrated groan when the woman seemingly disappeared, nowhere to be seen. Annoyed and not wanting to let it go, she rounded the aisles a couple more times before she conceded defeat. There was little chance of finding her out in the darkness either, so reluctantly, with one last glance around, she headed to the checkout to pay.

Tired now, and more than a little irritated, she'd been fortunate enough to go straight to a waiting member of staff and had no delays standing around in a queue, an advantage that comes with shopping later in the evening. The man at the checkout was of retirement age but worked quickly and with a friendly disposition, so much so that he also helped her pack. It was a simple gesture, but it didn't go unappreciated when all Chloe wanted to do was go home.

'St Stephen's Gardens, please,' she said to the taxi driver, as she hauled her bags onto the backseat.

As he pulled away, she noticed a flicker of movement near the exit where she'd just been standing. A moment of recognition. She snapped her head around and looked through the rear window, but there was no one there except an elderly woman pushing her trolley out into the car park.

It's okay. It wouldn't be him, she tried to convince herself. *He couldn't have followed me here, too...*

But maybe he had, and maybe he had brought his little

minion with him. She sat back and tried to relax. When that didn't work, she pulled out her phone and looked up how best to report her complaint to the police. It was time to let Danny know he didn't hold all the cards. Three options were available to her: visit a police station that would be open, which were very few at this time of night, call 101, or report online. She didn't have the inclination to visit a station or make a call, so she decided online would be best.

WITH HER PASTA meal cast aside on the sofa, Chloe scrolled the internet. She'd spent the last hour looking at charities that supported victims of stalkers and reading police articles on what to do when being harassed, staring in disbelief at the high number of incidents that occurred in this country alone. Scanning the self-help sections, she noted the advice to keep a diary of events, record every interaction for evidence, and not engage with the perpetrator. She knew she would find the last point difficult. It was impossible to ignore him when he confronted her; she just didn't work like that. She'd never hidden away from conflict, and with a nagging sense she'd brought this on herself, she felt a certain responsibility to figure out the solution, too.

She read through a couple of blogs and then immediately wished she hadn't when she learned about what abuse victims had suffered. Some women lived in the shadow of their stalkers for years, having to move and eventually change their identities to rid themselves of their pursuers. With trepidation, she told herself she wouldn't let it come to that. She was in control of this and needed to keep it moving. She could handle him, even if things got nasty. At least she hoped she could.

She ploughed on and found the website for her local

policing team and began the process of making her complaint. When she was done, she noted down her incident number and that she'd be contacted with the name and number of the officer responsible for her case, someone who would keep her informed of any developments.

When she heard a gentle knock at the door, the biting dread of knowing who it would be was almost too much to bear. Clutching her phone in her hand, she went to the door, keeping the lights in the hall switched off. 'Who is it?'

'You know who it is, Chloe,' Danny replied. 'Please open the door. I just want to talk.'

Her heart pounded in her chest. 'I want you to go away. I've made myself very clear.'

'Listen, I know I've freaked you out, today and at the gym, but I just want to put things right. Please.'

'You can start by no longer following me or sending an endless stream of texts.'

'I know, I know. I'm not handling this well at all.' The shape of his hand pressed against the glass as if reaching out to her. 'I've realised what I'm doing. I know I've alarmed you.'

'Yes, you have.'

'I'm sorry, Chloe. I know that you don't want to open the door, and I understand that, but I needed to come here to apologise. I felt another text would just look intimidating. Is that okay?' His voice was low and cracked when he spoke. 'Should I continue, or should I leave?'

She hesitated. 'Go on.'

'I get a little intense. I know that. It's been such a long time since I've found someone like you, you know? It's hard living in this world, with the constant reminder of everyone out there living their best lives when I'm so damn lonely.' He paused. 'The other night was just so nice, so easy, and I didn't want it to end. What I'm trying to say is that my loneliness made me a little crazy, I suppose, but I am sorry. Really sorry.'

She nodded. She did understand that, at least. She had been alone for almost a year, and sometimes it was so unbearable she thought she'd crumple to the floor and never get up. Her own dreams of a family had been ripped out from under her, and she'd had no voice in the decision. But she also knew she needed to remain resolute if she was ever to be happy again.

'I'm not a bad person, Chloe,' he said quietly, with some resignation. 'I just want a normal life and to be happy.' His tone was so sad, so desperate. 'Isn't that what everyone wants? I thought I might have had a chance with you, that's all.'

He was silent for a moment, except for minute noises that made her suspect he might be crying. She rolled her eyes and tutted. Anyone else would have ignored him or told him to leave, but she was not anyone else. She was someone who was on a path that offered no other route. She slowly released the catch on her door and saw him stripped bare of any arrogance or anger, only a relieved smile that she had given him this opportunity to see her again.

'Thank you, Chloe. Thank you for opening the door. I know you don't want me to come in, and I understand. I just wanted to explain.'

She sighed. 'I suppose five minutes won't hurt,' she said, and stepped back to allow him in. 'But after tonight, I don't want any more of this behaviour.'

'No, absolutely not,' he said as he crossed the threshold enthusiastically.

He followed as she walked to her sitting room and did what he was told when she gestured for him to sit.

'Please sit with me, Chloe,' he said as he shuffled along the sofa. 'I won't try anything.'

She glanced at the door and noted the small glass vase on the corner table next to the sofa, a weapon if needed, and sat on the very edge of the seat.

'Is there really no hope here, Chloe?'

She shook her head. 'You already know the answer to that.'

He nodded and for a long minute said nothing. He was so downcast, so lost, and she realised the hurt was cutting him deeply. 'But I don't want anyone else.'

She sighed. 'We can't always have what we want, and we can't force someone to feel something they don't.'

'But you can. I know you can. You just need to get to know me. Once you know me, you'll know I'm right for you.'

'I'm sorry, but I won't.'

He shook his head with a frustrated sigh. 'This is just like before.'

She studied him. 'Before?'

He nodded. 'Look, I guess I should mention there was someone else before you. Someone very important to me.' He smiled, remembering perhaps. 'I saw her, can't remember where now, some party or club, but she was with her friends, just dancing, laughing, drinking, without a care in the world.' He glanced away. Maybe still remembering, maybe feeling discomfort. 'She was so beautiful, and it was as if there was a light shining down on her just for me to see, illuminating her soul. Only I saw it, and it told me, "Here's my soulmate." I believed it – really believed it – and I knew that once she met me, she'd feel it too. That's what soulmates do, right? They find each other.'

Chloe thought about David, how she hoped it could be true. She hoped there were many soulmates for one person, if lucky enough to find them. 'How long were you with her?'

'About six months, on and off.'

'She obviously left an impression.'

'Oh yes, she did that, all right.'

Chloe nodded, remembering the Facebook posts. 'And are you still in touch with her?'

Now there was definite discomfort in his expression. A tender pain behind his eyes. 'No, not at all. She's gone now. It's over.'

'Perhaps that's for the best.'

He snapped out of his melancholy, his smile fixed in place. 'Of course it is. None of that matters now. It's clear that we couldn't have been soulmates, otherwise I wouldn't have found you. I can see that now.'

'Danny, it's not as simple as that.'

'Yes, it is,' he demanded.

She shook her head. 'I can't feel for you what you feel for me, and in a few weeks or even months you'll see it and realise this didn't matter at all. You'll be in a completely different place; I know it.'

'No, I won't,' he said with a sureness that was unnerving.

'Yes, you will. You'll look back at today and understand that I was right and that this was a mistake. I guarantee it.'

He sniffed and shrugged his shoulders. He clearly disagreed and was nothing more than a child right now. 'And now you want me to leave?'

'I think it's for the best.'

'Okay, but there's just one thing I need to ask before I do.'

She tensed and glanced at the art deco mantel clock above the fireplace. A wedding present from a distant aunt and something she loved. He'd been in the flat for five minutes. 'Go on.'

'I just need some water. Please.'

She became wary. His was a simple request but nothing was straightforward with him. 'Of course.'

She went to the kitchen, hurriedly filled a glass with water and went back to him, not wanting him alone in her room. 'Here.'

He took it from her and drank it down, placing the glass

carefully down on the coffee table in front of him when he'd finished. 'Thank you.'

She wasn't sure whether she ought to sit, so she decided to stand, to let him know this was over.

'Well, I guess I'll get out of your hair,' he said, rising to leave.

They made their way into the hallway.

'Goodbye, Danny,' she said as she opened the door.

He leaned forward to place a small kiss on her cheek but pulled back when he saw her flinch. 'See you around, Chloe.'

She locked up and hurried to the living room, feeling the need to rid her space of all traces of him. She plumped up the cushions on the sofa and took his glass to the kitchen, placing it in the sink. She returned and lit a couple of scented candles, wanting to replace his lingering aftershave, too.

11

The weekend started quietly, exactly as she wanted, and continued without any interruptions from Danny. Chloe wanted to believe that perhaps it really was over and kept herself busy by cleaning her flat until the place gleamed. With far too much nervous energy for her body to cope with, she'd pulled out furniture and cleaned behind, washed paintwork, polished ornaments, and scrubbed every scrubbable surface in her kitchen and bathroom. She needed to lose herself in something other than Danny, her feelings for Tom that refused to disappear, and the catastrophe of her life that had coiled into a knot of gut-wrenching anxiety.

Despite the silence from Danny tempting her into believing that he might leave her alone, within her heart she knew someone like him would not give up so easily. She needed to prepare herself for that.

With nothing left to clean or organise, she switched on the TV, wanting the Saturday night light entertainment shows to fill her flat with noise. It helped soothe her as she scrolled through her phone. When it beeped in her hand, the calm she had steadily reclaimed quickly faded. Glancing at her screen, she groaned in relief when she saw the notification was from Penny.

> Hey, you. Everything okay? Had a change of heart with that guy? Thought you were steering clear...

Clueless, Chloe immediately texted back, asking what she was talking about.

The notification pinged.

> Danny's posted a picture of your living room, if I'm not mistaken. Shared that he enjoyed spending a little quality time with his lovely lady. Take a look.

Penny added a screenshot of the post, which showed an image of Chloe's living room taken by Danny, his leg hitched over his other knee as if he'd settled in for the night.

Without messaging a reply, Chloe hit the button to call her instead.

'So, what's going on?' Penny said. 'Looks like he's very comfortable there. I thought this guy was trouble.'

'He is,' Chloe replied. 'And this is the proof. What you're seeing is a lie. He just turned up at my front door, all emotional and spouting a load of crap about being sorry and lonely. I took him in. I couldn't have him crying at the front door, could I?'

'Crying?'

'Yes, crying. Not much, but it was there. I explained that what he's doing couldn't continue. I think I was pretty firm. The idiot asked for a drink, and that's when he must have snapped the photo.' She anxiously rubbed her forehead. 'He's sending me a very clear message. In his eyes, this isn't over. It was just a game.'

'Why don't you message him or reply in the comments so everyone can see he's lying?'

'That would mean acknowledging him, and I don't think that's a good idea either. He wouldn't see it for what it is. He'd twist it into flirtatious banter or something, I'm sure.'

'Do you know where he lives?'

'No. Frustratingly, he knows everything about me, and all I have is his name and his mobile number.'

'And his Facebook profile,' Penny added. 'That's a start.'

'I suppose.' She switched the phone to speaker and pulled up his profile. The sight of it made her heart sink. His bio declared he was in a relationship, using her profile tag in the description to back it up. His posts were very different to a couple of days ago, more like before; more artwork and memes about finding love, finding your soulmate and that he couldn't be happier with how things have turned out. Anyone looking at his stream of consciousness would believe this was a stable, normal, and consensual relationship, rather than the fiction it was.

'Chloe, can you see his profile?'

'Looking at it now,' Chloe replied. 'Of course he wants the world to know what he's up to. Sharing all this shit about me.'

'You're a lucky girl, by all accounts,' Penny said.

'Aren't I just,' Chloe replied, as she clicked on his profile and hit the three little dots to report. 'There, that's a start,' she said, clicking through the harassment options. 'Who the hell does he think he is?'

'A complete loon,' Penny confirmed. 'Why don't you block him now?'

'Nope, won't do that,' Chloe said. 'I want to keep on top of what he's posting, especially since it's about me.'

'Good point.'

She scrolled a little more until she found the original,

grainy bedroom photo and the one in the club. He hadn't taken them down. Of course he hadn't.

'This man is something else.'

She reported the photos as well.

'He doesn't realise it yet, but he's made a mistake getting involved with me,' she said as calmly as possible. She had to. She had to show Penny she was in control of the situation, even if she feared her grasp was descending further into a darkness she didn't recognise. It frightened her. She'd been so stupid.

'You go, girl,' Penny sang. 'Don't discount the police either. This guy is away with the fairies.'

'Yep, I've done that, too.'

'Perfect.'

'Although I think I've probably invalidated it by letting him in. It'll be difficult to explain my actions about that.'

'You were doing what you had to do. They'll understand.'

'You reckon?'

She finished up with Penny and scrolled the internet again. Keeping evidence was very loose and hypothetical at this point because she had very little to provide. The only physical evidence she had were his texts, which, apart from the sheer number of them, appeared to be more desperate than aggressive. She took screenshots of what she had, thinking back to the research she'd done on this subject, aware that some cases – too many cases – ended badly. She forced those from her mind.

She worked hard not to let the stress get to her. Block it out. Pretend her life was not falling apart.

AT THE OFFICE, amongst the cluster of subdued colleagues, Chloe found Penny and Tom in the kitchen area. They both immediately stopped talking as she entered.

'Morning, guys,' she said as she pulled her mug from the cupboard, spooned in some coffee, and filled it with hot water. 'Is this private gossip, or are you willing to share? Unless, of course, *I'm* the gossip.'

'Yeah, sorry about that. I hope you don't mind. I was just filling Tom in,' Penny said sheepishly, her cheeks reddening.

'I'm just concerned,' Tom said, with a sincere smile. 'This guy's a psycho, Chloe. He was in your house. I can't believe the nerve of the man. But Penny said you've reported him to the police?'

She looked down at the steaming coffee in her mug. 'Yeah, I have. Although I think I've made a mistake. I mean, I did invite him in. What would they say? I've responded to his texts and some calls. Those are two things you absolutely shouldn't do. They'll laugh me out of the station.'

'Of course they won't,' Tom said gently. 'These things happen, and I'm sure there's not a rulebook that works for everyone in these circumstances.'

Penny's phone rang and she glanced down at her screen. 'Oh, have to take this,' she said, moving out from between Chloe and Tom. 'I'll catch you guys later.'

Tom moved closer, as Penny and the other stragglers, coffees in hand, slowly vacated the area. He gently rubbed her arm, the first contact she'd welcomed in a long while. The sensation made her skin tingle.

'I'm really worried about you, Chloe,' he said softly. 'You look worn out.'

'It's stressful, and keeping me up at night, as you'd expect. But he's gone quiet and made no contact over the weekend.' She scratched her head. 'I can't decide if that's a good thing or a bad thing. I'm guessing bad.'

Tom let his hand drop, but his fingers reached out and found hers, a quietly intimate moment. 'You're frightened?'

She gently let her fingers mingle with his, as she looked up at him and studied his eyes, soft and warm. 'He's a frightening person, but I'm okay, really. It's going to take a lot to spook me.'

'Let me help.'

'Thank you, that's really sweet, but I don't want you dragged into this. He's unpredictable and has done this before, I know it. I'm not his first, and that means he has a method of doing things. Right now, I'm guessing he's off in another world planning his next move. A world where I'm his girlfriend, or wife probably.'

The alarm and genuine concern in his eyes warmed her, and instead of breaking the gentle contact of their fingers, he held on more firmly.

'What about you?' he asked. 'What if you get hurt if he decides to get territorial and no one is there to help?'

'But to antagonise him now would be dangerous. For all concerned.'

A soft laugh escaped his mouth. 'You know what, Chloe, it would be worth it. And I can take care of myself.'

Her cheeks flushed. 'I'm sure you can,' she said, glancing over her shoulder to see if they had an audience yet. 'But you'd better be careful.'

'Oh,' he said. 'Why?'

'Keep talking like that and you'll have everyone thinking you care.'

'I guess I asked for that,' he said, amused. 'But I mean it, Chloe. You're special to me.'

She nodded and moved her fingers to take hold of his hand. 'I like this, here, with you. I feel safe with you.' She spoke cautiously, not wanting to do or say anything she might later regret, but after years of ambiguity regarding the pair of them, it was nice that her instincts had been correct.

He gently squeezed her hand in return. 'I'm glad. And I want to keep you safe.'

Why now? her heart cried. Danny, and now this – a potential for happiness that was about to slip through her fingers – was enough to break her.

CHLOE STRUGGLED to keep her focus on work. She bounced between exhaustion and extreme anxiety until every nerve in her body was frazzled.

At that moment, she was in a slump. Her stomach growled for food but she lacked the appetite to soothe it. She needed to leave, to go home, or anywhere she could disappear to, to think. She had Danny, her work, and now Tom to consider. He'd given away too many clues. Clues about his feelings towards her, which she'd suspected for a while. And now that she could no longer deny how she felt about him, her heart ached at the bad timing of it all. She rested on her elbows and held her head in her hands.

There was no time for a blossoming romance now. All her focus had to be directed towards Danny and what he'd do next. Everything was a mess, and she needed space to figure it out. She also needed sleep and some homemade food. A visit to her parents would sort her out, in her mother's care and getting her father's sensible advice. But it was a hopeless wish, because she couldn't risk Danny following her there. If anything were to happen to them, she'd fall apart. So it was home instead. Doors locked and the TV on to drown out any visitations.

She finished her most urgent tasks, packed up her laptop,

and took herself to Jeff's office. She knocked on his door and went in.

He looked up from his screen. 'Chloe. I didn't think we had a meeting today?'

She walked into the room. 'No, we don't, but I wondered if I might ask a favour?'

He smiled. 'What can I help you with?'

'I'd like to go home, if possible. I'm exhausted. Must be a bug or something.'

'No problem,' he said. 'Even though it's not like you to give up. You normally push through. Is everything okay?'

'Yes, I'm all right. Just sorting everything out, but today I'm struggling. I just think I need to go home and rest. It's been a fraught couple of days.'

'Do you want to talk about it?'

'Maybe, but could we do it another day? I'm shattered.'

'Of course. I assume you've completed any priority tasks today?'

'Yes, all done, and I've sent over the month-end report for you to check. Anything else can wait until tomorrow.'

'Okay, Chloe. That's great.'

Glad he hadn't made more of an issue about her request to leave in the middle of a working day, she went back to her desk and collected her things, keen to leave.

She said her goodbyes to Penny and the others as discreetly as possible and made her way to the lifts, meeting Tom on the way.

'Hello, where are you off to?' he asked, glancing at her bags and coat slung over her arm.

'Home. I feel shocking.'

'You need a lift?'

'No, thanks, I'll catch the bus. It'll be fine. If Danny does decide to come by the building, he'll do it later in the day when I normally leave. I should be pretty safe to get away undetected now.'

Tom frowned. 'It's really come to that?'

She shrugged. 'I have to expect the worst, but maybe the police report has helped. I don't know. I'm still waiting to hear. Maybe that's why he's gone quiet.' She pressed the button on the lift.

'I'll come down with you. At least I can see you out of the building safely.'

'Thanks, Tom. It's good to know I've got a friend.'

'Ah, no,' he sighed. 'I've been friend-zoned. That's the worst of the worst,' he said as they stepped into the empty lift.

'I'm not doing that at all,' she said as the doors closed. 'But I think we both know what's going on here.'

He nodded. 'You're very special. You always have been.'

She tensed; the moment spoilt. He wouldn't feel that way if she told him everything. If he knew the real her, the one who was spiteful, picking at the wounds in her heart that David had left there. 'I'm not special,' she muttered. 'I make mistakes like everyone else.'

'Hey, I didn't mean—'

'And you might change your mind if you knew the whole story. I'm not perfect.'

He hit the 'door-hold' button on the lift console, a trick to momentarily halt it. 'Chloe, I'm sorry. I didn't mean to upset you.'

'I'm not upset,' she said, letting the anger go. 'I'm sorry. I have a lot going on right now. I'm tired and stressed.'

'No, I'm sorry. The last thing I want to do is make things worse. I want to help, and I may not know everything about you, but I like what I know so far.'

He reached out and gave her hand a gentle squeeze. She wanted to grasp it, but she knew that if she did, she would never let go.

'But there's nothing you can do,' she said sadly. 'It's too dangerous.'

'Like I said, I can take care of myself.'

'Yes, but Danny has no rules, and he'll want to hurt whoever stands in his way. If anything happens to you because of me, I'd never forgive myself.'

'It won't happen, Chloe. I'm aware of what might be involved and it doesn't stop me from wanting to help. Let me?'

She let out a sigh. 'It's all such a mess. I can't take that risk, not now, when I feel what I feel.'

'And what is that?'

'That I would love to get to know you more, too. To be able to trust you.'

He edged a little closer until he was able to tip her head up to his. 'You can trust me with anything. But I understand, and I'm not going to put any more pressure on you because you have enough to deal with right now.'

She nodded, getting lost in his eyes.

'So, let's stick a pin in this for now. Us.' He smiled. 'There's always tomorrow.'

'I like that,' she said as she gently placed her hand over his. 'There's always tomorrow.'

All her thoughts were confirmed in one moment: the attraction, the desire for something more. All of it. Only this lift would know their secrets.

He nodded and hit the button again to crank the lift into action. 'But if ever you're worried or scared, call me. Okay?'

'Thanks, Tom, that means so much. And I will. I promise.'

Standing so close, she could just melt into him, take his face in her hands and place a gentle kiss on his lips. But that was not for now, and although she had begun to ache for him, she understood the necessity to keep him safe and away from danger.

The lift doors opened and they walked out, shuffling past the people trying to get in. They stopped at the turnstile.

'Are you sure I can't get you home? I can grab a fleet car in five minutes.'

'Really, I'm fine. I can't fall into that trap. Otherwise I'd never do anything or go anywhere.'

'Fair enough,' he said. 'If you're sure. But I'm around later, if you need me.'

'Sounds great. Perhaps I'll speak to you later, then.'

He smiled, and as she turned she let the memory of it embed itself into her mind. Something so warm, so sincere, was addictive. She knew she'd want more of it in her life.

She boarded the bus without a glance over her shoulder. Possibly a mistake, but she didn't have the energy to care if Danny was nearby. She'd become immune to the fear his presence usually stirred in her. Immune and tired.

She paid for her ticket and found a seat at the back of the bus easily enough, as the early afternoon travellers were light, the evening commute still several hours away.

She scanned the bus for him, but there was only an old lady sitting opposite, her wheeled shopping bag by her side, and further along, a mother busy wrangling two toddlers. She held them steady as they stood on their seats with their hands pressed against the window and talked gently to them as they nattered away about the colours and types of passing cars. Even the old man who ignored them all at the front of the bus, his face nestled deep into his newspaper and his wisps of grey hair visible behind the print, was reassuring.

12

The flat was cold, the heating not due to fire up until later in the afternoon, usually set in time for her arrival home from work. She locked the door, hung up her coat, then pulled up the app on her phone to override the timer. The boiler clunked into action from the airing cupboard in her bedroom. It wouldn't be long before the place was cosy again.

She kicked off her shoes just as a sudden awareness, a sense of threat, sent a tingle up her spine. She stood very still as the pulse of her heart rang in her ears. The flat was quiet, and surely empty, but she felt him. An essence of him, an energy. She hesitated by the door. Leaving now and calling the police was certainly the sensible option, or she could search her home and confront him.

Never one for choosing the sensible option, she settled on the latter choice. With clenched fists, she strode into the living room and glanced around, taking in every corner, every hidden nook. It was as she'd left it, and there was no sign of Danny and no disruption, except for a photograph of her parents that had been moved. She always kept it with other members of her family – aunts, uncles, and cousins – uniting them in print, even if the truth was that recent years had seen them scatter across the country for work, or to find a slower pace of life. But now, the photo was perched on her windowsill, away from the others.

Turning, she saw the sofa had the slightest imprint in the seat cushion, and she smelled the distinct aroma of coffee. Her mind racing, she hurried through to her bedroom. She felt him there, too, and panic ran through her. She scanned the room hurriedly. The white chest of drawers on the far side of the room exposed his presence, the drawers unevenly closed. Having been her and David's first attempt at flat-pack furniture, and probably only still standing by sheer luck and glue, she knew the only way to shut them properly was with a particular lift and push. They had been carelessly closed, perhaps in haste. She hurried to it and opened the top drawer – her underwear drawer. The disturbance of the garments was unmistakable. She opened other drawers and checked her wardrobe. All disturbed.

Heat rushed through her and she struggled to breathe. He'd been here. For how long, she didn't want to consider, but he'd walked into her home at some point since she'd left it and had inhabited her space unashamedly, touching her possessions, her clothing and underwear. She scratched her itching skin as though he had touched *her*, too.

Dazed, she fell to the carpet, trying to figure out how the hell he'd got in. Tears stung her eyes, and the sob that escaped her lips echoed in the empty room. But then came another consideration, and one that thrust her back to her feet.

What if he was still in the flat with her? What if he'd never left?

Heart thumping wildly, she cautiously checked under her bed, moved through every room, systematically checking every cupboard, behind every door and anywhere else that could house an adult male, until she was happy there was no way he could still be here. She should call the police, she should report this straight away, but first, she needed to focus on calming herself and steadying her trembling fingers. So she'd been right; this proved his absence was only temporary. Her home was meant to be her haven, and he'd wrecked it in one visit.

Chloe paused in the middle of the kitchen, tried to slow her breathing. Inhaling for four beats, holding it for four more, and finally exhaling until her heart rate calmed. Just like her counsellor had shown her. Strategies she'd learnt when she felt her life was caving in before her eyes. Her mouth had gone dry and she needed a drink, but she couldn't face the wine in her fridge right now. She couldn't risk it. A fuzzy head would not help her. Instead, she flipped the switch of the kettle and began making herself a cup of tea. It was the universal drink to help in any crisis, and today was no different.

Her eyes fell on the back door as she waited for the water to boil, and noticed it was open – only ajar – but open. She rushed to it and saw the splinters of wood where it had been forced. Horrified, she cried out as she pushed it shut. Although slightly misshapen, it closed with a little nudge, and she managed to lock it well enough for now. She leaned against the door as she focused on calming herself again. She'd need to look up locksmiths later to fix it properly and change the lock, just in case he had managed to clone the spare key that hung from the hook by the front door.

She picked up the phone to dial the police helpline when a notification flashed up on the screen. Danny. A new number, but the text was unmistakable. A saccharine greeting of love that sickened her stomach. He'd invaded her personal space and, not content with that, he now invaded her phone. She placed it down. She should take a screenshot, file it with the others and continue with her call to the police, but she was hesitant for a moment and drained by the effort it would take. And what would be the point? A government agency already stretched to the limit, what could they do with information based on her intuition and a forced door? She had no way of proving this was the work of Danny. How would they deal with her report of a few ruffled clothes and a misplaced photo? It was flimsy at best, but still, she knew she had to make the call.

Delaying the task, she went to her living room and switched on the TV, and when her phone rang out, she froze. But this time it was the familial pre-set ringtone of her mother. As though the parental bond between mother and child had alerted her of the turmoil.

'Hi, Mum,' she said as cheerily as she could. She didn't have time for this. She should be calling the police.

'Chloe, my lovely. How are you?'

Tears stung her eyes once again, and she looked to the ceiling to stop them from rolling down her cheeks. 'I'm good, thanks. You?' The police were her priority, but in this moment she needed her mother more.

'I know that voice,' her mother replied. 'What's going on?'

Despite her best efforts, the tears fell. She wiped them away with the cuff of her jumper. 'I'm okay.' She sniffed. 'Just being silly. Been a hard day, that's all.'

'Chloe, this is me you're talking to,' her mum replied with concern. 'Your voice has always risen an octave when you're upset, ever since you were a little girl. I can almost hear your chin wobble, too.'

'Ha,' Chloe said, through another sniffle. 'Can't get anything past you, can I? But, honestly, I have had the day from hell. I'm home and okay, though, really.'

She should tell her mother everything, but with all the

strain of recent months, Chloe didn't want to add to her mother's worry. Chloe had been enough of a burden, putting her mother through more than enough with David and the surrounding drama. All of it. She wasn't about to increase the level of concern by discussing Danny.

'That doesn't sound good. What can I do? Would you like me to visit? I can move my shifts around and be with you in a couple of days.'

The part of Chloe that would always feel like a child in her mother's presence wanted to scream out that yes, she'd love some quality time, letting her mother fuss over her and make things right again. But the adult in her knew that would be too dangerous. Danny could never find them. He could never latch on to them and insidiously infiltrate their lives. If anything was to happen to her parents, she would not be able to cope with the guilt. Being an only child carried the responsibility of knowing there was no one else to split this with, and so she would carry the weight of this alone.

'No, really, it's fine. You work hard enough at the hospital to be worrying about changing your shifts. You don't need to worry about travelling up. Besides, I still have to work and can't take any time. You'd be rattling around my flat.'

'Sweetie, that's all right. Janet owes me a couple of favours. There have been far too many times I've covered her shifts; it's about time she realised she's not the only one with a family. I can help, offer a little TLC until things get better for you.'

Chloe took a deep breath. It was so, so tempting and the agreement almost flew from her mouth before she had time to stop it. She just needed patience. Lots of it. There would be time to spend with her mum once this was over. 'I'm fine, and much better for speaking with you but...maybe I can come and visit in a month or so?'

'Okay, well, I won't nag. But, for now, I have a cup of tea

here and nowhere to go, so you can tell me about this day of hell.'

A knock on the door startled Chloe, and she leapt from the sofa.

'Mum, I'm going to have to call you back. Someone's at the door.'

She hung up and listened for Danny's voice. Another knock.

'Go away!' she bellowed. 'Leave me alone!'

'Miss Stark?' the voice said. A male voice, but not Danny, and not anyone else she recognised.

Cautiously, she went to the door and slipped the chain across before opening it a crack to see a uniformed policeman standing there. 'Chloe Stark?'

Embarrassed for her outburst, she clutched the door frame. 'Yes.'

'Hello. I'm PC Allan. I'm here to speak to you about the form you submitted regarding Danny Harris.'

The policeman was young, stocky, with fair skin and fat cheeks. His timely arrival meant her hesitation in calling them earlier was now irrelevant, but rather than reassure her, apprehension filled her mind. What if involving the police made things worse? What if it sent her down a path she wasn't sure she wanted?

'Ah, thank you for coming, but it's probably nothing, and you're probably busy with other things.'

'But it's bothered you enough to send in a report,' PC Allan said. 'So I'd say it's a little more than nothing. You did the right thing contacting us. We can help. Why don't you let me in, and we can discuss it in a little more privacy?'

Conceding, she nodded and opened the door.

In full uniform and clearly authentic, the policeman waited to be invited in.

'The living room is just through there,' she said as he

stepped over the threshold. She gestured for him to sit and did the same.

'So, can you give me a timeline of events?' he asked. He was young, probably newly recruited and, from what Chloe could tell from his focused attitude, keen.

She nodded. 'It's been a week now. It was innocent enough to start with, but now I can't get rid of him.' She hesitated. 'And, well, I suppose I was flattered by the attention initially. I've been trying to put my life back together, you see, and on the one night out I've had in ages, I bump into Danny. We talked for a bit, I went to leave, I lost my bag. I was annoyed, but it was not the end of the world.'

'And when did you see him again?'

'He returned it to me at my office the next day. I went for a drink with him after work, out of obligation more than anything else, and then...well, he's kind of got it into his head that we're in a relationship now. He's sharing all sorts over social media, and he's turned up here a couple of times, too.'

He nodded and used the end of his pencil to scratch his head, jabbing it through the wiry mop of pale brown hair. 'And how was his behaviour when he turned up at your house?'

Chloe heard the faint twang of a Scottish accent in his question. 'He's persistent, but not forceful. He knows just how much pressure to apply without giving me cause to call the police, but there's been a development. I think he's been here today, while I was out. Things have been disturbed.'

'Has anything been taken?'

'No, I can't see that I'm missing anything, but I know it was him. I just can't prove it. There's no one else that would break in and rifle through my belongings without taking anything of value.'

'I understand, but we need something more if we're going

to pursue it with him. Do you have any evidence? Something that he's left behind, maybe?'

'No, nothing.' *And that is exactly why I didn't want to call you!* she screamed within the privacy of her mind.

'And has he made contact with you today?'

She pulled up the screenshots on her phone and handed them to him. 'Yes, here. As you can see, it's all pretty intense. His usual – declaring his undying love, how I need to see sense, how we're meant to be.'

'But no admitting that he came here while you were out?'

'No, he knows better than that. It's best to keep me guessing, you see. That way I never fully relax.'

He sighed as he logged their conversation. 'I'm sorry you had to go through that. Unfortunately, for some people, this is a kind of game, I'm afraid. But let's see if we can help. We'll locate Danny and have a little chat with him, okay? He'll receive a warning and will be informed that any further incidents could see him arrested under the Protection from Harassment Act, so it's very important that you keep us up to date with what he's up to. If he stops what he's doing, and we certainly expect that to be the case, the report will be closed.'

'And what if he doesn't stop?'

'Let's see how this goes first,' he said and rose from the sofa, an imposing sight in her living room, his uniform and stab vest padding out his already stocky build. His radio sounded as he handed her a card. 'Anytime you need to chat, please get in touch on this number, or call 101.'

She took the card.

'Of course, if you feel at risk, at any time, it's—'

'999. Yes, I understand.'

PC Allan went to the door, and she gave her thanks again and locked up once more. It was a shame to think this had been a waste of time, knowing how tenacious Danny could be.

Irritated and jittery, she pulled out her laptop. It was time to continue her research on the topic of stalking and harassment. She found many articles on the subject. What her research quickly confirmed was that the matter was rarely resolved from the first police report and warning given. It was unrealistic to expect that. The psychology of the stalker was too vast to condense into one police procedure. And that took her to the many traits of a stalker. The intimacy seeker; the incompetent suitor; the rejected, resentful and predatory. All types came with their own threat, but the police still had their hands bound by law on how they could deal with each case. After reading, she felt content that, if ever asked, she could say she'd made a report. At least she had a record of his behaviour, too. Who knew what the future held for her, but at least she had that.

Chloe rubbed her eyes, tired from staring at the screen, and checked her watch. Forty-five minutes had passed since PC Allan left. Forty-five minutes of silence that still, in her mind, did nothing to prove she was alone. When the doorbell chimed, she jumped from her chair, heart racing.

She waited silently for his voice again, calling out to her, and flinched when the doorbell rang again.

13

'Chloe,' Laura shouted through the letterbox. 'Are you there?'

A groan of relief emerged from Chloe's throat. She went to the door, pulled back the chain, and opened it. 'Laura, quick. Come in.'

'Bloody hell, don't you answer your phone? I've been calling for the last five minutes,' Laura said as she strode through the door. 'I was worried.'

'Turned it to silent,' Chloe said as she shut the door, locked it, and put the chain across.

Laura noticed it. 'A little over the top, isn't it, Chloe?'

'Believe me, it's not. A lot has happened in the last few days. Were you alone out there? Did you see him?'

The confusion on Laura's face did little to soothe Chloe.

'Chloe, what's going on? What the hell are you talking about?'

'Danny. He's been bothering me again. I've had the police here and everything.'

'Really? Oh my God. It's that bad?'

'It's worse than bad,' Chloe replied. 'Have you got time to chat, or are you here on your way out?'

'Do I look as if I'm off to a club?' Laura asked, her face free of make-up, hair scraped into a messy bun, and dressed in a sweatshirt and old jeans. And although anything goes these days, Chloe knew Laura would never be anything other than completely polished for a night out.

'Okay, no judgements,' she said, under Chloe's scrutiny.

Chloe chuckled. Even in this mess, there was lightness in everything, if she looked for it.

'And if I were going out, I'd be taking you with me. You look like you need a night of fun,' she said, checking her up and down.

'That's a hard pass for me, I'm afraid. A night of fun got me into this mess,' she replied as she walked into the kitchen. 'I'll grab us a drink.'

'Perfect. And seeing as I'm driving, and you left me standing on the doorstep on this freezing cold night, I think that calls for a large mug of tea, please.'

'Jeez, you're such a drama queen, Laz. It was two minutes,' Chloe retorted as she pulled out two mugs from the cupboard. The blackness of night outside the kitchen window caught her attention, and the sudden sense it would seep through the glass and engulf the room stopped her from what she was doing. She went to it and pulled down the blind.

'Caught Tom earlier in the pub,' Laura began as Chloe handed her a mug. 'He had a lot to say about you. All good, I hasten to add. Really good.'

'We've had a couple of moments recently,' she said as she joined Laura at the table. 'Just chats, but...he's been great, actually.'

'Ah, do I see hearts in your eyes?' Laura goaded.

'No,' Chloe replied. 'There's nothing that's going to happen there, not right now. It can't.'

'You might want to tell that to your cheeks then, babe. They're glowing.'

'Shut it,' she said, touching her fingertips to her cheeks. There was no denying it. Laura was right – they burned.

'So, share,' Laura said, making herself comfortable. 'If psycho man has been outside, then I need an update. We can discuss Tom later.'

Chloe blew out a long breath. 'Whew, where do I begin? Let me see. Firstly, there's nothing more to discuss about Tom. Danny *is* a psycho. He's been texting, phoning, turning up at my place of work. Turned up here a couple of times, including just the other night. Had a few waterworks when I said we wouldn't work out, only to take a picture to share on social media. Oh yes, and since then I've had to report his Facebook account because it's full of me. We're in a relationship, apparently. I've just had the police visit, and I think Danny's been in the flat today, although I can't prove it. So you can understand why I silenced my phone. I'm not in the mood to read any of his texts or for him to start banging on my door. I thought you were him.'

Laura's jaw dropped.

'Exactly. I've been busy,' Chloe said.

'Oh my God, are you serious?'

'Of course I'm serious.' She circled her finger in front of her face. 'Can you see the shadows under my eyes?'

'I admit, you are pulling off a serious heroin chic vibe there. Supermodel style.'

'Nice.'

Laura smiled and shook her head, still in disbelief. 'But I'm sorry. I didn't realise things had escalated so much. The dude is seriously off the charts. I understand now why you didn't want to open the door.'

Chloe nodded. That meant a lot. Laura never apologised unless she truly meant it. It was easier to get blood from a stone than for Laura to say she was sorry.

Laura rolled her eyes. 'Jesus, the first time since David and it goes this wrong. Do you ever get a break?'

Chloe held up her hand. 'My name is Chloe, and I make bad choices.'

'Sweetie, you do nothing of the sort. We've all been there. Don't beat yourself up over it. You're just unlucky to have bumped into Mr Nutjob.'

'Luck, or the lack of it, had nothing to do with it.' Chloe grabbed the phone from the table and checked it.

Fifteen notifications. All from Danny. Wanting to know where she was, why she wasn't reading his texts, demanding to see her. 'Shit. He's angry.'

'He can't do this. It's unacceptable. This is your home. Call the police again. Get them back here.'

'I don't want to call the police,' Chloe replied. 'I'm saving screenshots of his texts, but, apart from that, I can't prove he was ever here today.'

'But he might come back. That's enough of a threat.'

'Well, then I'll deal with it when he arrives. There's no way to predict what he'll do next, but I'll understand if you don't want to stay.'

'I'm not going anywhere. We'll deal with him together.'

'I was hoping you'd say that.'

An hour slipped by, spent listening out for a door knock or phone call, but there was nothing. Complete radio silence. Somehow, it made Chloe more nervous. Where was he? They waited and waited, both on edge, and tried to distract themselves by watching a programme about climate change and the melting ice caps which, on reflection, was a mistake. An impending Armageddon when she was already stressed out to the maximum did nothing to calm her nerves.

'He's probably decided against coming over,' Laura said, after another hour.

Chloe nodded. Maybe his attention had moved elsewhere. Maybe another woman, another situation. Perhaps he had a harem of women in his 'care'. Chloe didn't know. But being a weeknight, Laura soon started making noises about work in the morning.

'I can stay, if you want me to,' she said.

Chloe didn't want to put her out and ruin her evening as well as her own. She also didn't want her to be involved. She felt the same about her friends as she did her family. They needed to be safe from his clutches. 'No, honestly, there's no need. I've got some pretty sturdy locks on the door. I'll be fine.'

'Are you sure?'

Chloe wasn't sure at all, but she wasn't going to drag her friend down with her. She stood. 'Yes, of course. Now get out of here and get yourself home. And make sure there's no one out there, okay?'

'Right, and my car is literally a hop away. I'll be fine.'

'And I'll watch from the window, make sure you're safe.'

'Listen to us,' Laura tried to joke. 'Two teenagers in a horror movie.'

'Just don't go striking up a conversation with a man with an axe or anything like that.'

'Funny.'

'Straight to your car, okay? Then doors locked.'

They moved out into the hallway, and Laura put on her coat and wrapped her arms around Chloe.

'I'll call you later,' she said. 'Make sure you're tucked up.'

'Thanks, Mum,' Chloe said with a laugh, as she opened the door.

They lingered, both looking out into the cold night,

clutching each other's hands. Laura looked at Chloe and, finding the humour, they both descended into laughter.

Hesitantly, Laura stepped outside. 'Okay, I'm doing this.'

Chloe lingered, watching her friend rush up the steps and hurry to her car.

'Go in! Shut the door!' Laura yelled, as she glanced behind.

'Okay, be safe!' Chloe called.

As the car fired up, Chloe shut the door and locked it, rushing to her living room. She opened the curtain a crack and saw Laura in her car, alone, and waving before pulling away.

Chloe fixed the curtain back in place and went to check all doors were secured again. She then went to the kitchen, grabbed a glass and the half bottle of white from her fridge, and went to her bedroom, leaving all the lights on.

She climbed onto the bed and checked her phone. Nothing. She couldn't figure it out. Where was he? She listened for any noise, but there was only the sound of the odd car, or the chattering of people as they strode by, fading in and out. He had ceased to bother her.

Clever. Get me all riled up and then leave me hanging. Bloody bastard.

She poured some wine and leaned back against the headboard, still dressed and not yet relaxed enough to consider sleeping. She sent her mum a quick text and then scrolled aimlessly on her phone.

CHLOE SNAPPED HER EYES OPEN, conscious and aware again. She was on her side, covers over her middle, leaving her top exposed to the cold morning air. The heating hadn't yet kicked in and she shivered, her arms cool to the touch. She ached and shuffled under the covers. At some point, after finishing the wine, sleep had taken her, but she struggled to remember anything since Laura had left.

In the dusky, grey dawn light of her room, she noticed the light was off. She pondered for a moment, having no recollection of doing that. She checked her phone – six-thirty – and she was relieved to see there were no messages from anyone, including Danny.

Her head pounded and hazy memories of the night filtered slowly into her waking mind, and she decided to give herself another fifteen minutes to warm herself up. She remembered speaking to her mum, the policeman's visit and chatting to Laura at her kitchen table, but after that, nothing. But a good dose of alcohol will provide dreamy oblivion, she reminded herself, and half a bottle could make things hazy. Especially since she had been so tired and had eaten nothing. And she realised, in her groggy state, that she was only in her underwear – no clothes – which would explain why she felt so cold.

When she scanned the floor for scattered remnants, it was empty of clothes. Instead, they were placed over her chair, folded with what looked like care. She could imagine herself dozily tossing them to the floor, asleep enough to have no recollection of it, but she was sure she would remember arranging them neatly because it would have involved the physical act of getting out of bed to undress. Activity enough to wake anyone, surely. But there was nothing to that effect she could pull forward in her mind. She blamed the wine again, and resolved to banish weeknight drinking for a while.

Frustrated and jittery, she turned on her lamp and dragged herself out of bed.

The lights blazed, and a scent filled the air, but the recollection of it hovered just out of reach, her brain struggling to focus. She turned out all the lights and went to the kitchen, where she filled the kettle, switched it on, and plopped a teabag into a mug. Exhaustion robbed her of her appetite and, again, she passed on breakfast, the most important meal of the day. She'd grab something at work perhaps, or stop off on the way, but she couldn't face it now.

Once she had managed a few gulps of tea, she readied herself for work. The process was lengthy, as she couldn't fight the need to rest.

With a deep breath and a quick check in the mirror, she opened her door and gasped. Two shopping bags had been placed on her doormat, full of groceries. Horror filled her when she saw the sanitary products placed on top of the shopping, the very same products that she'd bought. Her most personal items from the most private aspects of her life. A life he was now tracking by what she bought. Carefully, she inspected the other items and found they, too, matched exactly with the shop from the other night. He'd been there, watching, observing what she'd bought while she dashed around looking for that woman.

She felt dirty, tarnished by his watchful eye, and wanted to drop the two bags straight into the bin. But tossing the food away felt wrong, wasteful, even if it had come from the hands of her tormentor. So, unsure of what she'd do with it, and with a glance around, she carried it inside. She put the perishable items in the fridge and left everything else in the bag. She'd figure out what to do about this later – perhaps a food bank would take it – and whether it needed to be reported to the police.

Occasionally checking over her shoulder, she turned onto the main road and walked past the primary school that was yet to welcome its tiny students, then on to the station. Other commuters were doing the same, some rushing ahead and others lagging behind, and so she thought nothing of the footfalls behind her.

'Good morning, Chloe.'

She spun around to see Danny and his smile bearing down on her.

'You,' she hissed. 'What are you doing here?'

'Just making my way to work. The same as you.'

'But why here, now?'

'A perfect coincidence, but I can't say I'm disappointed. You look beautiful.' He reached out to touch her face but she swatted his hand away.

Anger filled her. 'Don't touch me. You need to leave me alone.'

'And I have,' he said. 'I didn't bother you last night when your friend visited. I thought I'd let you have an evening with her.'

'What?' she spat, exasperated and confused.

'It's okay, Chloe. I'm not going to stop you from seeing your friends. It's important to spend time with friends, even in a new relationship. I get that. I think it's healthy.'

'For the last time, we're *not* in a relationship,' she snapped.

'Well, now we're arguing,' he said, catching the eye of a man walking by. He smiled, and the man returned it with one of his own, a universal acknowledgement of the awkwardness of a very public argument with a significant other. He continued with no reaction to her outburst, despite people starting to stare. 'Chloe, Chloe, I get it. You're clinging on to your independence. It's totally understandable. I can wait. Take your time.'

She shook her head in frustration. 'No, you need to listen to me. Leave me alone. I'm serious. No calling, no visiting, and no shopping left on my doorstep. I've been to the police, and they will be visiting you with a warning.'

Her words were the dynamite to his next course of action. With little care, he grasped her arm and walked her to the edge of the pavement so that she almost collided against the building wall behind her. But as intimidating as it felt to her, he was careful to keep his body language light and inoffensive. 'That's not what you really want, though, is it, Chloe?'

'Yes, it is.'

He smiled, calm, unfazed. 'No, this is all a game to you.'

'You're the one who likes the game,' she countered. 'That's what I've been told.'

'Well, that's probably the first bit of information you've got right. I do like a game, especially one I will win.'

'Don't count on it.'

'Ah, but I will.' He rested his arm against the wall of the building. 'You're giving me the run-around and doing all you can to block us from happening. The threats, and now the police. Freezing me out. You like conflict, and you like to resist. It turns you on.'

A sound of disgust rumbled in her throat. 'Believe me, this is the last thing that turns me on. I want you to get out of my life and leave me alone.'

'No, you don't. Tell me your heart isn't pounding right now. Tell me you're not trembling.'

'Shut up.'

He smiled. 'You want me to pursue you and pull down the many barriers you've built up against me. And I'll do it, Chloe. I'm happy to do it because I know what you really want.'

'Then you'll be arrested,' she said, with as much defiance as her voice would allow.

He leaned in close. 'Do you really think I'm scared of what the police might do? Do you think that will stop me?'

Chloe had no words that could suitably convey the loathing she felt for him at this moment. When she noticed a couple of people glance their way as they strode past, she considered calling out for help, but she knew it would be pointless, and it may push Danny into doing something they'd both regret.

He held up his hands, breaking the mood, his sermon over. 'Okay, Chloe. I think we've discussed this enough for now.' He checked his watch. 'And we don't want to be late for work now, do we? Especially as you've already started the day badly, with all that wine you finished off last night. Your head must be pounding.'

Chloe's body began to shudder from adrenaline and fear. 'How do you know about that?'

He smiled. 'Chloe, please. I know how much you like your wine.'

'Just leave me alone, okay?' She stepped out of his space and walked away, quickening her pace to get as much distance as she could between them.

'I'll call you later, Chloe,' he shouted out from behind.

She managed to grab a seat on the train, despite it being packed, and it gave her the much-needed opportunity to calm herself with some subtle deep breathing exercises. It helped, and the crowded train began to soothe her once she felt safer amongst the commuters who looked on with indifference.

In the office, she sat at her desk and decided today, as far as her work was concerned, there would be no drama. She would concentrate on her tasks and then go home, and that would be it. A hot bath and then sleep was all that waited for her there. Lots of sleep.

Her phone pinged and she dreaded to look, but it was from Laura, checking in on her.

She messaged back and shared how he'd turned up on the commute. Someone walked by her desk as she typed. She didn't look, but his aftershave lingered in his wake and the scent of it allowed her mind to open and memories to rush to the forefront. Memories that took her back to last night and her broken dreams. An arm wrapped around her. Warmth beside her – his voice whispering so as not to fully wake her.

The wine.

She abandoned her phone, staring into the room as she remembered. He knew about the wine because he'd seen it while he was in her flat. He'd found it and tampered with it, likely adding a drug that would have knocked her out so he could spend the night with no resistance. He was the one who undressed her. He was the one who put her clothes on the chair. Her mind raced as she fought to remember, just as nausea rose like bile in her stomach.

There was no sex. I'd have known if we'd had sex.

She stood, her body taut and in an unstoppable action of its own. The sudden, unmistakable feeling of impending sickness made her rush to the toilets. Head down, she hurried, pushing open the large heavy door and slipping into a cubicle in time to empty the contents of her stomach. Retching hard, her muscles tensed as her body rejected the acidic bile. Her hair clung to her clammy skin as she managed a few fleeting breaths before another wave of nausea hit. After a few moments, her body stilled, she felt the unmistakable relief of the sickness passing. She stood up slowly and leaned against the wall of the cubicle to compose herself, taking long, deep breaths. Next, she ripped some toilet paper free and wiped her eyes and mouth before tossing it down and flushing it all away.

As disgusting as it was to remember any kind of intimacy between the two of them, she stilled, thought back to last night and let herself become aware of her body. She didn't remember feeling as if anything had happened this morning when she woke. There had been no pain, no feeling of intrusion. She felt untouched, and after a drought like hers she knew she would feel something in the wake of an encounter with him. Perhaps he wouldn't have risked it. He could have.

He had every opportunity to do whatever he pleased, but perhaps his plan was only to be in her space, quiet and unnoticed, until the next time. And she was sure he intended there to be a next time, so there was to be no more wine, and no food to be left open that could be tampered with. She would not allow herself to be exposed like that again. She would not be so vulnerable.

Stepping out and heading to the sink, she switched on the tap and cupped her hands, filling it with cool water to splash over her face and rinse out her mouth. She checked herself in the mirror. Grabbing a paper towel, she rubbed at the smudged mascara around her eyes and dabbed her skin dry. She shook out her hair, removing the strands that clung to her face.

When she was ready, she walked slowly back to her desk, stopping by the water fountain to fill a cup. She sat at her desk and focused on her breathing. This was okay. She could cope with this. She just needed to be careful, because if she underestimated him again, she might not get through this ordeal.

14

The lack of contact with Danny since their altercation on the street was as exhausting as having to deal with him constantly. It had been one day of respite from his meticulous attention, and she understood this would be a calculated plan to keep her on her toes. To never let her know when he was going to descend. Clever. Nasty. And effective. Chloe found herself seeking him out, checking his socials, wanting to know his whereabouts. A definite sense that if she knew where he was and what he was doing, she could control how she would react – a defence mechanism to keep herself safe.

At the end of the second day of radio silence from Danny, she decided to use the evening to spy on his Facebook profile while she waited for the locksmith to finally come over, after cancelling a couple of times. The timeline was reasonably quiet; a few shares of stupid memes, a few photos of the morning sunrise matched with an inspirational quote. It made her laugh how an unhinged person like Danny could sound so sane. But that was social media, full of plenty of other people who cowardly hid behind an online persona. He was active, going about his day in the normal way, only she wasn't part of it.

Why? Why would he claim to never give up on pursuing her, only to leave her alone entirely?

She was suddenly all too aware this process might be tipping into an obsession of her own. She had to remind herself of what was really going on here.

As she continued to scroll, a picture of Laura's face popped up on the screen, and it was the perfect interruption to end this line of enquiry. She answered the call.

'You will never guess who has just come to my place,' Laura said, her voice quivering.

Chloe sat forward on her sofa. 'Please tell me it wasn't him.'

'It was totally Danny. How does he know where I live?'

'I have no idea,' Chloe burst out. Now she understood this was just a reprieve; he was simply investing his time else-where, branching out to her friends and, possibly given the chance, her parents, too. But it told her this was far from over. 'Are you okay? He didn't do anything to hurt you, did he?'

'No, nothing like that. Actually, he was really charming and pleasant. It's only because I know what he's doing to you that I was even creeped out by it. God, he's a real charmer, Chlo. I understand how you fell for it.'

'Well, I didn't fall for anything, but I know what you mean.'

'He must have followed me home the other night. That's the only explanation I have.'

'Makes sense,' Chloe replied, deciding not to share that he very likely returned to her in the dead of night, broke in somehow, and slept beside her. 'But this is serious, Laura. What did he say to you? What was the reason he gave?'

'Well, he didn't buzz on the intercom or anything, he was just...outside, hanging around as if waiting for a car to pull into the bay. I saw him when I was about to go through the main entrance. He said he just happened to be in the area and, while he could be telling the truth, I call bullshit on that, even though I didn't let on at the time. Apparently, he saw me and remembered my face from that night in the pub. Thought he'd come over to say hello because he wants to get to know all of your friends.'

'Right. Fucking hell, the man is unbelievable.' She sighed. 'But you're okay?'

'I'm absolutely fine, if a little shaken up. It was creepy as hell, but once I was in the building I knew the concierge would stop him from trying to follow.'

'I'm sorry the stuff in my life is now affecting yours.'

'He needs to have some sort of restraining order.'

'He does.'

'And if he's just turning up here, how often is he hanging around your place? You need one of those video doorbells. Catch him in the act.'

'Already checked those out,' Chloe replied. 'Too expensive. I'd need one on both my doors and he'd only smash them up once he saw them. I know it. He'll find a way to do it so I won't catch it on camera, either. All it would do is put a dent in my savings.'

'But surely it's worth a try?'

'Maybe. I'll think about it.'

'Look, me and Gabby are off out tomorrow to celebrate it being Friday. Why not join us? Come out and let your hair down, away from his prying eyes.'

'That's not a good idea,' Chloe said, quick to reply.

'Why not?'

'Because Danny will only follow us and cause trouble, and partying is the last thing I'm up for right now. I think it's best for me to keep a low profile and just stay at home.'

'Chlo, you can't alter how you live your life to avoid him.'

'I know. And I used to think that, too, but not anymore.'

'Come on, we'll have some fun, and then you can stay with me. I know he knows where I live, but he can't get in, so he's no threat. And, anyway, he is more likely to go to your place than if we went out. And if he does turn up at the club, I'll be around to make sure he gets both barrels.'

Chloe smiled, glad to have such a loyal friend. 'You're the best.'

'I know I am. So get your glad rags ready, pull out that sexy black dress from the back of your cupboard and start living a little!'

'I'll think about it.'

'That means no, and I'm not going to take that for an answer. It's not an option, so be ready by eight, and we'll drop by in the taxi and pick you up on the way.'

'I'm serious, Laura. I don't think it's a good idea.'

DESPITE NOT WANTING to go out after an arduous day in the office and having dropped the unwanted groceries Danny had left on her doorstep at her local foodbank, she began the process of getting ready for a night out with Laura and Gabby. She ignored the niggling doubts in her mind, even though the feeling that this was a mistake wouldn't leave her be.

Standing with a towel wrapped around her head and body, she rifled through her wardrobe for something suitable to wear. Sliding the hangers along the rail, she found a dress she hadn't worn in a while, but, staring at herself in the mirror, she lost all confidence in what she was doing. She remembered very well the last time she'd worn it. It was for David's birthday, a night out after a strained evening of talks the night before. David never hid his infidelity, but what Chloe discovered too late was that, instead, he had hidden his love for Melissa. And that would prove their downfall.

Deciding not to let her anger and grief creep in and spoil a night out she already wasn't in the mood for, she focused on other outfits in her wardrobe and settled for a blue chiffon dress she'd worn for a wedding a couple of years ago.

The front doorbell startled her. She checked her watch. It was only seven, and her heart sank. It would be Danny. She had no energy for it, and this new challenge only reinforced her opinion that tonight was a mistake. But she remembered what Laura had said. If he was here, maybe it was better if she wasn't.

'Chloe,' Laura shouted, flipping the letterbox. 'It's me.'

With an eye roll, Chloe hurried to let Laura in, dressed to impress in a silver dress teamed with matching jewellery and black strappy heels. Hair perfect, nails recently done, she looked a vision of beauty. Chloe took a step back to let her friend in. 'You look absolutely gorgeous.'

'Thank you,' Laura said, as she hooked her clutch under her arm and studied Chloe.

Chloe looked down at herself, understanding. 'I know, I know. I shouldn't be coming.' She fanned out her dress limply. 'This is a crime to fashion.'

'No, you're just lacking confidence. You looked super-hot when we last went out.'

'That's because you critiqued every outfit I put on until you were happy.' Chloe sighed. 'I still don't think this is a good idea.'

'Nope, not good enough,' Laura said, grabbing Chloe's hand and dragging her back to the bedroom. 'I thought you might be having difficulties, or be ready to back out, which is why I've come early.'

'Laura.'

'Now, if you're going out for lunch with the in-laws, that

dress is great,' Laura continued. 'But we're not doing that. We're going out-out. Now, sit.' She sat Chloe down on the bed and went to the wardrobe.

After a moment of rummaging through Chloe's clothes, she grabbed a black halter-neck jumpsuit with the label still attached. 'You've never worn this?' she asked, as she ripped the label off. 'You looked fantastic in this in the shop. Why haven't you worn it? Actually, don't answer that.' She laid it on the bed and then returned to the wardrobe, swiping the clothes along the rail until she found what she was looking for. 'That teamed with...ah yes, this! I think you'll look great.'

She held out the gold satin belt that would cinch in Chloe's already petite waist and nodded.

'I'd forgotten about that,' Chloe replied. 'I must admit, it is lovely.'

'And you look totally gorgeous in it, so get to it.'

Chloe stood and changed into the clothes, desperate to put a stop to this but equally grateful that Laura was here.

Laura surveyed Chloe. 'Hmm, a nice set of heels and some jewellery and you'll be fabulous, darling.' She turned, went to the wardrobe again and sank to her knees. 'Now, I remember those killer heels. The little gold strappy numbers you used to have. Where are they?'

'In there somewhere. It's been an age, but they're there.' She kept her focus so her mind didn't drift back to the last time she wore them. It would have been with David, so she didn't dare to remember. 'So where are these killer heels going to take me? If I'm coming...' Chloe asked.

'Oh, yes,' Laura said, shoulder deep into the wardrobe. 'We're off to Loop. We may have to queue, I didn't have time to book, but it'll be fun and we haven't had a big night out for a while. I'm planning on taking your mind off everything for a couple of hours. I think you could use some of that.'

Chloe nodded. 'You're not wrong there.'

'And we can switch between the cocktail bar and the dance floor for some cheesy dance moves. Everyone needs a multicoloured dance floor in their lives, and tonight is no different. Ah, there you are!' She pulled out the shoes and rubbed the dust from them. 'Get these on and you'll be golden. Literally.'

'I wish I had your enthusiasm.'

Laura went to Chloe, dropped the shoes at her feet and then put her hands on her hips. 'Look, I know you feel like shit now, but we're going to have a good night. A few cocktails, a dance or two. Just what you need to let your hair down. And if it gets a bit much, we can chill out in one of the lounges until you're ready to continue.'

'Yeah, you're right,' Chloe said, glancing at Laura's perfectly manicured hands and then her own, free of polish, short and tidy. Boring.

'It's okay. They look fine,' Laura said kindly.

'Safe and dull, more like.'

'Honey, there's nothing dull about you,' Laura said. 'But why don't you come by the salon soon and I'll make sure you get the works. On the house.'

Chloe smiled. 'That's lovely, but I couldn't expect that. I'll happily pay.'

'I know you would, but it's the least I can do. You've been through a lot recently, so I think you deserve a treat. That, and a pitcher of Sex on the Beach in about, oh, an hour or so.'

'Yeah,' Chloe said with a sigh. 'That's about the only sex on the beach I'm likely to get for a while.'

Laura snorted. 'Well, at least you haven't lost your sense of humour.'

'Who said I was joking?' Chloe replied with a half-smile.

'Listen, babe, you never know what's around the corner. Now, let's get you finished up.'

She took time on Chloe's hair, styling it so that loose curls fell over her shoulders, and applied smoky shadow over her eyes, finishing with a nude lip gloss to balance it out. Spritzed with perfume, she was done.

'Right, beautiful lady, you look sizzling hot, and the Uber is going to be here soon, so let's get a wiggle on.'

'You're the best,' Chloe said, as she grabbed her bag and followed Laura to the door, fighting the ominous feeling that Danny could be capable of anything tonight.

When they reached the front door, she pulled Laura back for a moment. 'You will take care, won't you? I don't want you to get hurt, if anything should happen.'

Laura smiled sympathetically. 'You say that like he's going to know where we are.'

'He'll know.'

'Well, he can do what he likes. The little fucker can't dictate what we're allowed to do with our evening, and I can give as good as I get.'

Laura's phone beeped. She grabbed Chloe's arm and they walked out to the waiting car. 'Come on, let's not worry about it now. Gabby is going to meet us there.'

They got into the car and pulled the doors closed. 'Dering Street, please,' Laura said to the driver. 'The Loop Bar.'

15

Chloe and Laura pulled up to see Gabby already there and waiting outside the entrance to Loop. She squealed with delight at the sight of Chloe and rushed over to greet them as they got out of the Uber, pulling her into a hug.

'Chloe, you came,' she said. 'You look amazing!'

'As do you,' Chloe replied, casting her eyes over Gabby's gorgeous red bodycon dress.

They joined the long queue for the club and Chloe watched the revellers on the other side of the road, standing outside the Duke of York pub, enjoying a drink and a smoke in the cold night air. There was something about the atmosphere that appealed to Chloe more than where they were going, but Laura was trying hard to give her a good night out, and so Chloe would not let her down.

'Okay, so now I can share that you're all staying with me tonight,' Laura said. 'No arguments. Sam's on hand for cocktails. It's all arranged.'

She'd decided the itinerary of the night, and there would be no talking her out of it. It was a thoughtful gesture, Laura taking care to ensure her friends felt as comfortable as possible, but Chloe knew it was hopeless. It would very likely lure Danny over. She opened her mouth to speak.

Laura held up her hand. 'Nope. I know what you're going to say, so forget it. He already knows where I live. It makes no difference if you come to me. Besides, there's twenty-four-hour security, Sam's there, and I'm pretty good with a rolling pin, although I'm not sure we even own one of those.'

'There's no way you have one of those, lady,' Gabby joked.

'But my point is, we'll soon see him off.'

'That's right,' Gabby chimed in. 'He's got to get past all of us. If he does turn up, he'll take one look at our hungover, hangry selves and think better of it.'

'But—'

'No buts,' Laura said. 'I've got PJs, food, and enough skin-care products to shake a stick at. Everything else can be sorted in the morning.'

It was an appealing option, and Chloe wanted nothing more than to stay with her friends.

'I'm serious,' Laura said, a little more softly this time and with a hand on Chloe's shoulder. 'You need taking care of. Let us do it for you. And if it helps you relax and enjoy tonight, then even better.'

Chloe sighed. She couldn't disagree. There was no doubt it was just what she needed, so, with hesitance, she smiled. 'Okay, that would be lovely.'

'Yay,' Gabby and Laura chimed in unison, as Laura pulled them both in for a hug.

'Yay,' Chloe replied, hoping this was the right decision.

The club was alive with the beat of music pumping through the walls as they approached the entrance.

'Okay, I've got us a space at Casper's,' Laura said, once they were inside, her eyes glued to her phone. 'We can have a couple of drinks and a bite to eat. Sound good?'

'Definitely,' Gabby said. 'I'm starving.'

'We can either stay there, or go downstairs to Wonderland.'

'Or we could do both,' Gabby replied.

'Right,' Laura agreed. 'It's up to you, but wherever we're going, we're dancing. That's non-negotiable.'

Chloe didn't object to any of the plans they were making, and let Gabby and Laura figure it out between themselves. She waited as they discussed the benefits of either option, and couldn't help but glance around the room for a glimpse of Danny. She considered that maybe he wouldn't be aware she'd come out tonight, but quickly discounted it. It was just not possible.

The sight of Laura tottering towards Chloe and Gabby in her dangerously high heels, concentrating hard as she carefully balanced a tray of cocktails, made them all collapse into laughter. It felt so good to laugh, and it made Chloe realise how long she'd been humourless. Sad, even.

The night was easy, relaxed, and Chloe knew Laura had done well to suggest coming here. The cocktails she'd consumed warmed her and she felt loose, letting the alcohol guide her. She was even persuaded to venture onto the dance floor when their drinks were done, and let Laura take her hand and lead her. The beat of the music was infectious, as were the people already on the dance floor, waving glow sticks in the air like it was the '90s again. She moved slowly at first but soon found her rhythm with the others. It was good to be so free and not feel the need to look over her shoulder constantly. Even if he was here, she found she didn't care. He could watch from the shadows if he liked. She wouldn't stop.

Three tunes in, she felt a finger tap against her shoulder. She spun around, the part of her that was endlessly prepared to confront Danny ready to fight. But instead, she was greeted with Tom's smiling face.

'Hi,' he shouted. 'I didn't know you were coming here tonight.'

'Hey, Tom,' she said, relieved to see him. Happy, too. 'I didn't either. Laura and Gabby dragged me out.'

His eyes surveyed her, lingering in places where her skin was exposed. He tried to be discreet, but it was unmistakable. 'You look fantastic.'

'So do you,' she replied, liking his navy shirt, unbuttoned at the collar, and smart jeans. 'It's been a while since I've done this, but I am under strict instructions to have a good time, and I guess I am. Especially now.'

He smiled at the compliment. No longer dancing, they moved to the edge of the dance floor to avoid any elbows from interrupting their conversation.

'You here with anyone?' she asked.

He pointed over to the bar, where a group of lads stood, drinks in hand. 'That's the crew.' He smiled. 'Can I get you a drink?'

'Um, well...yes, that would be great, thanks.'

Laura and Gabby both waved at Tom, smiling as they saw him with Chloe. Laura came closer, with Gabby following behind.

'Oh, hi, Tom,' Laura began, with a sly smile. 'Fancy seeing you here.'

'Indeed,' Tom replied with a smirk.

Chloe clocked the sideways glances her friends gave each other and understood this had been a classic set-up. Laura had put two and two together and had decided to play cupid. Gabby seemed to know, too, which told Chloe that Laura hadn't wasted any time spilling the beans on their conversation about Tom from other night.

The music at the bar was not quite as loud, but they still had to raise their voices.

'Cocktail?' Tom asked.

'No, had a few too many of those,' she said. 'But a glass of white would be lovely.'

Tom nodded and called out the order to the bartender.

'Looks like you've had a good night, too,' she said while they waited, noticing his slow blink and the tiniest slur of words that gave the game away. It was endearing. She'd seen him drunk before at countless office Christmas parties, but this was different.

'You're not wrong, but it's much better for seeing you,' he said with a warm smile.

'I'm sorry about Laura,' Chloe said. 'It's clear what she's been up to, and I can tell you now that I didn't know anything about this little matchmaking scenario.'

Tom smiled. 'I didn't need convincing. Laura called and I jumped at the chance.'

Sadness swamped her at the regret she felt for not giving this more attention before. Why had she let Danny distract her from focusing on better things? A new relationship, perhaps, specifically with Tom. Why had she allowed it?

'That's so sweet.'

He must have seen the sadness, too, because he reached out and gently touched her hand. 'What's wrong?'

'I wish Danny wasn't around to ruin this.'

'He won't. He can't, because we won't let him. He won't be around forever.'

'I want him gone right now.'

'There's always tomorrow.'

'That phrase again,' she said. 'There's always tomorrow.'

'Ah, yes.'

'Where's it from?'

'My mother. An inherently positive person. She says that however bad your day, your mood, or your circumstances become, there's always tomorrow. An opportunity to start again.'

'I like it,' Chloe said. 'It offers hope. I could use some of that right now.'

'And good friends.' He handed her the glass of wine that had been placed on the bar for her.

'Cheers,' she said, taking the glass from his hand. 'I agree to that, too. Especially the really good friends. You know, the close friends. The ones who have not been friend-zoned.'

He gazed at her, picking up the hint. 'The friends who wish there was something more, and given half the chance would take something more?'

'Yes,' she agreed. 'Those.'

He smiled, and a spark of yearning ignited within her.

'You're beautiful, you know that?'

She leaned in a little closer and smiled. 'Thank you, Tom. As are you.'

'I'm so glad you came,' he said, his eyes fixed on her mouth.

'Likewise.'

Gabby and Laura approached, all smiles at the sight of them. Chloe was sure they were very pleased with themselves.

'We need to steal our friend back for a minute, Tom,' Laura said over the music, linking her arm through Chloe's. 'I think it's time we danced again.'

'Sure,' Tom replied. 'Go and have some fun.'

'We're looking out for her tonight.'

He nodded. 'Good. Then we all are.'

They all sashayed to the dance floor, leaving their drinks at the table, and Chloe let the beat move her. She danced, surrounded by her friends – people who cared about her, genuinely, and not some twisted ideal of it – and she loved them more in this moment than she had ever done before, if that was possible. She wanted to stay in this bubble, safe, warm, the alcohol blurring everything. She had blocked

Danny out. He was not welcome here. Tonight, she would live as she chose, with no repercussions from him. No threat.

She saw Tom at the bar with his friends, and while he looked reasonably engaged in a conversation with them all, his eyes kept darting back to her, as if compelled to watch her dance. She couldn't quell the butterflies jumping in her stomach, even if she tried. It felt good to be watched by him, and she found she wanted so much more of it. Perhaps it could happen. She might have another chance at happiness, and the thought of it manifested small buds of hope on the winter bark of her soul, growing to the music and the movement of her body.

Laura flung her arms around Chloe. 'I've missed you so much! It's so lovely to have you out with us.'

Laura moved and danced, and Gabby and Chloe matched her, laughing and cheering on each favourite song that was played until the drink and dancing left Chloe's bladder bursting at the seams. She let them know, persuading them she could do this alone, and made her way to the ladies room. The queue was long, the women rowdy and boosted by alcohol, but Chloe didn't care. She was assured by it. If a random man – or, more specifically, Danny – tried to infiltrate this area, Chloe could safely stand back and let these emboldened women kick him to the kerb. And feeling as high as she did, she'd probably join in, too.

The queue moved quicker the closer she got to the stalls, and soon enough she was deep in the melee of all the shrieks and laughter and the constant banging and locking of doors as a continuous stream of women, one in, one out, used the facilities. Hands washed, and lipstick reapplied, she walked out past the queue, hoping she would not need to visit here again this evening. The place was crowded now, probably at full capacity, and Chloe wove a path through the dancers and onlookers to where Laura and Gabby were still dancing. On the edge of the dance floor, Chloe felt the warmth of a hand on her shoulder and, sure it would be Tom, she turned with a smile, toying with the idea of a dance with him, their bodies touching.

But it was not Tom. To her horror, she looked directly into the eyes of Danny.

16

Danny was smartly dressed, looking like any other guy in the place. She ripped her shoulder from his hold and bellowed at him over the music: 'Get away from me!'

He looked disappointed, her anger not expected. 'I wanted to see you again, Chloe. You look so beautiful.' His eyes were much less discreet than Tom's had been, and she felt her skin crawl as he ogled her.

'Can we go somewhere? Talk?' He touched his ear, indicating the sound level was too much.

She shook her head. 'I don't want to talk to you. I never want to talk to you. Get out of my life. Do you understand?'

He grabbed her arm in an attempt to stop her from leaving.

She fought herself free and slammed her hands against his chest, barging him away from her. 'I said, leave me alone!' she yelled, and then turned and forced her way through the dancers, searching the sea of faces for Laura and Gabby.

He followed behind, shoving and pushing in order to keep up.

About to scream, she finally caught Laura's eye as she pushed people out of the way, ignoring their disapproval.

Laura immediately stopped dancing at the sight of her and Danny right behind. 'What the fuck!'

Chloe couldn't hear it, she only saw her friend mouth the words, but relief filled her as she neared Laura.

Laura strode towards them both. 'Chloe, are you okay?'

'I'm fine. I'm fine,' she said, breathless.

'I'm just here to see Chloe,' he shouted, a smile fixed in place, as if all of this was perfectly reasonable. 'I'm not here to cause trouble.'

'Just being here is causing trouble,' Laura shouted back.

Chloe moved to distance herself from him, but a sideways glance from Danny meant he saw it. He reached for her hand and gripped it. She wrenched it away, but in doing so she managed to smack it hard into a fellow clubber's arm as he walked past her.

'Sorry,' she said to the man. 'I didn't mean to do that.'

'Hey,' he barked at her. 'You want to be more careful, bitch.' After a death glare, he turned away.

Danny bumped into her as he launched towards the man, thunderous fury in his face. Chloe knew why. Danny would be furious that Chloe had been spoken to the way she had. He shoved the man, who returned one of his own, trapping Chloe between them as they tussled. Danny was ready for a fight, and one he looked well-matched to win. But his anger was intense and disproportionate for the situation, and he looked like he could kill this man given half the chance. Although the man was a low-life and probably deserved everything he would get, she wouldn't be responsible for him getting battered because of Danny's overreaction.

She shoved at Danny, separating the pair. 'Stop it, Danny!'

He moved quickly, red mist in his eyes, still wanting to land a glancing blow to the man. In doing so, he barged into her, knocking her out of the way, causing her to stumble and hold out her hand for balance.

'Chloe!' he cried, reaching for her.

She steadied herself, their scuffle likely to get them chucked out before too long. She saw Laura and Gabby in the commotion, trying to get to her, and then she saw Tom marching towards them, his friends towing behind.

He stepped between Chloe and Danny, and looked at the other man who was now pitching for a fight. 'Leave it, mate,' he said as he put his hand out assertively. They eyed each other for a moment, and when Tom wouldn't break the stare, the man conceded and soon moved on, shouting obscenities as he went.

'Who the fuck are you?' Danny bellowed.

'Not important, mate,' Tom replied. 'But you're gonna stop hassling her and get out of this fucking club.'

Danny's face was murderous, and Chloe was afraid of what he'd do next.

'I'm not going anywhere, *mate*,' Danny said, mocking Tom's tone. 'This is not your club, so I think I'll stay as long as I want. Mate.' He shoved Tom and waited, his stare demanding a response.

Tom reciprocated.

She couldn't let Tom be caught up in this mess. She wouldn't be able to live with herself if anything was to happen to him, but she also didn't want this – a centuries-old outdated ideal of two men fighting over her as if she were a mere possession to be owned.

'Stop it!' she yelled, as she struggled to separate them.

Gabby and Laura were making enough noise to catch the attention of the bouncers.

Two huge men approached, to the relief of Chloe.

They broke up the fight between Tom and Danny, and Chloe stepped back to allow them to deal with it. Laura wrapped an arm around her, and Gabby did the same as chaos ensued when other dancers got involved, and she let them remove her from the situation. A sudden emptiness hit her through the alcohol and adrenaline. She wanted to go home. She wanted the life she had before. She wanted its safe predictability.

Danny's posture was taut, unnaturally calm as he listened to the bouncers. This, when viewed with Tom's very visible anger, emphasised just how well Danny could manipulate a situation to his advantage. He was playing the victim, happy to create a fiction that implicated Tom as the instigator of the scrap on the dance floor. Tom's friends animatedly inter-vened, hastily giving their support, having watched it all unfold. One of the bouncers guided Danny to the edge of the floor, and the other continued to speak with Tom.

Chloe watched Danny being led away towards the exit by the bouncer, and only then, when he was through the door and out of sight, did Chloe breathe her relief. Tom was calmer now, too, and whatever he was saying to the other bouncer, it was working. At one point there was laughter. With a pat on Tom's shoulder the bouncer walked away, and Tom's friends surrounded him in discussion. Tom glanced Chloe's way and smiled apologetically.

Chloe went to their table and sat, and Laura and Gabby hastily followed.

'Let's get some more drinks,' Gabby said, trying to get the evening back on track.

'I don't want anything,' Chloe said, exhausted. 'But you two go ahead. I'm going to stay here.'

'Are you sure?' Laura said. 'We can stay with you if you'd prefer.' She glanced behind, towards the centre of the room and the crowd that now filled the space where the commo-tion had been. 'Looks like Danny's gone. I can't see him, and the bouncers aren't around either.'

'I know,' she said waspishly. 'I saw it, too.'

Laura placed her hand on Chloe's shoulder. 'Honey, are you sure we can't get you a drink?'

She shook her head. 'No, I've had enough.'

Sensing their friend's desire to be given some time alone, they cautiously collected their bags.

'Okay, but we're just going to be over there, and we'll be back in a second,' Laura said, pointing to the bar. 'I can still see you from there.'

'Christ, I'm not a child,' Chloe snapped. 'I don't need to be watched like one. Do whatever you want. I'm not bothered.'

Laura and Gabby glanced at each other and then walked away.

Tom was still with his friends at the side of the dance floor, but he broke off whatever conversation they were having and strode towards Chloe when he saw Gabby and Laura leave.

'Can I join you?' he asked tentatively.

'If you must,' she said with a shrug.

'I'm sorry about that. I know that was the last thing you needed. I just saw red when I saw Danny with his hands on you. I know how he's made you feel recently, and it made me angry.'

'I don't need you fighting over me. This is the fucking twenty-first century, you know.'

'Of course, and I'm sorry. The need to protect you came from nowhere. He's put you through so much. I couldn't help it.'

Chloe softened a little, feeling guilty that she had shown so little gratitude when they all just wanted to help. She smiled and looked at him, seeing the concern in his eyes. 'I know, I'm sorry. I'm so grateful that you're looking out for me. I'm glad you were there, and Laura and Gabby too. I can't believe I was so stupid to go to the toilets by myself.'

'But you should be able to do these things. Jesus, Chloe, that guy is a weirdo, and a dangerous one at that.'

In the loud club, with the music pumping and the crowd heaving, tears welled in Chloe's eyes. And right now, she didn't have the strength to fight them.

He noticed and wore a pained expression. 'I'm so sorry, Chloe. I didn't mean to make things worse.'

She shook her head. 'No, it's not you. I should have been more careful. I'm sorry, too, for putting you all in that situation. I mean, that man was an idiot, I don't care about him. But it scares me to realise I don't know what I'd have done if Danny had got to me just seconds before. He could have dragged me away, and in the dark and amongst the crowds no one would have noticed.'

'I would have,' he said with a smile, and it melted her heart.

'Tom, you're so sweet,' she said sadly. Whatever seedling of a beginning they might have had together was now ruined.

'What do you want to do?' he asked, gently wiping a tear from her cheek.

'I want to get out of here,' she said with no hesitation. 'I want to go home.'

'I can take you.'

'I'm supposed to be staying at Laura's but now it just feels like wherever I go, whether to Laura's or mine, there will be trouble.' She shrugged. 'It's inevitable. He'll be angry, looking for revenge for being thrown out against his will, which makes it worse. I can't deny that her apartment block is the safest option, with Sam there and the security, too, but still... the idea of bringing trouble to their door doesn't sit easy with me.'

He nodded, listening intently, and took a moment to consider. 'Okay, well, how about you come to mine?'

Her eyes shot to his.

He smiled and held up his hands. 'No funny business, I promise. Just a safe place to rest your head.'

'And you think we'll be able to stick to that plan?'

'I'm not going to lie, I'm very attracted to you, Chloe. But I just want to help. I have a spare room which I'm told is comfy, and we have the added bonus of Danny being clueless about where I live.'

'What if he follows us?'

'Then we'll make sure the taxi takes a few detours until we lose him. We can speak to the police when you're ready to report what's gone on tonight. I'm sure there's enough evidence now to charge him.'

Though still conflicted, she couldn't deny the appeal of disappearing for a night and forgetting about everything for a while. 'You're sure you don't mind?' she asked. 'I'm kind of a liability these days.'

'Of course I don't mind. It's the least I can do.'

'Okay,' she said hesitantly. 'That sounds great.'

'Perfect,' he said, looking up at his friends, chatting easily with Laura and Gabby. No doubt exchanging their opinions about the events of the night. 'Do you want to go and tell the others?'

Again, she nodded. 'Yeah, I can't just leave them without explaining. They'll go out of their minds if I'm not here.'

They shuffled up from the table, and Tom motioned for her to go first, following behind.

Laura noticed Chloe first, her smile fading to concern. 'You've been crying.'

'Yeah, I'm sorry for snapping at you both,' she said as Gabby joined them.

Laura took her hand. 'We didn't think anything of it. You're under so much pressure; I'm concerned about you.'

'I know, and I'm sorry tonight has ended on a downer. I know you wanted it to be perfect.'

'Hey, don't worry about that. We had some fun, before Danny arrived, and Tom's here now. What do you want to do?'

'I'd like to leave. I'm sorry. Do you mind?'

'That's fine. Let's round up our things and we'll grab a taxi.'

Chloe placed her hand over Laura's. 'No, honey, not like that. I can't come to yours now.'

'Why?' Laura asked, dismayed.

'I love you so much for what you've done for me tonight, but I won't bring trouble to you.'

'But Sam's at home.'

'I know, but Danny will be irrational, I'm sure. Wherever I go, he goes, and if he knows I'm with you, he won't stop until he gets to me. If he realises I'm not there, he'll leave and try to find me elsewhere. Do you understand?'

'But you can't go home,' Laura said. 'If he's angry, it's more dangerous to be alone. You need to call the police. Come back to mine. Please.'

'Well, yes, I will speak to the police, obviously, and...this is a little awkward, but Tom's offered me his spare room.'

Laura's gaze moved to Tom, her interest awakened. 'Has he now?'

'It's somewhere neutral, that's all,' Chloe said. 'Danny won't know where he lives, and I can't face another confrontation tonight.'

Laura nodded her agreement, but failed to lose the knowing smile that tipped her lips. 'Okay, that sounds like a solution. Tom will look after you.'

'What about you?' Chloe asked.

'We'll be fine. We'll make sure Sam comes down to meet us from the taxi.'

Relieved, Chloe felt the tension melt away. 'Yes, that sounds like a plan. A really good plan.'

Laura placed her hand on Chloe's arm and pulled her aside. 'Listen, I just wanted to check that, you know, you have everything you need for a stay at Tom's?'

With an eye roll, Chloe understood exactly what Laura was hinting at. 'I'm sure I will be fine. I'll be staying in his spare room, but I appreciate the thought.'

'Okay, it's sweet that you think that way, but you – gorgeous you – with him, both with alcohol in your system and enough electricity to power the national grid? Well, it's the perfect storm.' She rummaged through her bag, unzipping a side pocket. 'Here, take this,' she said as she handed Chloe the square foil packet. 'It's old, but not that old. It'll do the job.'

Laura astutely picked up the confusion on Chloe's face. 'It's from my life before Sam. You know I don't play away from home.'

Chloe nodded. 'I know,' she said, tucking it into her bag. She wouldn't need it, but if it appeased her friend to have it, where was the harm? 'That's sensible, I suppose.'

'Yes, it sure is,' Laura said as she pulled Chloe into a motherly hug. 'Now, you take care and get out of here.'

They walked together to Tom and his friends.

Tom waited for Chloe in the foyer of the club while she collected her jacket. At her request, they remained inside until the taxi pulled up, hurrying out when it arrived, keeping their heads down. Nerves crept in, and Chloe jumped at every shout and call on the street, expecting to see Danny racing towards her.

'It's okay, Chloe. I won't let anything happen,' Tom murmured by her side, pulling open the door of the taxi.

She nodded, and only exhaled when they were safely in the car and pulling away, finally leaving the club and chaos behind.

17

Chloe gazed out of the window as the driver turned into a street of terraced houses, all matching in a uniform design of attractive white bay windows, the front door on the left, and a handful of steps leading up to each one. The road was well maintained and lined with trees.

'This is nice.'

'Thanks,' Tom said. 'When I decided to step fully into adulthood and leave the house-shares and rentals behind, I chose this place. That was four or five years ago now and, you know, if we're talking investments, the property has a garden and has good links to the city, blah, blah, blah. You know, the standard agent pitch.'

'Well, I can see why. It's a lovely street, and I bet those trees look exquisite in the spring.'

He shrugged. 'Uh, yeah, I guess they do.'

She smiled as the driver pulled up next to a parked car, and Tom handed him a couple of notes.

'Cheers, mate.'

They both got out of the car, and she glanced around, checking for any signs that Danny had followed them here.

'There's nothing to worry about,' Tom said, when he realised what she was doing. 'I've been checking the mirror all the way here. There's been no car tailing us.'

He strode to her as the car pulled away. 'Are you sure about this?'

She nodded. Her mind was fuzzy, but one thing she knew was she didn't want to be alone.

Tom gestured for her to go up the steps to the red front door. 'After you.'

He opened the door for her, and she stepped inside. The exposed floorboards and long hallway led to a carpeted staircase ahead of her.

Tom pulled off his coat and took Chloe's. 'Just through there on the left,' he said, hanging the coats on a Victorian-looking coat rack by the door.

She walked through to the living room. The bay window had its white blinds pulled down to shut out the night, and the lamps he'd left on for his return filled the room with a cosy hue. She liked it a lot.

The exposed brick fireplace, the only pop of colour in a white painted room, was large and, from what she could gather from the remnants of log and ash in the grate, it still worked. She imagined the flames that burned there and turned away from it, calming the shudder that trembled her body. Focusing elsewhere, she liked that he'd kept the ornate ceiling architrave and centre rose but had a large modern light fitting hanging from it to balance it out. Old and new, together.

'You have a really nice place here, Tom,' she said after a moment, wanting to break the tension creeping up on her. It had felt like a good idea to do this at the club, but now she was here, the reality was awkward.

'Can I get you a drink?' he asked.

'Some water would be great, please. I've had my fill of alcohol for one evening.'

She followed him into the kitchen, a long galley with double doors leading to what she assumed was the garden, currently hidden by darkness. Knowing Tom, she knew it would be well cared for.

She leaned against the metal countertop, almost clinical in its look, only broken up by the stripped wood-effect cupboards above and below.

'This is very unusual,' she said, running her hand over the smooth, grey metal.

'The guy who had this place before me was a chef, so I just got to benefit from his choices. I never bothered to change it, especially as it works so well.'

'Are you lining up another career? Has the world of corporate banking left you jaded?'

Tom chuckled. 'I guess part of me will always be jaded with banking, but no. No second career as a chef for me. I can burn air.'

He pulled out a bottle of sparkling water from the fridge and filled two glasses. Handing one to her, he gestured back towards the living room. Not sure where to sit, she crossed the room to gaze at the photos arranged on the white shelving either side of the fireplace. Pictures of him with friends – the glowing, slightly sunburnt nights out from holidays abroad and celebrations around dining tables – and with family.

There was no mistaking his parentage. Tom, the image of his father, whose distinguished Nordic features, blue eyes and grey-blonde hair, made him very attractive; his mother, equally as attractive, with a flash of grey that ran through the front of her shoulder-length hair, deep dark eyes with cute wrinkles in the corners as she smiled, and honeyed skin. A sister, with the same blonde hair curled around her face and dark eyes like her mother. But Chloe couldn't guess her age. She was almost the same height as Tom, who completed the image of a family content in each other's company. They were laughing, at what looked to be a happy occasion, from their attire a wedding. Tucked at the back stood a photo of him with friends she recognised from other shots, but in this one his arms were wrapped around a young woman. They were all bundled up in coats and scarves against the blue-pink light of a crisp midwinter's sunny day. The woman snuggled into him, resting her head on his chest as they all smiled at the camera, their noses pink from the cold. She was beautiful, her long raven-coloured hair shining in the light as it tumbled over her shoulder.

She thought of David and the compliments he gave when she was at the centre of his world. How he had told her how much he loved her hair. How he said it looked like the colour of sand on a beach at sunset. Golden. He used to touch it, idly run his fingers through it as she lay in his lap watching a film, or in bed discussing their plans for their future together. Turns out, as Chloe discovered, what David really loved was brunette hair. A particular long-haired, brown-eyed brunette specifically, with a full pout and a heart that just needed to be loved. His words, not hers.

She turned to Tom. 'Nice pictures.'

'Yeah, had some fun over the years,' he said as he joined her. 'Lots of good times.'

She nodded. 'You look like your dad.'

'And he doesn't let me forget it, believe me,' he said with a smile. 'Said he should donate his genes to science because they're so pure and perfect. It was his duty to allow other people to benefit from his wondrous looks and his ability to create a carbon copy of himself.'

'So he kept his modesty, then,' Chloe said wryly.

'Totally,' Tom said with a smirk.

'That's a very attractive woman,' Chloe said, pointing to

the group photo and the woman with her arms around Tom. She shouldn't have said it, it was none of her business, but she couldn't help herself. She needed the details of what might be going on there.

'That's Claire,' he said. 'And whatever we had was over a long time ago.'

'Oh,' Chloe said, hugely relieved. 'That's a shame. She's very beautiful.'

'She is, but that's not the reason I've kept the photo. It's a great group shot, and I wasn't going to take it down just because she's in it. That would make me bitter, and I'm not.'

'That's a great attitude,' Chloe said. 'Bitterness is a horrible thing. It can eat you up if you're not careful. Stop you from moving forward.'

'Oh, don't get me wrong, at the end she gave me every reason to be, but, for the most part, we were like any other couple – good times and bad, the usual – until one day she decided our paths were no longer aligned.' Chloe couldn't help but smile as he made exaggerated air quotations. 'She said she "needed to find herself" and, at that point, I realised my feelings for her were not strong enough to fight to keep the relationship going. One of those things. We're still friends, though, but probably only because it's long-distance. She's in Thailand now, teaching English at a local school.'

Chloe smiled and tried to keep an air of equanimity despite her heart thumping. It crept up on her now and then. It liked to remind her of everything she was doing, all the mistakes she was making. 'Sounds lovely. Very rewarding.'

'She is very happy,' he said, pointing at the sofa. 'Please, sit. Make yourself comfortable. It's been a hell of a night. You must be exhausted.'

She joined him on the pale brown leather sofa, sitting at the furthest end.

An awkward silence descended. The rush of emotion in the club had died down during the taxi journey.

She smiled at him. 'I am so grateful for this, Tom.'

'You're welcome, Chloe. Happy to help.'

'I won't stay long or keep you from your weekend plans.'

'I don't have any. I'm in no rush. Stay as long as you'd like.'

The room was quiet, peaceful, and she realised she hadn't had any texts from Danny. For now, she wouldn't worry about what that meant. She would enjoy her haven with Tom. She imagined Laura and Gabby and the hangover they'd have tomorrow and was suddenly grateful for the glass of water in her hand.

'Laura was telling me about the first report you gave to the police,' he said.

She sighed. 'Yeah, for all the good it'll do. He had a warning and was told he'll be arrested if he oversteps again. Tonight was probably that overstep, but I know someone like him will always manage to wiggle out of it somehow. I just don't want to think about how he'll do it.'

'The man is a psycho.'

'I'm in over my head, that's for sure. Some days I think the only option is for me to run away.'

'Don't say that, Chlo,' he said, reaching his arm out to affectionately tap her on the shoulder.

'So you'd miss me, then?' she said with a smile.

He nodded, smiling too. 'Of course I would. I would miss your face. Your smile.'

'That's sweet,' she said, glancing down. When she dared to look up and found his gaze, she was sure it had never left her.

He moved and gently took hold of her hand. 'I think you know how I feel about you, though.'

She nodded, as electricity began to buzz between them and her body stirred, a silent call, reaching out to his. She let their fingers link together, the sensation producing a small gasp from her lips. It was what she wanted, this with him, and what she feared, all in one rush of emotion.

Suddenly uncertain, she withdrew her hand, leaving his empty. 'I should get some more water.'

She stood and rushed to the kitchen, going straight to the sink to clumsily pour fresh water into her glass. She turned to find Tom standing in the doorway.

'I'm sorry,' he said. 'I didn't mean to make you uncomfortable. And I didn't bring you here for anything other than to give you a break from him. You know that, don't you?'

'Yes, of course I do,' she said, having no reason to doubt him. He might have wanted more – he made no secret of his desire – but he would not trick her into it, or take advantage. He was better than that. 'And you didn't make me uncomfortable. I can do that all by myself.' She drank a little water from the glass. 'Tom, I hope you know that in any other situation I wouldn't be so cautious. I really like you, too, and getting to know you better would be something I'd like very much.' She placed the glass down and wrapped her arms around herself. 'But I'm a walking disaster at the moment.'

'No, you're not. None of this is your fault.'

'I wish that were true.' She ran her hands through her hair and looked to the floor. 'Everything is messed up. Everything is so complicated.'

'Do you want to talk about it?'

'No, you might end up hating me. And I can't risk losing you because of it.'

He shook his head, sympathy etched on his face. 'Why would I do that?'

'I haven't handled this well. I've mucked up and made it worse.'

'I could never hate you, whatever has happened, and I'm not going anywhere.'

Her heart melted, and she wanted to run to him, hold him, to feel protected in his arms. 'I thought I had everything ahead of me, you know?' she said. 'Married life and all that. We weren't perfect. God knows, we were far from it. But I knew what my life was. And then, in the blink of an eye, it was all gone.'

'I'm so sorry, Chloe.'

'For a while I was lost, drifting, not knowing how to move forward. The betrayal, the grief. It consumed me. I should have taken the time to heal. To really heal. Maybe then I could have moved on.'

'What do you mean?'

She shook her head. She'd said too much. Now wasn't the time. 'It doesn't matter. Let's not do this now. I don't want to bring the mood down even further.'

'You know I'm always here if you want to talk,' he said gently.

'I know. But tonight I just want to forget.'

He walked to her and placed his glass in the sink. 'Okay, well, are you hungry? Because I have a serious case of the munchies.'

'Maybe a little,' she said with a shrug.

'So glad you said that. What do you fancy?'

'Whatever you're having,' she said.

He held out his hand. 'Then come with me, my lady, and I'll prepare you a midnight snack. The king of all midnight snacks.'

He got to work and pulled out a bowl and pan from the cupboard and eggs from the fridge. 'Okay, maybe I was a bit over-ambitious with my statement, but I do make a mean omelette. Just saying.'

She laughed and leaned against the counter as he busied himself.

'Oh, no, no. You don't get to watch. You're helping. Come here.'

She sidled up beside him. 'Yes, chef?'

He grabbed an egg and hit the side of the bowl. 'Number one.' He grabbed another and handed it to her. 'Your turn.'

She cracked the egg into the bowl. He repeated the action with a third, then mumbled something about a whisk and began haphazardly opening cupboards.

'Aha!' he said, pulling out an electric whisk. 'I knew I'd need this one day.'

He plugged it in at the wall, angled the whisk into the bowl and clicked the button. It circled into action, began to wobble, and then clattered into the bowl with some speed. The gelatinous mixture exploded into the room, hitting every surface possible, including them both. He reached for the plug, expletives rushing from his mouth as he yanked it from the socket, and did as much damage limitation as he could as the appliance slowed to a stop.

She gasped as she looked down at her clothes, splattered with the mixture, and then at him – and burst into laughter.

'Oh no,' he said, rushing for the towel next to the sink. 'Here, let me.'

He gently wiped her down and then tended to himself, all while hurriedly apologising as they laughed like two kids. Then he folded the towel in half to use a cleaner edge and focused on her face, wiping the mixture from her cheek.

'Stop,' she said, giggling. 'I think it's gone now, along with my make-up.'

He stood close. She looked up at him and the little dots of mixture splattered over his face. 'Here,' she said softly, taking the towel from his hold to gently wipe his face.

Close up, and able to take in every feature, she saw how perfect he was, from his forehead to his chin. Kind eyes, perfect mouth. Still and silent, they remained this way, eyes locked and her lips aching with the desire to kiss him.

'I can do another omelette,' he said quietly, his face close to hers. 'If you're hungry?'

She nodded, still lost in his eyes.

With his thumb, he gently wiped away a trace of the mixture from her hairline. 'It'll only take a minute.'

'Okay.'

Their breathing quickening, he tossed the towel aside. Their lips collided, crushing, seeking what they desired. She wrapped her arms around his neck as a sigh escaped her mouth into his. His hands wrapped around her waist, pulling her to him, the kiss lingering and deepening as their tongues explored. He held her close, keeping her steady. She melted into him, into the kiss. It was firm, expert, and she yearned for more.

He pulled back, his lips swollen and wet as they both panted for air.

'We should stop,' he said breathlessly. 'This isn't why I suggested coming here.'

'I know,' she breathed.

He held her face in his hands as his body skimmed hers. 'I can't lie, I am so fucking attracted to you, and I think I have been since the first day we met. But I won't take advantage of you, Chloe. I will be your friend first, if that's what you want.'

She should have said yes to remaining friends. A sane person would agree, but there was no fighting it – this was always going to happen if the circumstances ever allowed, and in this moment she realised how much she wanted it. So much that she could no longer focus on anything else.

'I know, Tom,' she breathed. 'I know. But please kiss me like that again. I want this. I want you.'

He nodded, and she was ready when his lips touched

hers, warm and insistent. She fell into the moment, understanding that whatever her body craved it would be granted.

He manoeuvred her gently towards the stairs, stumbling, hurrying. Lips touched; hands explored impatiently. In his bedroom, his fingers reached for the clasp of her halter neck, unclipping it and letting it fall at her feet. She was naked except for her underwear, and his eyes widened as he beheld her, his fingers caressing her skin.

'Beautiful,' he murmured. 'Just like I knew you would be.'

He nuzzled her neck, his tongue exploring her skin, and she swayed and moved with each gentle command. Lost in his touch, spellbound, and wanting more, she relished the shudder that seized her body. She let her fingers glide over his taut, soft skin as she unbuttoned his shirt and slipped it over his shoulders, catching the sandalwood and sage drifting from his skin. His body was toned, his shoulders broad, and she wanted to explore every part of him. He reciprocated, gently trailing his fingers over her body.

'You're stunning,' he breathed, as his lips brushed against her skin.

She let out a soft sigh as he walked her backwards towards the bed. She lay down and let him remove her underwear, arching her back to assist. His mouth was on her before she had time to prepare, and she gasped as he found her breasts, sending jolts of pleasure as her body revived itself with forgotten sensations. It had been so long since David and their easy marital sex. This was unfamiliar. Someone new to discover, and it was thrilling.

She trusted him. The only man she trusted in this strange time in her life, and she didn't want it to end. Their hands roamed, bodies touched, hungry for more, sending them on a new journey.

She arched her back in pleasure, their eyes locked on one

another. His fingers ventured lower, and she adjusted her legs a little to show that, yes, she wanted this.

Mouths joined, she felt his gasp as his fingers explored, in awe of her body, and for a moment she felt cherished. Wanted. She moaned at each caress, delighting in the tender touch. The coupling of two people, bound by an intimate vow. Her hands wandered, too, over curves and muscles. Her body tensed, feeling the embers of pleasure flicker into flames. She remembered what Laura had given her, and with a hazy thought she spoke.

'I need my bag,' she whispered.

'Why?' he murmured, through kisses.

She looked at him.

'Oh,' he said, understanding. 'Don't worry, I have one here.' He grabbed what he needed from the drawer of his bedside table and returned to kiss her deeply.

She relaxed into the moment again and moved beneath him, giving silent consent. Their moans combined as he sunk himself into her, with only the movement of their bodies and the breath of whispered promises filling the room. They moved in unison, alive with the discovery of newfound desire, and kept the rhythm as the tension built, taking her closer to the edge of her climax. Her body hungry, it sought the release it yearned for until splinters of pleasure tore through her, pulsating jolts that rolled through her body. He watched as she came undone before his eyes, in the street-lit darkness of his room, and it wasn't long before he followed, groaning low against her neck as he found his own blissful release.

Exhausted from pleasure and alcohol, they slumped together, their breaths quick as they came down from their high.

'I can't think,' she murmured, after a moment. 'Feels like the world has stopped.'

He moved to lay beside her, pulling her close into his arms. 'It hasn't stopped turning. It's brand new, that's all. For both of us.'

She sighed and snuggled into him, wanting to believe. No more words were spoken, only kisses, until she slipped into sleep.

18

Chloe woke to Tom's bedroom shrouded in inky darkness. And silence, too, except for the soft sound of Tom's rhythmic breaths. Her eyes adjusted and found his silhouette, the cover draped over his lower half, exposing his long, sleek back, and his arm resting against his body. She wanted to touch him, to nuzzle his skin until he awoke, and to arouse him again. Instead, she yawned silently. Sleep hadn't refreshed her, but the pleasures they'd shared in the night had been worth it. Theirs was a three-act play. The hurried passion, the journey of discovery, and finally, the expertise, their bodies knowing exactly what to do to satisfy the other.

But while she wanted to revel in this new beginning, something inside prevented her from giving into it completely. This was a complication. They'd laid themselves bare emotionally, and now she knew exactly how Tom felt about her. She felt the same, but the responsibility of keeping him safe from Danny and the harm he could do if he ever discovered what had gone on was heavy around her neck, like a dark doom-filled prophecy.

Chloe shifted, and the movement set off an explosion in her head. She moaned and clutched her forehead, even though it wouldn't help. Grateful that it was the weekend and there was no need to rush, she slowly pushed the covers back and sidled out of the bed. She needed to hydrate and maybe find a packet of painkillers to tackle the herd of elephants trampling over her brain. She dressed and tip-toed to the kitchen as the swell of nausea pooled in her stomach.

Grabbing a glass from last night, she ran the water until it was ice-cold and filled it. She drank, letting it refresh her, and then gazed out of the window at the grey morning sky.

She heard the padding of his footsteps behind her, and smiled when Tom gently brushed her hair aside and pressed his lips against the nape of her neck.

'Morning, Chlo,' he murmured, still sleepy.

'Hi.'

He wrapped his arms around her, and they stood in silent contentment until she was sure she'd float away on the peace that bloomed inside her.

'A penny for them,' he said.

'What?'

'Your thoughts.'

She turned to face him, resting her hands on his chest. 'I didn't know how much I wanted this, you, until it happened. Last night was perfect.'

'Couldn't agree more,' he said. 'And I can't believe how I nearly blew it by acting the way I did in the club.'

'You were only looking out for me. I understand that, and whilst I shouldn't condone what you did...I really kind of liked it.'

He raised a brow. 'You did?'

She nodded. 'I feel safe with you. Taken care of. It's nice.'

'Happy to help,' he said.

'Keep that to yourself, though. I have a reputation to maintain.'

'Secret's safe with me,' he said. 'So, how can I be of service now, my lady?'

Sadness appeared like a cloud hovering above them both. 'Ah, well.'

He tipped her face up to his. 'That doesn't sound good.'

She hesitated, nervous to share her thoughts. 'As much as I want to continue with this, it might be best for me to go.'

He struggled to hide his disappointment. 'No, don't say that. We have the whole weekend ahead of us.'

'Believe me, I don't want to, but I'm scared. What if Danny finds us?'

'I don't care if he finds out. I'm a big boy. He's not going to hurt me.'

She shook her head. 'I know that, but he doesn't play by the rules, and it would be a mistake to underestimate him. Can you say with all honesty that he won't find a way to hurt you? Can you guarantee that?'

'Well, no, but—'

'Then what choice do I have?' She looked up at him. 'I believe him when he makes threats, and you should, too.'

'The police know he has form. We'll call them, report what he did last night.'

'The police can't be with us twenty-four-seven. He'll find a way. And what if he's already out there watching, waiting, deciding on his next move?'

'Let's take baby steps,' Tom soothed. 'He hasn't come here yet. He's not banging on the door, so let's assume he's in the dark right now. Take a moment to think about this.'

'I think about nothing else.'

'I know,' he said as he pulled her closer and rested his forehead gently against hers. 'And I'm here for you, if you'd let me in.'

'I love that you feel that way, but I think this is something I have to do alone. It's my mess, my error of judgement.'

His arms enveloped her, making the choice more difficult.

'You're not alone. Far from it. Trust me and let me prove it.'

Resting against the warmth of his body, she tried to trust, wanted to trust. 'It's my fault,' she whispered.

He gently stroked her hair. 'How is it your fault? You're not responsible for his behaviour.'

'But you don't understand. I invited him into my life. I started it.'

He hushed her, held her a little tighter. 'You can't think like that.'

'But I do, because it's the truth. I was a fool. I didn't care if he could ruin my life because I didn't think I had a life worth living, so I was reckless with it. But now...now everything is different. I wish I could go back and change what I've done. I've been so careless. Other people are involved. You, Laura, and I'm not convinced he won't find my parents. I'm scared to confront him about it. The responsibility is too much.'

'Chloe,' he whispered. 'It's okay.'

Feeling as though something was unravelling inside, the tears – the bulbous drops of emotional desperation – fell from her eyes and trailed tracks down his chest, one after the other. She'd wanted to be strong and had tried for so long to achieve it, but she was tired of holding back the fire. The barriers were down, and she no longer had control of herself. He held her and let her release what she needed to, gently soothing her, holding her tight.

When the torrent of emotion had passed, he sat her down and ran a paper towel under the tap so she could dab her face. The cool towel against her hot blotchy skin was needed, and as she calmed, a sense of balance returned.

He crouched in front of her, wiping away a stray tear.

'Chloe, I know what you've been through with David, and I know the responsibility you feel to do the right thing, but if you can, let me take care of you. For a while at least.'

'I want to stay with you more than anything—'

'Then stay,' he said, his eyes searching hers.

'Tom,' she whispered, as she let his hand cup her cheek.

'Give us more time, Chloe. Just an hour if need be. Let all the problems stay out there for a while. Be here. With me.'

He placed a gentle kiss on her lips, and that was all she needed. That, and the way his eyes searched hers, intensifying her hunger for him. She couldn't help but respond, knowing her plan was doomed. She'd crumbled at his first words of persuasion, even though she'd wanted desperately to resist. She couldn't leave. She wanted Tom as much as he wanted her, and the knowledge left her open and ready to admit her feelings for him were far deeper than she'd allowed.

'Yes,' she murmured, as he kissed her again, leaving her defences at her feet. 'I'll stay.'

CHLOE SHOWERED and dressed in her jumpsuit again, having managed to clean up most of the mess from last night, and drank the coffee Tom made for her while she waited for the taxi. She could take the tube – it would only be a ten-minute ride at this time of the morning – but she was far too old for the morning-after-the-night-before walk of shame, and too tired to worry about Danny's whereabouts or how he'd react if he saw her in last night's clothes.

Tom made a good effort of an upbeat mood, but his prolonged hold of her hand and the hunch there was much more he needed to say told Chloe this was not what he wanted. At all. She was reluctant, too, but she had managed to persuade him that her returning home was for the best as the sun hung in the midday sky. Going home now was the only way she could protect him from all the crazy in her life.

The journey home was quiet, and she successfully avoided being drawn into a conversation with the driver. When he pulled up to the kerb, she checked up and down her road before getting out of the car. No sign of Danny.

She rushed down the steps and pushed the key in her front door, swiftly slipping inside and locking it securely behind her. She moved through her home with precision, checking all the doors and windows for signs of an intruder. Only when satisfied he'd not broken in again did she feel ready to switch on her phone and face the flood of messages she knew he would have sent. She'd turned it off in the early hours of the morning, not wanting anything, specifically Danny, to disrupt her and Tom's moments together. Danny would not infiltrate or tarnish her time with him.

The screen lit up with countless messages. She logged on to discover twenty from Danny and one from Laura. Danny's were threatening. He knew she hadn't been home. He'd obviously been here, but from the exasperated tone of his messages, he was unaware of her location. That was comforting at least, and she let out a huge sigh. But when she checked Laura's message, her heart sank.

Fate had given with one hand and taken away with the other. Danny had been to her apartment block several times and had stood in the grounds calling out Chloe's name. Laura, Sam, and Gabby had watched the commotion from their living-room window, bemused but not afraid. He was no threat, apparently, and with nowhere to direct his anger, he was only an irritation to the other residents. After thirty minutes of shouting for Chloe and an altercation with the building's security team, he was removed from the grounds.

She called up Laura's number. 'Laura,' she said once her friend picked up the phone, 'I'm so sorry. Is everything okay?'

'It's fine, honey. He was just a nuisance and looked quite the loser.'

'This is what I wanted to avoid. I'm so sorry you're caught up in this. I really hadn't anticipated how far his reach would be.'

'Don't be silly. Of course you didn't know. How could you? He's a crazy dude. But we're safely tucked up here. My head is banging like a banshee still, even though it's...what, four o'clock in the afternoon? Bloody hell, Gabby, what were we drinking last night?'

Gabby's response was muffled, and probably rambling, if she was as hungover as Laura. Always the lightweight, Gabby went out with good intentions to pace herself but would always drink too much too quickly, paying the price for it the next day.

'I'm glad you both got home safely, even if you have got the mother of hangovers.'

Laura relayed the conversation to Gabby, to which there was another mumbled response.

'Can you apologise to Sam, too?'

'He's all right, don't worry about him. He was totally invested, ready to go out there and confront Danny himself. Said it was better than anything that was on the box. Anyway, where are you now?' Laura asked. 'Home or at Tom's? And is there a nice little juicy something to share with your best buddy? I jolly well hope so, or all my effort would have been in vain.'

Chloe's cheeks burned so hard she was sure Laura would feel the heat through the phone. 'I went to Tom's, as we agreed,' she replied. 'And I wanted it to be platonic...'

'Fucking hell, please tell me there's a "but" coming.'

She bit down on her lip, unable to stop the grin. 'Yes.'

Laura hollered and then promptly groaned. 'Ugh, bloody hangover, but forget that. I'm thrilled! So, tell me, what was it like?'

Chloe couldn't conceal her smile. 'It was lovely. Really lovely.'

'I knew it!' Laura exclaimed. 'The drought is officially over. So, details, please.'

'A lady never tells.'

'Chloe,' Laura warned, 'I'm hungover. I haven't seen Sam since last night because he took himself off to the gym really early, which means I haven't had my morning...attention. I'm a little bit testy. I need details. Now.'

Chloe chuckled. 'Okay, well, he's gorgeous, has a body to die for and knows *exactly* what he's doing. I'm very, very satisfied. But that's all I'm saying!'

Laura squealed, triggering a string of expletives from Gabby in the background.

'But it's more than that. He's kind, and funny too.'

'And completely into you.'

'Perhaps.'

'Ha,' Laura cried. 'I knew you two just needed a little nudge.'

Chloe sighed. 'Yes, well, thank you for that, and I am really grateful, but it has muddied the water a little.'

'How so?'

'Danny. Can you imagine what he'd do if he found out?'

'You need to concentrate on getting that little creep out of your life once and for all, Chloe. Just don't let Tom slip through your fingers. He's one of the good ones.'

'I know, I know. I'll do my best.'

Her phone began to ping throughout their conversation until Chloe couldn't concentrate on anything else and made her excuses to go. Glancing at the phone, she groaned.

> Chloe, my patience is wearing thin. You cannot treat me like this. I will be waiting for you tonight.

She should ignore him. Go and do everything she needed to do: another shower, fresh clothes, and something to eat. But something made her reply. Anger or desperation, she wasn't sure.

> No, Danny. You will not call me. You will not come to my house. I will call the police the minute you do. Leave me alone.

His reply came back almost immediately.

> We'll see. I'll see you tonight. We need to talk. Circumstances have changed.

She took a screenshot of all the messages and then tossed the phone down on her sofa. That would have to be enough for now. She needed time to think, to plan what she would do next. She kicked off her shoes and carried them to her room, discarding her clothes into the laundry basket on her way. She stepped into the warm shower and lingered there as the water cleansed her skin.

Finished and dressed in a faded Rolling Stones T-shirt and jeans, she decided to make eggs to replace what she'd missed last night.

She switched on the TV, letting the Saturday bonanza of cookery shows fill the silence just as her mobile buzzed again. Wearily, she checked the number. It was a local landline. Cautiously, she answered.

'Hello, Miss Stark?' the man said. 'It's PC Allan. How are you?'

'I'm okay. Well, I'm still struggling on, and I guess that's as good as can be expected.'

'Has Danny been in touch at all?'

'He found me in the bar last night. There was a confrontation, but they chucked him out. This morning I've had a
couple of texts, more of the usual.'

'Well, that's interesting because I have some news, too,' he
began. 'We've been to see Danny.'

19

C hloe froze. Was that the change he mentioned? Had he been charged? Was this over? If so, she didn't know how she felt about it. Was it enough? Would he return? The thought that they'd been to his home also crept into her mind, intriguing her. A small part of her wanted to know exactly where he lived, what his house looked like, and if it showed signs of his true nature or if it looked just like any other home – normal, tidy, lived-in.

'What did he say this time? I bet he denied contacting me.'

'Actually, he called us.'

'What?' she gasped.

'He wanted to report the altercation last night that you've just mentioned.'

'Yes, I was going to report it, too,' she said hurriedly, embarrassed that it hadn't been the first thing she had done since leaving the club.

'We went to his home and had a chat with him. He had some pretty nasty bruises on his face. Looked like he'd taken a bit of a beating. Claims he was on the dance floor when your friend Tom got a little physical, and when Danny was thrown out, Tom followed, manhandled him into an alley and assaulted him.'

'What? No! That's not how it happened. I was there.'

'Well, unfortunately, we have a statement from Danny telling us otherwise and, because of that, we have to follow up on the information provided.'

'But I'm the victim here. He's the one harassing *me*.'

'I'm sorry, but in regard to this incident, we have to treat Danny as the victim. We will need to speak to a Mr Tom Rivers.'

'But that's ridiculous,' she said, panicked. 'He came on strong with me, and my friend intervened, that's all. After that, I left with Tom. I have no idea how he got those bruises, but it wasn't at Tom's hand. You can ask anyone there.'

'Well, yes, that's what we're trying to establish now. Were you separated from Tom after the confrontation? Did he disappear at all?'

Fear caught in her throat, and she thought she might cry. She steadied her mind and thought back to the club. She'd sat at the table and saw Tom talking with his friends, but she hadn't taken notice of his exact movements. He could have slipped out, but she didn't believe he would do that. There was no time, either, and if Danny did get the beating that PC Allan says, surely she would have noticed signs on Tom – bruised knuckles, blood on his shirt.

'Not that I saw, no,' she said, her voice shaky. 'He was with his friends, which I'm sure they'll confirm. So what now?'

'It depends on whether Danny decides to press charges.'

'Wait, so he harasses me, bothers my friends, and we have to wait to see if he decides to press charges? Are you serious?'

'I'm sorry, Chloe. I know this is hard to take, but he has reported a crime and we have to take that seriously.'

The anger pumping through her veins was hard to

suppress, and she began to tremble. 'So when will I be informed of what he intends to do?'

'If he doesn't press charges, we'll file a crime report with the basic details: who was involved, the time, place, and any other details, and if the victim was supportive of an arrest or not.'

'So he holds all the cards? He gets to decide if he'll destroy our lives or not?'

'I know this is very difficult for you, but we need to follow up. I'll let you know any updates as soon as they come to hand. I am on your side, Chloe. I know how people can play the system, but there is a procedure to all this.'

'I understand,' she said as tears tumbled down her cheeks. 'It's not right, but I understand.'

'I would suggest you keep the messages he's still sending you so that we can build the case against him. But in the meantime, I am going to need the contact details of all the people that were involved.'

'Okay,' she said, sniffing and wiping her nose. 'But please, Tom wouldn't hurt anyone. He was just looking out for me.'

Once PC Allan hung up the phone, she decided the confines of her home were too much to bear. She needed space to breathe, and peace, even for just a moment, and opted for another journey. Somewhere unknown to Danny, and a place he was unlikely to follow. She grabbed her keys and phone and threw them into her bag, and hurried out of her flat to rush to the station, jumping on a couple of tubes until she was at Waterloo. Checking the train times, she glanced at her watch. She could take the two-thirty train to Ash Station in Surrey to arrive an hour later, perhaps a little more once she'd walked from the station. She went to the ticket machine and selected the route she needed.

Waiting on the station platform, her phone rang out, startling her, but soon enough she recognised the ringtone from her mother.

'Hi, Mum,' she said.

'Hi, my darling,' her mum replied. 'I wanted to check on you. See how you are. You seemed so stressed when I spoke to you before. Everything okay?'

'I'm okay,' she said, then conceded defeat. 'Well, actually, I'm not, to be totally honest.'

'What's going on?'

'I'm tired. Of everything.'

'Ah, Chloe,' her mum said sympathetically. 'Define "everything".'

'Oh, you know. Life. Work. Things seem to be getting worse rather than better.'

'Oh, sweetheart. So where are you now? I hear noises.' She paused. 'Wait, are you at a station? Are you visiting? That is just what you need. Some time out.'

'I wish I could,' she said as she took a breath and readied herself. 'Actually, I'm going to see David.'

Her mother was silent for a moment, and Chloe heard the soft sound of her breathing. 'Are you sure that's a good idea, sweetheart? It's taken you a long while to get to where you are, as far as he's concerned. I don't want anything to unsettle you, especially with the stress you're under.'

'It won't unsettle me.'

'But I think it's time to leave the past in the past. Exactly where it belongs. He can't help you.'

'I know that, but I still want to go. It's just something I have to do.'

'You always were impulsive when it came to him. You relied on him too much.'

Chloe would have been angry if her mother had been mistaken, but everything she said was true. 'I know that, too, but even so, I just feel I have to do this to be able to really move on. One final time. I need some clarity; everything is so chaotic here.'

'I understand. Of course I do. And it won't hurt, I suppose, if it makes you feel better. I just want you to look after yourself. It sounds like you haven't been doing that recently.'

Chloe sighed. 'You're right; I haven't. In fact, I've been very foolish. That's why I need to do this. I need to draw a line under it and then I can leave the past in the past, like you said. I just need to explain that to him. There's a kind of... finality when saying something out loud. Do you know what I mean?'

'I couldn't agree more,' her mum replied 'I'm proud of you, sweetheart.'

'Thank you. And things will get better, I promise. I just have to make a few things right again.'

'Just take care of yourself,' her mum replied. 'Be sensible. I love you, my darling.'

'I will, and I love you, too.' Chloe hung up the phone and dropped it into her bag.

The train departed on time, and Chloe knew she would enjoy the hour's journey in peace. So much had happened recently that she needed this time away from her life, just for a moment – away from her friends, from work...even Tom. As much as she loved having their support and care, she needed space to think, really think, and clear her mind. And she had so many thoughts, she worried they'd consume her.

But this was a positive step in the process. She needed to visit David, but not in the pleading, desperate way she had when he first left her, begging him to return. And not afterwards, either, when all the damage had been done. She needed to tell him about Tom. Especially Tom, and because of him this would be her final visit. She no longer had room for David in the future she hoped for herself.

The train slowed to its stop at Ash train station, and she

rose from her chair and waited by the door with the scattering of other commuters. She walked through the small, pitched-roof station and past the level crossing, coming to a little flower stall that had pitched up on the pavement. As she had to pass by, she stopped and selected a small posy of yellow roses sitting amongst other bunches in a green bucket on the ground. They were bright and just as cheery as the woman on the stall who chatted easily while she wrapped the flowers for Chloe, her grey hair and lined face giving away her age. Chloe paid and thanked the woman, tucking them into her bag, careful to keep the flowerheads upright to avoid being crushed.

The sun was high, and for a late winter's day surprisingly warm. Something she appreciated, having rushed out without a jacket. The sun's beams scattered through the budding leaves of the trees, casting dappled shadows against the ground. Birds chirped, and everything about this moment was of calm serenity. It would be fleeting, she knew that, so she was careful to appreciate it. Keep it locked in her memory.

The ten-minute journey brought her to the familiar wall topped with hedging that would lead her to her destination. She walked through the tall iron gates attached to brick pillars on either side of the pathway. The landscaped gardens were empty of people today, and quiet, and she felt the peace that surrounded this place envelope her as she approached the headstone of David's grave.

'Hello, David,' she said softly, wiping away the stray leaves that had fallen from the tree above. 'I'm sorry it's been a while.'

20

Chloe let her bag fall at her feet, crouching down to pull out the weeds that had taken root since her last visit. She tossed the withered flowers away, along with the weeds, and pulled the fresh roses from her bag. She placed them in front of his headstone. Just as she'd done on every visit since his death.

She grabbed her bag and pushed it flat so she could sit by the mound of earth that covered his final resting place. Earth that was still to settle within Ash Cemetery, home to eleven fallen from World War I, nine from World War II, and now her husband. Or rather, her estranged husband, David.

Threads of grass had begun to claim the area but the winter months had blighted its growth, leaving traces of the cold earth beneath exposed. The wreaths that had laid here, sent by family and friends on the day of the funeral, had long since withered and died. Now, the visits she made when she could kept his grave tidy and well maintained. Of course, it wouldn't only be her that visited his grave. His parents and family would also come, but when, she didn't know. They had never done it together, in-laws and daughter-in-law, united in

grief. They didn't have the necessary words to fix the discon-
nect between them, and she had accepted it was unlikely to
ever be repaired. She only ever visited alone, but she
preferred it that way. She could talk and share her news as if
he could hear her. She hoped that, somewhere, he would.

The headstone was suitably classic – white marble with
appropriate wording in black letters – *loving son and husband*,
despite his decision to leave her to be with Melissa a month
before he died. Nobody wanted to remember the bitterness,
though. Only reminders of affection would be left to fade into
history.

Melissa was laid to rest here, too, although Chloe couldn't
remember where. What she did know was her family were
close enough to this area that this would be their chosen
cemetery, too, and although Chloe had visited her grave
briefly in the weeks after the funerals, she had not been back
there since. Why would she?

She began to arrange the flowers in the little vase at the
base of the headstone. Whilst she worked, and without warning, the insidious sense of doom signified the onset of a flash-
back crashing into view. It caught her off guard, and she had
to sit back and focus on her breathing, the memories
plunging her back to that awful night. The phone call at five-
fifteen a.m. on the twentieth of August last year, pulled her
from sleep, the tortured sobs of David's mother down the line
revealing his death. The final blow to her already fractured
world.

A fire had ripped through Melissa's house during the
night. Ferocious, it tore through the house as if it were a
tinder box, and by the time the fire service arrived they were
faced with an inferno. Chloe had been informed the crowd
that had gathered outside to watch as the crew worked
together to get the fire under control praised their actions
and their exemplary service. But murmurs began to emerge

that they did not expect to find survivors after the fire had ripped through the house as it had. It had become clear that very little could be done to help anyone trapped inside. But the crew continued, extinguishing the flames until David and Melissa's charred remains were eventually discovered in her bedroom, wrapped in a macabre embrace.

In the investigation that followed, the cause of the blaze was found to have originated in the hallway, an accelerant found, likely put through the letterbox of the front door. It quickly engulfed the area and blocked their best means of escape. David and Melissa had retreated to the bedroom, charred fabric found around the doorway indicating they had tried to block the gaps in the door with clothing and bedding while they waited for help to arrive. The barrier they'd tried to create was no match for the heat and toxic smoke that seeped into the room, clogging their lungs and depriving them of the oxygen they needed to survive. They would not have been conscious when the flames destroyed their bodies to such an extent that the only means of identification was via their dental records. Chloe had found that information merciful and oddly comforting. It meant they didn't suffer.

She wished for that, anyway. She hoped it was a quick death and not the long, drawn-out, painful death by suffocation that had haunted her dreams for months after the funerals, and after every visit to his grave.

The perpetrator was found, arrested, and ended up in court. But a questionable alibi, a lack of any real evidence, and a jury that was far from unanimous meant that justice was not served. Two lives lost, and Chloe's shattered, and the person responsible walked free. Case closed.

The memories faded, and her mind stilled. Back in the cemetery again, she continued with the flowers until her anguish calmed.

She ran her fingers over the soft petals of the roses,

ensuring the brightest and freshest heads stood at the front of the arrangement.

'I hope you're happy wherever you are,' she said. 'I hope you're at peace.'

She sat back on her bag again and picked at the blades of grass at her feet. She sighed, and a small smile formed on her lips. 'And I want you to know that I've found someone. I didn't expect it either, but they say that things happen when you least expect them, don't they? I really needed it, too. I was lost for a while, caught up in my grief, and I made some bad decisions because of it. Landed myself in a bit of trouble, if I'm honest. But I'm about to put it right. Anyway, I really like him, David. I think we might be a good fit. It's Tom, from work. You may remember him from an event – or maybe you don't – but he's thoughtful, kind, and he's there for me. I really think I could be happy with him. I really do. And that's all I want. I just want to be happy.' She gently laid her hand on the earth. 'So, I think it's time I let you go now. To live my life again.'

The breeze gently rustled in the trees surrounding her, creating a wispy sighing sound that soothed. 'Thank you,' she murmured, wanting to believe it was a sign. She laid her hand on the marble. 'I guess this is it,' she said. 'Goodbye, David. Rest peacefully.'

For a blissful moment, it was just Chloe, the breeze, and the peaceful surroundings, but the unmistakable feeling of being watched crept over her; a sense she had become very attuned to – people being close to her. Danny especially. She had him to thank for that, and it prompted her to check over her shoulder. In the distance, across the path and standing amongst the headstones, was a figure. A woman, from the way she held herself. Chloe recognised her immediately. The same woman from before, outside her office and in the supermarket. Chloe turned, and at the point of their eyes meeting, the woman turned and fled, hurrying away.

Flushed with anger, Chloe jumped to her feet. 'Come back and face me, you coward!' she yelled, following the pathway towards the woman.

The woman, however, took little care and hurried amongst the gravestones, but Chloe still gained on her, fury pushing her on. The woman glanced behind again, an expression of fear on her face. Why would she be scared? She was following Chloe, after all, not the other way around. Within a moment, the woman was gone, moving through a tree-lined pathway that gave her the protection to disappear. Chloe slowed to a halt, breathless, and her skin clammy from sweat.

'What the fuck is going on?' she said breathlessly, as she surveyed the area for any sign of the frustrating woman. Nothing. She had disappeared again.

Who was she? A past love of his that had her own history of stalking? Or a family member, someone who knew what he was capable of but with a familial need to protect him? Who, damn it?

Frustrated and angry, she marched back to David's grave and blew it all away in long breaths. She needed to remember why she was here. She paused, paid one final tribute, and collected her bag. She checked her watch. She'd been here just over an hour. It was time to head back to the station. If she hurried, she'd catch the 4:55, and if she happened to see that woman again, she'd be ready to give her a piece of her mind. She walked along the path that cut through the middle of the cemetery, periodically checking over her shoulder. She was alone still, the only indication of her visit the immaculately arranged floral display on David's grave.

Her phone beeped, startling her. Filled with irritation, she looked at her screen. Danny. Demanding to know where she was. This would anger him, a second time of evading him in as many days. She'd hoped David's grave would be a stalking-free zone and she was proved right. She could only hope it would stay that way. Because, with Danny, there was seemingly no part of her life he wasn't prepared to trample over.

Pulling away from the station, Chloe looked out the window, whispering another goodbye.

HE HAD ARRIVED as he'd promised, but then he always kept his promises. He was committed to his current object of desire, and she was a fool if she thought he'd ever let go.

'Hello, Chloe,' his calm voice sounded through the door. Calm but purposeful.

She hovered on the other side. 'What do you want?'

She heard the voice of the policeman in her head, telling her not to engage. *Do not enter into conversation.* But it was difficult when he angered her, standing only feet away.

'I want to talk, Chloe. We need to discuss what's happened. It can't go on. I can't be attacked for being in a relationship with you.'

She had to purse her lips together because if she didn't bitter words would spill from her mouth. She sighed. He wouldn't leave until he'd seen her. He wouldn't go until he'd said what he wanted to say. Slowly, she unbolted the door, opened it to see his mood was dark, matching the bruises around his eye and cheek and the scab from his split lip. The injuries were fresh. And confirmed what PC Allan had told her.

'What have you done?' she asked. 'Because there's no way my friend would have done that to you.'

'Friend? Is that what he is?'

'It's none of your business.'

'It doesn't matter. None of it does. I won't let it come between us, Chloe. I won't press charges. I mean, I could.

Look at me. The police were very sympathetic.' He edged a step closer.

'Stay where you are.'

'Or what?' he goaded, ignoring her instruction and moving closer, forcing her back into the hallway. 'I'm not your enemy, Chloe, but you may want to review the other people in your life. I can't keep you safe from people like that.'

He reached out to touch her hair, and she flinched and pulled back. 'Don't touch me.'

'Oh, I think I can touch what's mine,' he said.

'I'm not yours, and I'll never be yours. I don't care if you live or die.'

'Oh, you should, my love. If you want your friends to enjoy the rest of their day.'

'Are you threatening them?'

He laughed. 'Of course not, but we need to discuss the situation with that man. What's his name, Chloe? Tom?'

'Don't you dare.' She wanted to reach out and hit him.

'I know you get ahead of yourself when you need to let your hair down, but I can't allow it to go on. You must understand. Not now you're with me.'

'Leave him alone.'

He gently brushed his thumb over her cheek and she swiped it away. 'I will. No harm will come to him. But whatever's going on will stop now. We can't have anyone else in this relationship.'

'There is no—'

'And I am prepared to overlook this misdemeanour and forgive you. Just this once, Chloe. But please don't push me. I don't want to get angry with you. I hate it when we fight. I'm not a violent man. I don't want to hurt anyone. It's you. You make me possessive and jealous.'

She inhaled, needing the air in her lungs to calm her. 'I want you to leave now.'

He smiled, as if this problem was not a problem at all. 'I've done so much for you, and you don't even notice.'

'Well, now I want you to leave me alone.'

'Ah, there it is. You think you can discard me once you're done with me. But you know that's not how it works, don't you?'

'You think you can own me?' she said, refusing to cower away from his overbearing posture.

'I already do.' He smiled. 'You're mine, and you will stay mine until I decide otherwise. We all know it. Even Tom.'

'What if I go to the police and tell them about this little conversation? Let them know you're still bothering me. Threatening my friends. One little call and your police warning will become an arrest. You'll never see me again. What then?'

'Well, yes, I can't stop you from doing that,' he said. 'But it would be a mistake.'

'I disagree.'

'Chloe, please don't be so naïve,' he said, exasperated. 'You think this attention will disappear once the authorities are involved? Nothing will stop me. Me and you, we're meant to be together. You want me to prove how much I love you. That's what this is all about, isn't it? Playing hard to get. Letting me in here, but not allowing me to touch.'

It was the first time he'd used those three words – *I love you* – and the sound of them tumbling out of his mouth turned her stomach. 'You couldn't be further from the truth.'

'And I will prove it to you. I really will. Even though it'll never be enough, I will be a slave to it.'

'You stand here, in my hallway, telling me how it's going to be, as if I have no say, no choice.'

He smiled, nodded his head in agreement.

'You think you have all the power.'

'I know it, that's why.'

'Do you?' she asked, looking him in the eye. 'Do you really have all the power?'

A frown furrowed his brow.

'You should be careful what you think you see,' she warned. 'What's staring you in the eye. Because things might not be as they seem.'

'I see exactly what's going on. You're fighting us, and I understand that,' he continued. 'Your marriage breakdown hit you hard, but it's okay to start again, with me. I'll treat you better than your ex ever did.'

Surprised and furious at where he intended to take this conversation, hearing him dismiss her marriage and David rocked her soul. He had no right to bring David into this. No right at all. She breathed hard and with anger controlling her, she slapped him across the face.

'Don't you say that,' she spat. 'You're not fit to say his name. He was a thousand times better than you, do you understand? A thousand.'

Danny grabbed her wrist hard, anger flashing in his eyes and pursing his lips. 'Don't ever do that again,' he warned under his breath. 'Do you understand?'

'I hate you,' she murmured, squirming from his grasp. 'You know that, don't you? I really, really hate you.'

'But, Chloe, don't you see? Hate is a passion as powerful as love. And everyone knows that the line between them is fragile.' He smiled. 'So go ahead and hate me if that's what it takes. I'll take that from you, too.'

Fear and anger swirled within her until she was ready to snap. 'Get out of my flat,' she said through gritted teeth.

He tilted his head as he surveyed her, appearing to make a decision. After a moment of silence, he spoke. 'I guess there's been enough drama for one day. I'll be seeing you again, Chloe. Soon.'

She shut the door on him and locked it, keeping all the

frustration and anger within herself until she heard his foot-falls on the steps up to the pavement. Only when he was gone did she release a breath.

'Damn it,' she cried as she turned and leaned against the door. This wasn't supposed to happen. Her friends should have never become involved. She knew staying at Tom's was a bad idea. She knew going out at all was a bad idea, but she'd done it anyway and now she was paying the price. 'Damn it.'

She went to the window. She couldn't see him. Maybe he'd gone, but would she ever really know? She looked over towards the little garden in the centre of the street and noticed the small orange glow fading in and out. The molten end of a cigarette. He'd found a perfect vantage point oppo-site her flat covered in darkness and smoked while he waited. She leapt back from view and wrenched the curtains shut. The burden of it all became too much, and she marched to her bedroom, falling onto her bed.

Lying on her side and pulling her legs up close to her chest, she wanted to cry but her eyes were dry. All that remained was an emptiness she still couldn't shake off. She wanted to run from here, to her friends, her mother; anywhere to feel protected from the monster under her bed. But she couldn't do that. She'd brought this monster into her life and now it was she who had to protect her loved ones from him instead. She thought she could handle someone like him. She thought she had it all under control. But it was clear she'd opened Pandora's box. It was a stupid mistake, everything was a mess, and if she could go back in time and change it, she would. She would give anything to change what she'd done.

Chloe scooted off the bed and returned to the window, nudging the curtain so she could see out. No glowing cigarette. He'd gone. She strode to the bathroom, pulled down the blind, and discarded her clothes. She jumped into the shower, desperate to get the touch of him off her skin.

When she was done, she made herself a large mug of tea and grabbed her phone. She needed to speak to her mother. For two reasons. The first, because she needed to check her parents were okay and hadn't been visited by Danny or anyone out of the ordinary. And second, because she felt alone and scared and desperately needed comfort from the people who knew her best.

The conversation was long, and while it did offer the comforting salve her soul required, Chloe's questions in return resulted in a gentle inquisition from them, too – why did she want to know their movements? What was going on? Was she okay? She deflected them all as best she could and avoided the fact they would know she was not being entirely truthful. Still, she hoped she had managed to allay any fears.

The positive she took from the call was that it was clear Danny hadn't paid them a visit so far. Whether he knew where her parents lived and had a plan for them was something she couldn't be sure of, and the fear of the possibility flipped her stomach. But for now, they were safe.

Considering it might be best if they were out of the harm's way, she steered the conversation towards holidays, and how they should take one now that semi-retirement offered more time on their hands, and a caravan on their drive meant they could take off at any given moment. She didn't think they'd take the bait, but when they showed interest in the idea, Chloe worked harder than a skint holiday rep working on commission to persuade them that an unplanned holiday was a fantastic suggestion. Anything to get them away from Danny and his plans, even for a week or two.

After the call to her mum, Chloe messaged Laura and Gabby, checking in, hoping to head off any further questions. She left out the Danny drama because of it. It was unnecessary and would only worry them further, so she kept it to herself. This was something she needed to do on her own now. It was the only way to keep them safe.

She wanted to message Tom – it was him she thought of now, him she wanted – but she stopped herself. She needed to keep whatever bud of affection about to bloom between the pair of them out of Danny's grasp. It was then that she knew something else had shifted in her. The net binding her to her past, and David, had frayed a little more, allowing threads to snap. David was no longer at the forefront of her mind. That spot was now reserved for Tom. He'd thawed her icy heart, and if she'd only let him in sooner, maybe none of this would have happened. She would have been far too busy nursing a blossoming relationship to ever become entangled with Danny.

21

The trudge of Monday morning arrived and, with it, the face of every commuter standing with her on the train, the heavy weight of responsibility etched onto their faces. Sunday had been a quiet day. She'd had a couple of silent calls and was sure she'd heard activity outside, but that was it. She hadn't ventured outside of her flat, hadn't even opened her curtains, not wanting to catch Danny outside or in the gardens opposite, watching. Forever watching.

She'd wanted the quiet, needed the time alone, but trapped as she was in her own home, there was no longer any peace. Her mind never stopped, always thinking – over-thinking – and there was no release from it. Even sleep was a roulette as to whether her anxieties would crawl into her dreams, or if she'd be granted the black void of nothingness.

She stepped off the train at Farringdon and moved along with the sea of commuters when she saw a figure standing further along the platform in jeans, trainers, and a black bomber jacket. A woman, the same woman who had followed her before, was not walking with the other travellers but lingered, head down, a black baseball cap covering most of her face and hair.

Chloe had convinced herself she must be something to do with Danny – a little cohort – one of his supporters. Perhaps there were several, all wanting to do his bidding for a crumb of affection in return. Well, she wasn't having any of it. She'd stand up to Danny, and she'd stand up to his little foot soldier, too. With little left to lose, Chloe sidled into the cover of the crowd and walked by unseen.

Then she turned back, ready to catch her off-guard. Chloe watched her search the crowd, her head bobbing as she tried to locate her target.

'Looking for me?' Chloe asked as she approached.

The woman turned, her eyes wide and mouth open. She turned and ran, fighting through the crowds without a glance behind.

Chloe ran after her, no longer caring that she should be boarding the connection that would take her to Blackfriars and work, if she was to make it into the office on time. She needed answers, and she needed them now.

Hurrying, she pushed through the crowds, following the woman who did the same. Her mind raced in time with her feet. She needed to think. What was she doing? Where was this woman going? Straight into the arms of Danny?

Out of the station and on to Farringdon Road, the woman didn't let up as Chloe followed. But Chloe had a strategy in place. She made sure to keep behind at least a couple of people so the woman would believe she had lost her and relax a little. Perhaps slow down. Although Chloe was fit enough, she was out of breath and starting to sweat.

After ten minutes of this, the woman slowed to a stop and did a three-sixty for any signs of her follower. Chloe rushed towards the nearest building, hiding within the doorway to watch what the woman did next. She paused, too, and waited for her breath to level out, looking confused more than anything. She seemed to be deciding what to do when her phone rang in her back pocket. She answered, spoke gently, and was now focused on whoever was speaking to her. She glanced towards the road and the bus stop nearby.

Chloe remained where she was, her heart thundering in her chest. She glanced at her watch. She'd be a no-show at work and was already on a very tight rope with Jeff. This might just tip him over the edge. But as she pulled her phone from her pocket to text Penny, the woman headed to the bus stop and waited in the queue of other passengers, still talking on the phone.

Had Danny summoned her? Knowing it would be madness to follow her if he had, Chloe found herself drawn to the woman. She had to know more of what was going on here, and perhaps it included where he lived, which would be all the better. The number twenty-five bus to Whitechapel Station pulled up and the woman jumped on. Chloe watched. She could only do this if the woman was to disappear up to the top deck. There was no way she could get onto the bus unseen if she didn't. But fortune smiled on Chloe as the woman paid for her ticket and climbed the stairs. Decision made, Chloe strode over quickly and lingered behind the other passengers waiting to board.

She moved to the back, finding the seat in the furthest corner. She sunk down to hide, the pungent odour of urine surrounding her, and she realised why this part of the bus was empty. She made a concentrated effort not to check the floor beneath her feet for the source of the smell. She already regretted her decision. If Danny was wherever this woman was going, how would he react if he saw her? She was walking into danger. No one was aware of her location, either.

She pulled out her phone again and typed out a quick text to Penny, letting her know she was heading to

Whitechapel and to help her out with an excuse to give to Jeff. A dental problem. Anything, as long as she let her know the story so their versions matched.

After twenty minutes and several stops along the route, the bus pulled over again and passengers rose to stand.

Chloe leaned forward in her seat, ready to move, and waited for the woman to appear. She slunk back when she spotted her at the bottom of the stairs by the doors. Only when the bus had stopped did Chloe stand, keeping herself behind the wall of people now shuffling down the aisle.

The woman alighted and did not look back, her stride purposeful. She had a new task. Chloe followed. She walked for another five minutes until they were in a residential street, then headed towards a block of flats. It was old, from the sixties at least, but it was well kept and probably in a nice neighbourhood, not that Chloe was familiar with the area, the landscaping well-tended. The woman approached the entrance to the building; Chloe needed to be quick to find somewhere to hide as she watched. Finding a collection of shrubs, she crouched down. The woman hit the buzzer, spoke, then pulled at the door. Panicking, Chloe stumbled out from the shrubbery and then back again, as she thought about what to do. There was no way she could follow behind, she'd be seen, and no way to enter the flat by herself. All she could do was wait with frustration as the door shut and locked again.

She remained where she was, wracking her brain. Would Danny be up there? Would he have seen her already, lurking in the bushes like a stalker herself? Which, she considered, was exactly what she was in that moment. She'd come so far and risked so much to turn around now, even as she heard PC Allan's voice ringing in her head about this not being the right way to go about dealing with a stalker. But what choice did she have? She'd suffered Danny barging in on her life; she couldn't deal with a second person, too.

By chance, a man wandered towards the entrance, a phone held to his ear. Chloe waited until she was sure he was going to open the door before tailgating behind, pulling her phone from her bag as he punched a code into the keypad to unlock the door.

Chloe followed behind, her phone held to her ear, mimicking him, only hers was a fake conversation as she reached out her hand to take the door he held for her.

'Thanks,' she said with a smile. 'You're a lifesaver.'

'No problem,' he replied, and climbed the concrete stairwell two steps at a time until he disappeared out of view.

She was in, but what now? Heart fluttering, and so deep into her barely laid plan she was sure she'd drown, she looked up through the stairwell snaking above her. So many floors. So many flats.

She cautiously climbed one flight of stairs. She could check each floor, and if it led to nothing she'd return to the office and retrace her steps back here another day. With more back-up, too. The sound of a door opening and women's voices echoed on the landing above her. Chloe glanced through the balustrades to see the woman appear in the doorway, quietly speaking with another woman. The other was ghostly thin, her long hair unkempt and lank, and she wore shapeless old clothes that hid her wisp of a figure.

Shit. Panicking, Chloe hurried back down the stairs to the very bottom and tucked herself into the shadowy void to the right of the staircase. She crouched and clamped her mouth shut, focusing on breathing as quietly as she could, frantic that she'd be heard. When the footsteps grew louder as the woman descended, Chloe was sure her heart would expose her hiding place as it pounded in her throat. She watched the woman leave, completely unaware of Chloe's presence, and waited until she had disappeared from view before she emerged back into the daylight. She stood in the hallway again and brushed the concrete dust from her black suit jacket where she'd pressed herself against the wall to hide.

She considered her choices. She could leave right now and make her way back to her office and very precarious job, or she could go up the stairs, knock on that door and find out exactly who that poor waif of a woman was. She had so many questions that needed answering but what she wanted to know, after looking at the state of the woman, was whether Danny was keeping her there against her will. Certainly, he'd be capable of it, and if that was the case, then surely it was Chloe's duty to act. To help.

Steeling herself, she reached for the banister and climbed the stairs. If Danny was there, she'd turn and run as fast as her legs would allow, and if he wasn't, she'd get the chance to speak to the woman. It was incredibly dangerous either way, but she couldn't turn back now. The dark blue door loomed closer until Chloe watched her hand knock against, it as though she was not connected to the limb in any way.

She waited and listened to the sound of soft footfalls approaching from the other side.

'Who is it?' the woman asked with a shaky voice.

'Hello,' Chloe said. 'I'm sorry to bother you, but I'm lost and wondered if you could help me.'

'I can't help you,' the woman replied. 'Now, please go away.'

'Please,' Chloe said, desperately.

The door clicked and opened just an inch, revealing the thick chain that held it securely. The woman's eyes were dull, as though the life had been drained from them, and dark shadows hung beneath, her skin almost translucent. 'What do you want?'

'I...I'm sorry to bother you,' Chloe stammered, not sure

what the hell she was doing. 'But I couldn't help but overhear you had a visitor a moment ago.'

'What?' the woman replied, a little taken aback. 'I'm not sure what's it got to do with you.'

'I guess I just wanted to check you are okay.'

'Ah, so you took one look at me and thought "She must be in trouble because she looks so awful" – is that it?'

'No, not at all,' Chloe said, even though she had hit on the truth immediately. 'I'm not here to cause trouble, I know it's none of my business, but—'

'You're right, it is none of your business. Now please go away and leave me alone.'

Instinctively, Chloe placed a hand on the door to stop the woman from closing it. 'No, please, wait. That woman who visited. Well, the truth is that she's been following me, and not just her. A man, too.'

That sparked an interest in the woman's eyes and she pushed the door a little, released the chain, and opened it fully. 'Stay right where you are,' she warned.

Suddenly and inexplicably, Chloe was afraid. If he were to suddenly appear, there would be nothing she could do about it and would likely be trapped here with this other woman. 'Actually, I should go...'

'No, wait,' the woman said, reaching out to hold onto Chloe's arm, exposing her skinny forearm and a long, thick, angry-looking scar that ran the length of it. 'Who's been following you? The man, I mean.'

Chloe hesitated, stared at the scar and then moved her gaze to the woman's penetrating eyes. Her stomach plunged. 'Erm, well—'

'Let me guess,' the woman said. 'He's tall, dark-haired and handsome, but won't take no for an answer.'

'Yes.'

'Danny?'

Oh God. 'Yes. That's him. Danny. You know him?'

The woman nodded and dropped her hand, her gaze roaming to her scar. She gently placed her other hand over it, protectively or to conceal, Chloe wasn't sure. 'I know him well.'

'How long?'

'Just shy of two years. From the moment he came into my life to the moment he finally left.'

'He pursued you for nearly two years?'

'Not quite. Not at first anyway. We were in a relationship.'

'Oh,' Chloe said.

The woman nodded. 'Yeah, I know, how lucky was *I*?' she said sadly. 'He was so charming at first, I was bowled over and failed to see the many red flags. Or maybe I chose to ignore them, I don't know. But relationships to him can mean many things. Consensual. Non-consensual. It doesn't matter. If he wants you, he'll do whatever it takes to have you. Nothing will stop him. And then when you want to leave, well, he will dish out the punishment according to the crime.'

'What happened to you?' Chloe murmured, her voice cracking.

'This,' she said, pointing to her arm. 'And this.' She pulled back her long brown hair, exposing her left ear, revealing the crescent-shaped scar running along her scalp behind it.

Chloe couldn't breathe. Danny did this to her, this woman, his other woman, because she defied him. Much like Chloe was doing now. 'Oh, Jesus,' she whispered.

'He pushed me down the stairwell. Said he tried to stop me from slipping but I felt his hand firmly push my back before I fell. The concrete and metal did their worst. I was lucky not to break a bone. He called the ambulance and stayed with me while we waited, hovering over me, telling me what a fool I'd been to slip like I had. He even laughed, said he could see the white bone of my skull through the flap of skin that had been ripped away and how fascinating it was to see the inner me.'

Chloe fought the urge to vomit. She thought she knew what he was capable of – but this? This was just another terrible string to his bow. She glanced at the concrete steps and the damage they would cause.

'No, not these steps,' the woman said. 'Where I used to live. Although the steps there were much the same as these. You don't need much of an imagination to see the damage they'd do.'

'So you were leaving him?'

'Absolutely. Had my bags packed and was ready to go on the day of the "accident".'

'When was this?'

'A year or so ago. I can't really remember.'

'And did you report it? Was he arrested?'

'You're joking, aren't you?' she snorted bitterly. 'He visited me in hospital with the largest bunch of flowers and sat with me, happily chatting with all the nurses until they left us alone. Then he began telling me how terrible the accident was and how terrible it would be if it happened again, and probably worse the next time around, too. He also told all the nursing staff how unstable I was when negotiating stairs. That was a lie, of course. I was perfectly capable, and led an active and healthy life before I met him. But, of course, that didn't fit his narrative, so he made sure the account he shared was more suitable, if a complete fabrication. I had the odds stacked against me. So, no, I didn't report it.'

'I'm so sorry.'

'Not your fault.' She gently rubbed at the scar on her arm.

Through the emaciation, Chloe saw she had once been pretty, very pretty. Her eyes, although dull, were a charming blue, and the chestnut hair that now hung limply would have once been an impressive mane when styled and cared for.

Chloe hoped with all her heart that, with time, she'd return to how she was before she met Danny. But looking at her now, she was not so sure.

'My parents helped me get away,' the woman continued. 'That's why I live here now. I'm going for surgery in a few months. They're going to pay for these scars to be repaired cosmetically at a private clinic so they're less obvious, but that doesn't help the scars in here, does it?' she said, tapping at her temple. 'It doesn't help the fear, the inability to leave my home in case he finds me.'

'No, it does not,' Chloe said. She needed to keep her nerve – she could easily crumple if she wasn't careful. 'And are you getting the support you need now?'

'Yes, I am. Everyone has been great, although some days it's more difficult than others.'

'I understand. I really do.'

The woman nodded.

'And he doesn't know where you are?'

'That's right, not right now. Unless you blab to him.'

'I will not be doing that, believe me,' Chloe said. 'You may not know me, but you have my word. I promise I'll keep you safe from him.'

Again, she nodded, and the sadness that radiated from her made Chloe's heart clench with sorrow. The horror of what this woman had gone through, Chloe could only imagine.

'I hope not. I don't want to move again.'

'And that woman? The one who was just here.'

'I can't talk about her,' the woman snapped. 'So don't ask, okay?'

Chloe held up her hand. 'Okay, of course.'

'I need to go now,' the woman said, looking more exhausted than before. 'I hope you're looking out for yourself. I can see why he's interested in you. Just his type.'

'Wait,' Chloe said as the door closed. 'What's your name?'

But that was it. She stood there for a moment to let the shock subside. She'd learnt so much in these last few minutes, but as far as the woman who was following her, absolutely nothing. She turned and walked down the steps, imagining the horror of being shoved down them and the resulting fear and pain. This was a game to him, but it could be because he never suffered the consequences.

He should never be allowed anywhere near another woman for the rest of his life, and yet he's out there, living whatever life he chooses, while that poor woman is a prisoner in her own home.

Thinking quickly, she disabled the location services in her phone settings so she'd be invisible to Danny, just in case he was tracking her. Then she messaged Penny as quickly as her trembling fingers would allow to let her know she was on her way to the office.

She'd keep her promise to this woman and not reveal her whereabouts to anyone. Especially Danny.

22

Chloe left the building and retraced her steps back to the high street. She had no idea how long it would take to get back to the office, or if she even had a job now, but she'd go anyway and take it from there.

She wanted to throw up, her stomach queasy with anxiety. She had poked at a hornet's nest and was in so deep she felt sure only one of them would get out of this alive. But she had to continue. She couldn't give up. For herself, for that woman and all the other women he'd tormented in the past, and for all the women he'd be free to harass in the future. Once she was back within the safety of her office, she'd start by calling the police.

Hot, and too clammy for the weather outside, Chloe pushed open the door to her office.

A text pinged to her phone. Danny.

> Where are you, my love? I didn't see you
> arrive at work this morning.

She stared at the words, relieved. He couldn't have followed or tracked her. The woman would be safe. Despite his apparent affection, he'd be frustrated, knowing he'd lost her again, but she ignored the text regardless. Better to say nothing at this point.

Her mood darkening, she headed straight for the lift bank, not wanting to make eye contact or share pointless greetings with the other staff members. In a bid to remove the memory of the woman's haunted expression, she focused her attention instead on the woman who'd been following her. She needed to find her again. She needed to talk to her, understand exactly what was going on. The lift was silent as she struggled with the thoughts that crowded her mind.

She walked to her desk and caught sight of Tom in the corner of her eye. He looked stunning in his smart suit, and her mind, even in its ragged state, still recalled the memories of their perfect night together. The way her stomach flipped just glancing at him across the room should have made her happy – this new potential relationship in its infant stages, fragile and in need of nurturing – but it did not. It caused more anxiety. She'd fallen deep already. He was the antidote to the current poison in her life, and despite the very real sense this was right for her, that *he* was right for her, she considered the consequences he could suffer by association. She should back off, let things cool down between them. It was the right choice. She had so much to do before she could allow herself to begin with him. So much to do.

'Good morning, Chloe,' he said. Formal but friendly, his eyes were on hers, glinting with the secrets they shared.

'Hi.'

'Just thought I'd check in. See how you're doing.'

'I'm doing okay,' she said with a faint smile. Mistake or not, she decided not to mention her eventful morning. 'Did the police visit you?'

He nodded as he leaned against her desk. 'Yeah, they did. They were nice guys, actually. They see this sort of stuff all the time. They have little to go on, as everyone has backed up our version of events, and apparently Danny's not pressing charges. They're not taking it any further.'

She held her hand against her chest in relief. 'That's great news. I was so worried. Can you imagine what Jeff would do if he found out?'

He gently nudged her arm. 'I'm not intimidated by that old fool, and I've been here long enough to be rather indispensable now. Well, that's what I tell myself anyway.'

'I just would hate for your plans or your career to be ruined because of this horrible mess.'

Serious now, he reached out. 'Chloe, you haven't got anything to feel guilty about. I knew what I was doing. I did what I did because I wanted to. And that means accepting the consequences of crossing someone like Danny, too. What you witnessed was all that happened. I just wanted to fight your corner. You seem so alone right now, but I never left that club and I didn't cause those injuries.'

'I knew it.' Her voice quivered, and she swallowed hard, fighting the tears. 'You have too much decency to sink that low. And your friendship means a lot to me right now.'

He frowned. 'Friendship?'

'You know what I mean.'

Chloe spotted Penny striding towards them and took a step back from Tom, certain their closeness wouldn't have gone unnoticed.

'Good morning, you two,' she said cheerfully, with the lightness of someone who had no idea how dark her boss's life had become. 'What have we got going on here?'

'Nothing, Penny, just catching up.'

Penny eyed them suspiciously. 'Uh-huh.'

Chloe looked at Tom. 'Shall we catch up later? Finish going over that report?'

'What do you say to lunch?'

'Sounds great.'

Chloe pulled her laptop from her bag and opened it as Tom went to his desk.

Penny turned to her. 'You dodged a bullet this morning. Jeff's diary shows an all-day meeting so you're lucky no one noticed your absence.'

'Thank God,' Chloe replied with a sigh. 'And I really appreciate you helping me out. I know I shouldn't put you in that position.'

'It's fine,' Penny replied. 'I'm happy to help. Is everything okay? You look a little stressed.'

'Believe me, you don't want to know. Just this business with Danny. It's wearing me down.'

'I'm not surprised.'

'But I have some catching up to do, so if you don't need anything...'

'Got it. But I'm just over there if you need me,' Penny said before turning to leave.

Chloe pulled out the card PC Allan had given her and punched in the numbers. It took her through to a switchboard with multiple options. She selected each one and then waited on hold for the next available operator. She thought back to what the woman had said to her. How she'd not reported the terrible assault out of fear that he would return and do something much worse. What if that turned out to be her fate, too? She needed him off the streets, but the arrest had to be solid. And she needed to ensure she would still be alive at the end of it, with no chance of him evading the punishment he deserved. The hold music filled her head, her blood cold as ice. Then she hung up the phone. She needed to think this through first. She needed to be sure.

After a futile attempt to focus her mind on her work, she admitted defeat and went to meet Tom in the office café. Her mood was destroyed, and she was left with a ball of nerves and tension.

'You okay?' Tom said, with a cautious expression as Chloe sat down at his table.

'I'm running on nervous energy, but I just have to get through today,' she said, as she placed the coffee and sandwich on the table that she'd grabbed on her way over to Tom. 'I think I have a headache looming, too.'

Tom placed his palms on the table in an open stance and looked at her, his voice sincere and quiet. 'Chloe, I need to ask you something before we go any further.'

'Yes, of course,' she said, quickly filling with dread.

'It's about earlier.'

She pulled at the sandwich wrap unenthusiastically. 'What about earlier?' She took a bite of the food and instantly regretted it, her stomach churning.

He took a breath. 'Okay, well...you're going through some stuff, which I understand, and I'm behind you in whatever way I can be.' He ran his hand through his hair. He was uncomfortable. 'But, well, was Friday night just a one-time thing for you? An itch to scratch out of curiosity?'

She chewed and swallowed the food as quickly as she could, then reached out to touch his hand before remembering where they were and retracting it. 'What? No, of course not.'

'Because I get it, if it was. You've got enough going on and I'm not about to add to your stress.'

'But you're the only thing keeping me going,' she replied. 'What made you ask?'

'You kind of friend-zoned me earlier at your desk.'

Her heart sank. She was hurting him by blowing hot and cold and she hated herself for it. He didn't deserve to be treated like that with no explanation.

'I'm so sorry. I've had one hell of a day, that's all.' She

rubbed her forehead in an attempt to ease the headache that had begun to pound. 'I've managed to hold onto my job by the skin of my teeth, and Danny, well...that's a gift that just keeps giving.'

He smiled softly at the roll of her eyes. 'So talk to me.'

She shook her head and a sad smile crossed her lips. 'I can't. I wish I could, but I can't.' She reached out and held his hand, not caring how it would be perceived by others. 'I wish I could give you the answer I want to give. The one I feel in my heart. I feel so good when I'm with you, everything feels just right, and I haven't felt like this for a very long time.'

He held onto her hands. 'Okay, so let's do this together. We'll get rid of Danny together.'

'I am the focus of his attention, and anyone else is just a distraction that would need to be removed. You would be the distraction, Tom. You. And the reason it scares me so much is because my feelings for you are far deeper than I was prepared for at this stage. I couldn't cope with another loss in my life.' She caught his eye. 'I couldn't cope with losing you. That's why I'm trying to make sure you don't get caught up in this. And earlier was my clumsy attempt at that.'

He looked at her, too, a heartfelt fire in his eyes. 'I feel the same, Chloe. The exact reason why I want to help. It's not cool these days for a man to say he wants to protect a woman, but that's exactly how I feel. Not in a caveman-drags-woman-by-hair thing, but because I care.'

She smiled. 'Actually, I think it's really cool that you feel that way. It's lovely and I'm grateful. I feel less alone with you in my life. You give me strength.'

THE SECOND POST had been delivered when she returned to her desk, and amongst it were two cards – one in a pink envelope, one purple, both marked 'Private and Confidential'. Cautiously, she opened the pink one. Inside was a beautiful card with elaborately painted flowers, the words 'To the One I Love' written in a romantic, swirly font. Inside, it read:

> You're still resisting, Chloe. I understand. But I will never stop until I have your absolute devotion, and when I have that, you'll see I'm right and how happy we can be.

She shivered. This was to be expected. A process. Everything she'd looked at online highlighted that this was the path a stalker would take: unrelenting messages, contact, intimidation, control. And worst case, possible violence. But then she had plenty of evidence of that.

Hesitantly, she picked up the smaller purple envelope and tucked her finger under the seal to rip it open. Inside was another card with a poem on the front expressing what it meant to love the recipient. It was blank inside, except for the initial *D* and a kiss.

She threw both in the wastepaper bin by her desk and kept her breathing steady. She fought against the tears and tried to focus on the mundane correspondence, tossing the junk mail into the same bin, hiding the cards from view. It was important for others not to see these items from Danny as much as it was for her.

A note from reception was tucked within the post, informing her that flowers had been delivered and were ready for collection. She called down and rejected them, telling the team to do what they wanted with them, she didn't care. And then she continued to bury herself in work, needing to make amends for going AWOL this morning.

Despite her exhaustion, Chloe left the office on time. She knew public transport was no longer a safe option, so she ordered an Uber and waited in reception until she received the notification of its arrival. Not cheap, but safe, and if it ate into her pocket, she'd take the hit.

As the car approached her flat, she was sure she caught a flicker of movement in the gardens opposite. When the driver slowed to a stop, she thanked him, jumped out of the car, and strode quickly down the steps to her front door. She hoped the driver would linger a while longer, and maybe she should have asked him to do just that, but she heard the engine revving as it pulled away to disappear down the road before she could get her key into the lock.

Footsteps echoed in the still night air.

Chloe fumbled with her keys, unable to work her hands. She didn't dare look over her shoulder. He would be there. Of course he would be there.

Louder, the footsteps were close, his feet hitting the pavement of the street above. 'Do you need a hand there, Chloe?' he asked, his voice low and quiet.

She ignored him and continued to struggle with her lock. *He's not there*, she repeated over and over in her mind.

He was right behind her now, so close. Just as she expected his hand to fall on her shoulder, the key turned and the door opened. She leapt inside and banged the door shut, not once looking behind, too terrified to acknowledge the monster. She crouched down, hiding from the distorted shadow that lingered through the glass in the door, and didn't move until it had disappeared.

23

I f there was ever an emotional state that made a person feel like a ghost, Chloe was suffering it. With morning an unwelcome arrival, she dragged herself out of bed and trudged to the bathroom. It was as if her feet were fighting their way through treacle. She couldn't remember when she'd last eaten a proper meal, and her constant thirst highlighted her dehydration. Danny hadn't contacted her at all overnight or this morning. His usual tactic.

The absence of the builders was welcome, at least.

Pulling open the fridge, she found some bacon hiding at the back of the shelf and grabbed it. She took out the half loaf of bread in the tub and removed the slices from the bag. Choosing the ones that had the least amount of mould, she picked off any residual blooms as best she could and chucked them onto a plate. She should go to the shops, replenish her stock, but she knew she couldn't because he would only follow her there, and if it wasn't him, it would likely be that elusive groupie in his wake. She considered an online grocery shop, but it would have to wait – she didn't feel up to it right now. She felt a momentary niggling regret at having given away the items from Danny's shopping gift – but then realised she couldn't have used the food. Whatever she'd eaten would likely have stuck in her throat. Getting rid of it had been the right thing to do.

Her mind drifted away, as she leaned against the counter-top, as it did so easily these days, until the piercing beep of the smoke alarm snapped her out of her reverie. She looked down at the oven and the smoke curling from the burnt bacon she'd left under the grill.

She grabbed a tea towel and wafted it up against the alarm until the siren stopped, then returned to buttering the bread and tipping the charred bacon remnants onto a slice. With her hashed-together sandwich and a cup of tea, she walked into the living room.

As she forced down the poor excuse for a sandwich, a sudden crash and splintering of glass resonated throughout the flat, launching her from her chair. The plate in her lap dropped to the floor and her heart pounded in her throat. The unmistakable sound of the kitchen door opening, its familiar creak and the whine of hinges, froze the blood in her veins. Tiredness made her mind fuzzy, but this was not her imagination. This was terrifyingly real. With only a couple of walls separating her from Danny – because, of course, it would be him, no one would be unlucky enough to have a stalker and a burglar to deal with in one day – her mind had only seconds to process and plan. Footsteps crunched slowly over glass on the laminate floor. Grabbing her phone, she rushed into the bathroom, slamming and locking the door behind her.

Standing in the middle of the room, she waited, listening for the sound of movement as he inhabited her flat. Sure enough, muffled footsteps against the carpet approached and she sensed his presence as though there were no walls separating them. Shallow breaths escaped her mouth.

'It's only me, Chloe,' he said. He was close, right outside the door. 'You're quite safe.'

She heard movement again and looked down as the round brass handle turned slowly, menacingly.

'You have to understand why I've done this,' he continued. 'Your mixed messages are pushing me to the very limit. First you invite me in, and next you change the locks.'

'Fuck off!' she yelled. 'You broke in. Kicking the door in not good enough for you this time?'

'Are you sure you want to test me like this? Do you think it will stop me? Because it's pointless to try.'

'Leave me alone, do you hear? I have my phone. I'm calling the police right now.' She punched the screen three times and listened for the operator.

'Oh, you do that, my love, and I'll make sure they get the right version of events from the other night. How Tom assaulted me.'

'Shut up!' she screamed, trying to think.

'And you don't want that for him, do you?' he murmured, mockingly sad. 'That would be very damaging to his reputation if I were to press charges, would it not? All those years he's given to that company, all gone because of an arrest. And it would be all your fault, Chloe, because you failed to stop him from coming into our lives.'

The responder asked again for the service required. Chloe paused.

'Think hard, Chloe.'

He was right. The bastard was right. Of course she couldn't do that to Tom. She only ever wanted to shield her friends from this. She swallowed, clearing her throat to speak. 'I'm sorry, my mistake. I hit the wrong buttons,' she said, not listening to the operator's curt response.

She hung up. Feeling trapped in her own home with no one able to help, there was nothing left to do but face him.

Inhaling deeply, she unlocked the door to see Danny standing there, triumphant.

'I thought you'd see sense,' he said.

'I want you to get out of my home, right now.'

He smiled, a nasty leering sneer. 'You don't get to call the shots, my love. I won't be leaving here until I'm ready.' His eyes wandered over the lines of her body, particularly where her pyjama top gaped and hung to one side, exposing her left shoulder, and dangerously – by the glint in his eyes – the curve of her breasts beneath the fabric.

Disgusted by this, she flipped the T-shirt back, lifting it higher to hide any skin.

A voice came from the kitchen, calling out, surprising them both.

Without hesitating, Chloe rushed past Danny towards the kitchen. 'Hello, I'm here.' Her voice was high, desperate. 'I'm right here.'

She found her neighbour, John, standing in the middle of her kitchen, looking around at the mess and broken glass of the door. 'I heard a smash,' he said, looking at her. 'I didn't want to intrude, but I thought I'd better come and see if you're okay.'

Her mouth open and ready to ask for help, he held up his hand. 'No, don't come any further into the room, you'll rip your feet to shreds.'

She stayed where she was, Danny close behind her now, the outline of his body against hers. She said nothing, the moment for help was gone.

'My fault,' Danny volunteered, laying his hands on her shoulders. Careful to apply just the right amount of pressure, an unspoken command, telling her he was right there and she was to behave. It could have looked normal to John, cosy even, and certainly nothing like the enemies they were. 'I thought Chloe was out, and I've left my keys somewhere. I had to get in.'

'You've moved in, then?' John asked. 'Only I haven't seen you around here that often.'

Danny moved past her and held out his hand to John, his shoes crunching. 'Where are my manners?' he said. 'I'm Danny, Chloe's...friend.'

John's expression relaxed, and he took Danny's hand and shook it, clearly warmed by his good manners. 'John. Nice to meet you.'

Chloe could have screamed at the charade playing out before her. Jesus, how did someone like Danny manage to charm everyone he met?

'Yeah, I've been trying to get hold of Chloe. No response, of course. She is always so forgetful. Then I thought she might be in trouble.'

'Why would she be in trouble?'

'No reason at all, John,' Danny said. 'I just worry, that's all.' He shifted his gaze to the empty wine bottles in the recycling box, silently steering him towards what he wanted John to see, however misleading that was. 'You know how it is.'

Chloe stared at him, doing little to hide the hatred she felt for him at this moment. But if John was here to witness this, she could use it. This would be helpful evidence for the day when she'd finally deal with Danny, the man who had caused her so much pain. So for now she was silent, in fearful obedience. She'd let the situation unfold and allow John to jump to his own conclusions.

'I guess, on reflection, it is a bit dramatic,' Danny continued, 'and I appreciate how it looks, but I'll cover the cost obviously. I could have a chat with one of your builders.'

The warmth in John began to fade and suspicion crept in as Danny did all the talking. 'Is that right, Chloe?' John asked. 'Are you okay?'

Danny soon shut it down by gregariously placing his arm around John's shoulders, guiding him back out through the door. 'Anyway, thanks for dropping by and checking in, but I've got it from here, John.'

Danny watched him leave and offered a wave when John checked over his shoulder, and then he turned his attention to Chloe. 'He's nice.'

'I want you to get out of my flat right now,' she snapped.

'Ah, come on, Chloe,' he said with a smile. 'No need to be like that.' He raised a brow as he considered his options. 'Maybe I will. Or maybe I'll go and have a little chat with the neighbours, work on him some more. I'm sure old Johnny boy has put two and two together and come up with five. People like him are so predictable.'

'Just get out of my home.'

He reached to the floor and picked up a long shard of glass, dangerously knife-shaped. 'I'd say he thinks this is a lovers' tiff gone wrong. It happens to the best of us. Life is stressful. Relationships can be stressful. Not ours, of course, but he doesn't know that yet. He's only just met me.'

He played with the glass, examining the edges, turning it carefully in his fingers until a line of blood appeared on his thumb. Unbothered, he simply raised it and covered the wound with his mouth as his eyes moved to her.

Her heart hammered in her chest as she waited for his next move.

'I have been gentle with you, and patient. Jesus, have I been patient. Waiting for you to see that we are meant to be together, but you still don't get it, do you? You think you can lead me on and I'll just go away when you've changed your mind.'

'I never gave you any indication that I was interested. I was polite, that's all, and you took it the wrong way.'

He nodded. 'Oh, is that how we're going to play it?'

'I have no idea what you're talking about.'

He sighed. 'You see, that's disappointing. You know what happened. How you made me believe we could be together.'

'No, I didn't! But that doesn't matter to someone like you, does it? You just chose to do whatever you wanted. You follow me, call me, send stuff to my place of work. And here, you turn up, intrude, walk into my flat. Is that when you decided to drug my wine? Is that the only way you can get women to sleep with you?'

He crossed the kitchen to her, so close she felt his breath on her face. She faced up to him despite the terror of what he'd do next. 'I see what you're doing,' he said, 'You want to argue. You like goading me.'

'What did you do to me?'

He sighed as the fire faded from his eyes. 'Chloe, Chloe, Chloe,' he said as he released the glass from his fingers and brushed away any residue. 'I would not do anything to hurt you. I only wanted to be with you, surround you, hold you close while you slept.' He touched her face with his thumb, leaving a wet trail of blood on her skin. 'It was beautiful, but when the time comes for us to consummate our relationship, and it will come, you will be willing and compliant. I'll have your devotion first, and then I'll have your body.'

Her stomach turned. She thought she'd vomit right there on the kitchen floor. 'That'll never happen,' she spat. 'Never.'

He grabbed her arm, the threat clear in his eyes. 'Don't push me, Chloe. Otherwise I might change my mind and take what I want right now.'

She stared into his eyes and thought of the poor woman from before, trapped in her flat with her terrible scars. There would be no reasoning with him, no point to prove. He lived outside the usual confines of human interaction. This, to him, was normal. The usual rules did not apply. What she needed now was for him to be out of her space before things got out of control. A surreal calm descended upon her. Manipulation was an ugly trait, but it was part of this game, and it was time to match his with her own.

She took a moment to breathe, nodded, and even managed a smile. 'I'm sorry.'

Delighted at the change in her attitude, he smiled, too. 'You're tired, I understand,' he said. 'And you're always so argumentative when you're tired. I need to learn that about you.'

She'd let him have that one.

'You need to take better care of yourself. The day is only beginning and you look done in.' He looked down, gesturing to the scattered glass at their feet. 'And now you have all this to clean up.'

'You're right, of course,' she agreed, hoping her fixed smile would adequately hide her clenched jaw.

He liked that, his lip twitching into a smile. 'Okay, well, I think we're done here. I'll go now, leave you to sort this. I'll catch up with you later.'

'You don't need to do that,' she muttered.

'It's what any good partner would do, and I'm here for you, Chloe. Only you.' He walked by her and out into the hallway, opening the front door.

She murmured her 'goodbye' and calmly closed the door behind him. She focused on her breathing. She could do this. She could handle him.

She went to the living room and stood at the window, looking out onto the street. Danny made what appeared to be easy conversation with John, who had now been joined by his wife, Louise. Danny was conciliatory, his hands outstretched, palms upward facing – probably giving a very reasonable explanation as to what was going on. Feeding them lies. He made Louise laugh, and John smiled, but the way he watched Danny, his sideways glance as he listened, suggested to Chloe that he didn't trust him as much as he was letting on. She continued to watch as they shook hands.

John and Louise turned to walk back to their home, and Danny turned to look up, his gaze focused directly on Chloe's window, as if he could see her, standing right there, his eyes penetrating through the glass.

'Shit,' she hissed, as her stomach dropped and her heart pounded. She took a step back, but not before she saw the smirk on Danny's face as he turned and walked away, lighting up a cigarette as he went.

AFTER AN AGE of waiting for someone to come out and replace the glass in her door, combined with the task of cleaning up the mess he'd left her with, it was close to midday by the time Chloe was ready to leave for work, and she knew she'd have trouble once she got to the office. She'd called ahead to Penny to explain, but Jeff was at her desk when she arrived and his face told her that all sorts of crap was coming her way.

'Morning, Jeff. I'm so sorry I'm late. Someone vandalised my door. I had to make sure it was secure, and the bloody guy took his time coming out.'

'Morning, Chloe. That sounds very challenging.'

'Yes,' she said as she pulled her laptop out of her case. 'But obviously I'll make up the time.'

'Yes, about that. I wanted to catch you straight away. We need to talk. My office. Now, please.'

Silently and with a small nod, she placed her bag under her desk and quickly followed behind.

Jeff gestured for her to sit as she walked into his office and closed the door. 'I'm sorry, Chloe, but it seems recent outside influences that have been affecting you are now affecting the business.'

Her stomach sank. He said no more as he sat in his seat behind the desk, but she knew what this was about. He'd have to have been living under a rock to not know what had been happening in her life. Mortified that he should have a glimpse into her world, heat filled her cheeks.

'I'm so sorry. Things have been difficult, and I know he's been a bit of a nuisance here a couple of times, but there's not been any real harm, surely?'

'I guess it depends how you look at it, but I can see that it's also affecting your concentration. Your work is slipping.'

'Oh my goodness,' she said, blinking back the surprise. 'I thought it was just the one report that was incorrect.' She scrutinised his expression and found it did nothing to show his understanding, or the truth of the situation.

'Well, yes, perhaps. But you missed a meeting yesterday and have not yet replied to an email from one of your clients. They came to me asking where you were.'

'Oh,' she said despondently. She hadn't even noticed.

'And when we mix that with the frequent visits, calls, and now emails from this chap you're seeing, we have to get involved.'

'He's not my chap,' she snapped. Then winced. 'Sorry.'

'It's okay,' he said.

'He's been sending emails?' she asked.

'A string of them this morning alone. IT had to get involved, again.'

'Again?'

'Yes, and unfortunately it's come to light that this is not the first time he's done this.'

'Oh no. I'm so sorry.'

'And he came to the office yesterday. Got a little heavy with one of the guards. We just can't have that kind of impression at the doorway. Our reputation cannot be damaged like that.'

'Please,' she said, sitting forward in her seat. 'Please let me sort it out.'

'I would let you, but so far you haven't managed it successfully. Now, it's come to the attention of the chief and he's not happy. He wants to contain it before it goes any further.'

'Will he give me any time to deal with it?'

He didn't respond. She understood why and couldn't help but loathe his cowardice.

'Chloe, we think it might be best if you took a little time away from the company. A little time to sort yourself out.'

'No, don't say that. Give me another chance to put it right.'

'It's just for a while. We want you to take some leave. A month, perhaps.'

'I can't believe it,' she sighed. 'All the years of extra hours and commitment I've given to this company, and the first time I hit a problem they want me out.'

'Look, Chloe, they – we – do not want you out. We want to support you.'

She nodded and pursed her lips together against the vitriol that would spill out otherwise. 'And is this unpaid leave I'm supposed to be taking?'

'No. Under the circumstances, we're prepared to offer you paid leave, to show that we value you as an employee and we support you in getting your life back on track.'

He has no idea what I'm doing to get my life back on track, she thought bitterly. *And the price I'm paying.*

'We think it's a very generous offer, but you need to do the work, Chloe.'

'Clear my name, you mean.'

'Chloe, I understand the amount of pressure you've been under recently. I don't want to lose one of my most valued members of staff and I really think this will do you some good. Give you the space you need.'

'I suppose this has killed any hope of the promotion now?'

He smiled, but it didn't hide the sense of the inevitable. 'We can discuss that again when you're back.'

'And there's no negotiating this?' she asked. 'The leave is mandatory?'

'Yes, it is.'

She sighed. Never had she thought it would come to this. The idea had crossed her mind recently, but she didn't imagine it would actually happen. Danny had spread his reach far into the corners of her life and it dumbfounded her how she'd let it.

'So when does this start? Today? Can I at least notify my clients?'

Uncomfortable, he shifted in his chair. 'I think right now is the best time.'

'Now?' she cried, unable to comprehend.

He nodded.

Anger buzzed around her so much she could almost hear it. She couldn't bear the thought of being escorted out of the office as if she were a squalid misconduct case. 'Well, can I leave by myself at least? Or am I to be paraded through the office like an outcast?'

'I have to come with you. You'll need to hand over your pass card once you're through the turnstiles at reception. But we can make it as discreet as possible.'

'Oh, God. Not only the office, but I'm to be escorted from the building, too.'

Jeff stood and walked around his desk, resting against the side. 'I'm so sorry, Chloe. I really didn't want it to come to this, but my hands are tied.'

Tears threatened, burning her eyes, but she blinked them

back. This was not the time. She nodded and stood, not willing to give him conciliatory words to ease his conscience. 'Okay. Let's get this over with, then.'

He moved to the door and waited for her to walk out before shutting it behind him.

They went to her desk, and she packed up her laptop and collected her bag, resting it on the desk as she collected other items from the desk drawers that she didn't want to leave behind. Right now, she wasn't sure if she ever wanted to return, but all she could do was keep the searing pain of hurt under control until she got home.

Penny watched from her desk, her mouth agape, her hands frozen over her laptop keys. It didn't go unnoticed by others, either, who discreetly stopped what they were doing to watch this little soap opera unfold. When she saw Tom hurry through the department, she felt the dam holding back her tears begin to splinter and break without her control.

'Chloe?' Tom said as he drew near. 'What's going on?'

'It's okay, Tom,' she said, her hand raised in a reassuring manner. 'I'll speak to you later, okay?' She didn't stop. She couldn't.

'But—' Tom stammered, as he rushed to walk alongside them.

She slowed and rested her hand on Tom's arm, ignoring the stares. 'I'll call you later, okay?'

He nodded, bewilderment and concern in his eyes.

She smiled at him and glanced around at the confusion on everyone's faces before turning away, not wanting it to be the last thing she saw in this place. Somewhere she loved to work and saw herself being part of for years to come.

In the atrium, she caught sight of the reception team watching as she handed over her badge, and when Jeff glanced at the laptop and held out his hand, the humiliation reached peak level. All that needed to happen now was for her clothes to fall off and this moment would be complete.

'Thank you, Chloe, and you know we are here for you,' Jeff said, fiddling with her lanyard. 'I'll have HR send you some information on the benefits you can take advantage of: counselling, CBT, that sort of thing.'

She nodded. With nothing more to say, she turned and walked towards the doors, numb from the inside out.

'I'll be in touch,' Jeff called out. 'I'll drop you an email.'

She ignored him and pushed through the door.

Standing outside of the office entrance, Chloe hesitated. She had always known that dealing with Danny was going to be difficult, she didn't mind admitting it, and she'd prepared herself as much as she could. She thought she could separate her private life from her professional one, but he'd found his way here, too, and that was something she hadn't accounted for. She didn't know what to do next. To go home would be to risk seeing Danny, and to visit her parents could jeopardise their safety. Laura and Gabby would be at work, and she couldn't keep dragging them further into this mess; this can of worms she was now frantically trying to contain.

A voice shouting her name carried on the breeze, brought her back to the present. She turned to see Tom rushing towards her.

'What's going on?' he asked, brushing his hand against her shoulder. 'I've just passed Jeff on the stairs in a thunderous mood.'

They moved to the side of the pavement, closer to the building to let people pass them by.

'That makes two of us, then,' she began. 'Jeff thinks a bit of time away from the office would do us all some good. A month's paid leave. Apparently, Danny is causing problems at the office, too, and my productivity is slacking because of it.

I'm embarrassing the company, so I'm out of the game until I can sort this out.'

'What?'

'It's a nightmare that I couldn't argue against, Tom. Danny has disrupted the office one too many times, and I know my output has been at an all-time low. What could I say? I don't have a leg to stand on. I just feel a bit betrayed. Although, paid leave softens the blow a little, I suppose.'

'Jeff's an idiot,' he snapped. 'He needs to grow a backbone and stand up to those sad old men who make up the senior managers.'

'Five years, Tom. Five years of hard graft, and all for what?'

'You're right. This is out of order,' Tom replied. 'A new low.'

She shrugged. 'I know, but look at it from his point of view. The damage to their reputation by association is a concern. You know what the socials are like. Danny just has to make something go viral, include the company, and then boom, it all becomes toxic opinions and cyber lynch mobs. Jeff's just doing what he has to do.'

'Chloe, you're one of their best. The department depends on you, and that promotion is all but yours.'

'And I could get riled up about it, too, or I could just get on with it.'

He checked his watch. 'Bloody hell, why is there never enough time? Look, I have to run, but I'll call you later, maybe pop over.'

She smiled. 'I'd like that, but maybe somewhere neutral.'

'Okay, and then we can figure out what we can do.'

'Tom, this isn't your responsibility.'

'I don't care. I want to help.' He glanced towards the entrance of the office. 'We'll speak later, yeah?'

'Okay,' she mumbled, and let out a defeated sigh.

24

The afternoon spent on her sofa, with nothing to do but scroll the internet for terrifying stories of women being stalked, had been quiet and unproductive. Too quiet, in fact – as if she had stepped into another dimension. And for Chloe that did not invoke a sense of calm serenity but a feeling of something much more foreboding. An impending drama from Danny and whatever else he had planned.

But she also yearned for Tom, wanting the working day to be over so she could see him, or at the very least, speak to him. No one made her feel as safe as he did. She thought of him – the look in his eyes when they last spoke, the warmth in them, the concern. He had a big heart, and somehow she'd managed to get to the centre of it.

A text from Danny popped up on the screen, breaking the moment.

> Did you miss me? Or are you missing something else?

Small tendrils of fear spread across her chest, which she

managed to suppress despite finding it hard to breathe. Chloe's fingers trembled as she typed out a text.

> What the hell have you done?

She stared at the text as it was delivered and waited for his reply.

> Do I have your attention now?

She could have cried out and hurried to throw her coat on.

> Don't you hurt anyone. Do you understand? I'm calling the police.

She waited, her breath shallow and fast as she stared at her screen. 'Answer, you bastard!'

> I warned you, Chloe. I told you I would not tolerate you straying again. I suggest you run along and check on your loved ones. Someone might need you soon.

With a cry, she dashed out into the street and ran at full speed to the end of her road to hail a taxi. Jumping in, she barked out Laura's address, making it clear how much of an emergency it was. Whilst they weaved through the traffic, she pulled up her mum's number and called.

'Hello?'

'Mum!' she cried. 'Are you okay? Where are you?'

'I'm at home, darling. With Dad.'

'Is anyone else there?'

'No, sweetie, just our neighbour, who has popped round for tea.'

'Listen to me, if anyone knocks on the door, you must not answer it. Okay?'

'Why ever not?' her mother asked, disquiet in her voice. 'What's going on?'

'I can't explain now, but there's someone out there harassing me. I just want to make sure he doesn't get to you, either.'

'Oh my goodness. Are you okay?'

'Yes, I'm fine, but I've got to go.'

'Chloe, you need to explain!'

'Mum, I really don't have time. Please, just do as I ask. Don't answer the door or phone to anyone. Do you understand? I'm in a taxi heading to Laura's right now. I've got to check she's all right, too.'

'I don't like this. You sound so panicked. Let me help. Or call the police, let them deal with it.'

'I can't, Mum. He knows where she lives. He's been there. She's an easy target. Oh God, he could be hurting her right now.'

'Right,' her mum said assertively, 'I'm calling the police. Stay in the taxi when you get there. Wait for them to arrive.'

'No, Mum. No!' Chloe spat out the words and heard her mum sigh.

'Chloe.'

'Honestly, I'll call you later. Let you know I'm all right. If I need the police, I'll call them myself.'

Her mother's need to keep her safe would not override Chloe's need to protect her friend. She mumbled something in agreement, knowing it was a promise she would struggle to keep.

The taxi approached Laura's house, and Chloe thrust a twenty at the driver and climbed out of the car, calling out her thanks as she went.

She hurried to the apartment block and slammed her

hand against the intercom at the entrance. 'Laura, are you there? Open up.' She repeatedly jabbed at the button, willing her friend to be okay.

'Chloe?' Laura said from the intercom. 'Come up.'

The door buzzed as Chloe tugged at the handle and rushed inside. She climbed the two flights of stairs to where Laura was waiting for her.

Chloe rushed to her. 'Are you okay? Has he been here?'

'Who?'

'Danny. Has he contacted you today?'

Confusion mixed with concern highlighted Laura's face. 'Of course not. He hasn't been around here since the other day. I thought he'd disappeared.'

'No, no. I don't understand.' Chloe shook her head and stepped back. 'Gabby. What about Gabby? I'll never get there in time.'

'No, no, sweetie,' Laura soothed. 'Calm down. She'll be fine. She's gone away with Rob for a couple of days.'

Chloe struggled to order her thoughts. 'But...but...'

Laura held Chloe's shoulders. 'She's in France. She's fine.'

Chloe pressed her hands to her temples. 'I need to think.' She wandered in a small circle as it hit. Horrified, she stopped and stared at Laura. 'Oh God,' she gasped. 'Tom.'

'What?'

'It's after five. He should be done for the day. Danny couldn't have got to him, could he? Could Danny have followed us the other night after the club?' She reached into her bag for her phone. 'I need to find Tom.'

She called Penny.

'Hey, you,' Penny said, concern in her voice. 'You okay? Do you want to talk?'

'Maybe later, Pen,' Chloe replied hurriedly. 'I just need to check there's been no incidents at the office.'

'Everything is fine,' Penny replied. 'Except it's not the same without you here. I miss you already.'

'I miss you guys, too,' she said. 'And Danny hasn't shown up?'

'I haven't seen him.'

'Okay, good. Have you seen Tom?' Chloe asked, trying to control her breathing.

'No, he hasn't been in the office all afternoon, actually. What's up?' Penny asked.

'I don't know. He said he'd be in touch, but I haven't heard anything yet.'

'I'm sure he's fine,' Penny said. 'Probably working from home.'

The unease in the pit of her stomach didn't move. 'Well, if he calls, can you ask him to ring me?'

'Of course,' Penny said. 'And then you can get me up to date, too.'

Chloe hung up and looked at Laura. 'He's not been at work.'

'Look, don't worry. I'll take you to his place. I'll grab my keys, just a sec.' She rushed to her bag lying by the collection of her and Sam's shoes, and hastily rummaged through it, pulling out a chunk of keys. 'Let's go.'

They rushed out of the building and wound their way to the block of garages tucked out of view as Chloe tried to call Tom.

'He's not answering,' Chloe cried as terror clenched her insides.

Her phone pinged. 'Thank God.' But relief soon turned to horror.

> Chloe, do you understand me now? That it'll only ever be you and me?

'Shut up!' she shouted as they drove.

'Chloe, you need to calm down,' Laura said. 'You don't know anything has happened to Tom yet.'

'I've put everyone in danger. I've been a fool! This mess is all because of me. Stupid me. He's been supporting me, helping me. Something I needed, and this is how I repay him?'

'Please just calm down. You are not responsible for that crazy dude.'

Chloe put her head in her hands. 'I've been so stupid. I realise nothing matters now other than you guys and Tom. Oh, Tom, I'm so sorry.'

Laura rested her hand on Chloe's leg. 'Honey, it's okay. He'll be okay. I'm sure Tom can take on a little shit like Danny.'

Chloe nodded and made an effort to slow her breathing, inhaling and exhaling deeply. They spent the rest of the short journey in silence, save for a few moans from Chloe at any red light or obstruction in the road.

When they finally pulled up outside his house, she felt the ominous doom as she approached. She hurried up the steps, rang the doorbell and leaned over to the window, placing her hand against it so she could peer in. The room was empty. The house seemed quiet, and she couldn't decide if that was a good thing or not.

She rang the doorbell and tried him on the phone again. 'He's not answering,' she said as Laura approached.

'Try again,' she said.

Chloe felt the panic rise. 'What if he's in there, hurt?'

'Is there someone you can call? Someone who could let you in?'

'No. No one. Except...' She thought it through. 'Maybe I should call the police.'

Laura took hold of her shoulders. 'No, no. Slow down. We need to think first.'

'I can't. I need to know Tom is okay!'

'Why wouldn't he be?'

Chloe swiped the screen of her phone and showed Laura Danny's text.

'Shit,' Laura replied.

'I was always careful to make sure Danny didn't know about Tom's home. We checked the night we arrived here. He warned me, told me that I couldn't stray.' Pacing, she looked at Laura. 'That's it,' she said. 'He must have seen us talking outside the office when I left today. He said he couldn't accept it. He's hurt Tom.'

She called him again. If leaving multiple messages was what it would take to get him to call her, then that's what she'd do. The phone clicked, and she stopped, listening for his voice. 'Tom?'

'Chloe.'

'Are you okay?' she hurried. 'What's happened?'

'I'm at home.'

'What? But I'm here, too. I've been banging on your door.' All the emotions rushed at once, and her lip began to tremble. 'Are you hurt?'

'Of course not. Look, hold on, I'm coming down.'

She hung up as she and Laura waited for him to answer.

He pulled the door open moments later, dressed casually in jeans and a T-shirt, completely unharmed.

When he saw the state Chloe was in, he reached out for her. 'Hey, hey. It's okay.'

Laura breathed her relief when she saw him, too. 'See? No damage done.'

'I was just so worried,' she sobbed. 'I thought Danny had hurt you.'

'No, of course he hasn't. I decided to work from home for the rest of the day. I couldn't bear to look at Jeff. I never hear anything in that back bedroom.'

Laura placed her arm around Chloe's shoulders. 'This one has been going out of her mind. Couldn't get hold of you. More issues with Danny. I think she might need a drink.'

Tom smiled sympathetically. 'Come in, both of you. I can sort that out.'

'Ah, no, not for me, but thanks,' Laura said. 'I make it my mission never to be a third wheel. I'll get out of here and leave you two to it. I should get back.'

Chloe let Laura wrap her arms around her and pull her into a firm hug. 'I'll call you later.'

Chloe nodded. 'Thanks for helping me out. I'm sorry I'm such a mess.'

Laura squeezed Chloe's shoulders in a last gesture of affection and glanced at Tom. 'Take care of her, okay?'

'My pleasure,' Tom said, as he held out his hand for Chloe.

Chloe walked to him and turned to Laura, checking she was safely in her car before allowing Tom to close the door.

In the privacy of his hallway, she wrapped her arms around him, something she'd wanted to do for so long. 'It was terrible. I thought...I thought, oh God, you don't want to know.' She hugged him hard and he reciprocated, his arms warm as they wrapped around her.

'Hey, it's okay,' he said soothingly.

'No, it's really not,' she said, burying her head in his chest to breathe him in. 'I thought he'd got to you, I thought he'd hurt you and I couldn't handle it. It was awful.'

'He hasn't been near, I promise.'

She looked him deep in his warm, sincere eyes and knew this was what she wanted. It had never been clearer, and she would fight to have it. She cupped her hands around his face and placed her lips to his. She felt his reaction, his surprise, and then his desire as he sank into the kiss, savouring her, giving away all the clues as to how much he wanted her, too. It was perfect.

'Wow,' he breathed. 'I wasn't expecting that.'

'I'm sorry, I'm sorry. I'm not being fair to you. One minute we're pulling clothes off each other and next I'm telling you I can't commit. Now I've come here and thrown everything up in the air again.'

'Let's stop right there,' he ordered gently. 'You have nothing to apologise for. You have only ever been honest with me about how you feel about us and where we're going, and I appreciate that. Claire never was, and I realise that there is no foundation for a relationship without honesty.'

'But that's where I failed. There's so much more I need to tell you.'

'You haven't failed, Chloe. I've known all along there's something more going on that you're battling alone. But I also know there will be a reason for it, more than just simple dishonesty. I know who you are.'

She hung her head and let a sob escape. She didn't deserve his kindness and his understanding, but she held onto them, knowing they were the only things she had left.

He took her hands and held them. 'I want you to know that I'm here, and I'll wait until you're ready to share it with me.'

'I want to tell you, so desperately. I want you to know everything.'

'And you can't?'

She shook her head. 'No. Not right now.' Now, she looked him in the eye, wanting her answer to reach his soul. 'I want to be able to tell you everything. I want you to know me, inside and out. Then and only then do we have something we can build from because that's what I want, Tom. I want to be in your life however I can, but this has to be over with first.'

'Then I'll wait.'

'You'd do that for me?'

'Of course I would. You know how I feel about you.'

She reached out and hugged him again, grateful. Forever grateful.

'You're shaking,' he said, checking her over.

She nodded.

He smoothed his hand over her hair, sending a tingle through her body. 'Come on, I'll make you something to drink, and you can relax for a minute and then decide what to do next.'

He took her hand and led her to the kitchen. She sat at the table and felt her pounding heart ease up a little as she watched the birds through the glass back door, gathering on the feeding table in his garden. So soothing to watch animals in nature, just getting on with living their lives, while a whirlwind seemed to surge through hers.

'Coffee, tea, or something stronger?' he asked, bringing her back to the present.

'I don't know. Coffee, I think, thanks.'

She checked her phone and the countless messages from Danny. He may have started the game by sending her on this pointless mission, but she'd won it by being here and out of reach. There was no more time to delay what she needed to do, but she allowed herself this moment with Tom before she would do it.

Tom busied himself with the drinks and, numb from shock and adrenaline, she watched him work. In a strange daydream her mind popped up a thought as to what it would be like to share lazy weekends with him, to share these precious inconsequential and private moments. To be part of someone's life when they're at their most relaxed.

He joined her at the table and placed two mugs down.

She wrapped her hands around the hot mug of coffee and let it warm her fingers. 'Thank you.'

He lightly tapped the table, a nervous gesture that exposed his desire to speak. 'Chloe, I just wanted you to know that whatever has happened, I'm not going to turn my back on you. You know that, don't you?'

She reached across the table and took his hands in hers. 'I do, and I'm very lucky. I'm not sure I deserve such blind faith.'

'No, I think you do,' he replied. 'I watched the fall-out from David and Melissa, and all I wanted to do was whisk you away and make you smile again. It's been such a long time since you did that.'

'I kind of got caught up in that fall-out, too.' She felt the spear of guilt. 'But I've come to realise that what David and I had wasn't as solid as I had believed. He didn't really commit; it was just a fleeting idea at the time, to get married in a whirlwind. It suited him until he changed his mind. And then he just...moved on.'

'Well, I think he was mad to let you go.'

'But he lived for adventure, excitement, and it soon became clear that marriage wasn't always about that. There were bills to pay, shopping to do, and all the other boring things that make up a life. He soon looked for other adventures when it got too much.' She paused for a moment and let the silence give her the space to prepare what she needed to say next. With a sad smile, she spoke. 'I just wish I'd got to know you better, before Danny crashed into my world.'

He smiled, and it felt good to say these things out loud, but it also came with a burden. She checked her watch. 'I should go now before he realises where I am and who I'm with.'

'Is there no way I can persuade you to stay a little longer – plan what you need to do next?'

'I can't. If I stay, I'll crumble. I'll fall into your arms and involve you even more in this mess. I need to finish this, and I need some distance to do it. It's going to get worse before it gets better. I can feel it.' She held his hand. 'When this is over, please just tell me you'll listen to what I have to say. That's all I ask.'

'I'll listen, Chloe. Happy to.'

She leaned forward and placed a clumsy kiss on his lips, and he grabbed her, prolonging it for as long as he could.

She rose from the table and walked to the door.

'How are you getting home? Will you be safe?' he asked, as he stood with her.

'It doesn't matter now, but he won't hurt me. He thinks he's in love with me.' The sound of the words hurt her, and Tom, too, by the wince on his face. She hoped she could repair the damage this might cause.

'I will call you as soon as I can,' she said as she pulled open the door.

He nodded, closer now. 'If you need me, I'm here for you. You know that, right?'

'I do, and I'm so grateful for it. I've felt so alone for so long when I should have been with you.'

He smiled sadly. 'There's always tomorrow?'

'Yes, you're right,' she agreed. 'There's always tomorrow.'

She was careful to check her surroundings and take the necessary detours when she left Tom's. Danny couldn't know this place. Ever. After walking up to the main road and having created a safe distance from Tom's, the relative anonymity of the bustling main road of shoppers and cars meant she no longer cared if Danny was there or not. In fact, she wanted it. Whatever he wanted to do next was fine with her.

25

Chloe switched on her phone and listened to the beeps of multiple messages. She glanced around, sweeping the area for anything suspicious, but she found nothing. Maybe she had eluded him, or perhaps he was here and better at this than she was. She checked her phone.

'Oh, Mum. I'm sorry. I should have called you sooner,' she said, remembering what she'd promised. It was over an hour since they had last spoken and guilt filled her. 'I was at Tom's.'

'Chloe Rose Stark, I've been going out of my mind!' her mum replied. 'I've left countless messages.' Muffled sounds at the end of the line confirmed her mum was relaying the information to her dad that all was well. She wished it was.

'Sorry, Mum. I didn't think.'

'Sweetheart, it's okay. I'm just so relieved to hear your voice. I was so worried. What the hell happened? You mentioned a situation, but, Chloe, to hear your voice like that was terrifying. Talk to me. I need to know what's going on.'

She nodded, taking the heat like she was a child again.

'Okay, well, I met this guy a couple of weeks ago and things have got a little out of hand. He's persistent.'

'Define "persistent",' her mum interrupted.

When Chloe had got her mum up to speed, she waited for her response.

'Chloe, this sounds extremely serious. Have you spoken to the police?'

'I have filed a report. They are aware.'

'That doesn't sound an adequate response to what happened earlier. You're going to be calling them again, yes?'

'Of course. They're well aware of Danny.'

'That's his name, is it?'

'Yes,' Chloe said cautiously.

'And do you have a surname?'

'Mum, you don't have to go all detective on me.'

'I just want to know who this maniac is that you have to protect us from.'

'Like I said, the police are dealing with it.'

'I think you should come home. Get some distance between you and him.'

'Oh, Mum, there's nothing I'd love more, but I have to deal with it here. He's everywhere. I can't be sure he won't follow, and I can't risk exposing you. If he knows where you live, who knows what he might do.' She had been walking while talking and had come to the station. 'Look, I've got to go now, but I'll call later. Promise.'

'But what about your father? He wants to speak to you about all this.'

'Mum, I can't. Would you get him up to speed?' She couldn't face relaying the information again, giving every little detail so he could analyse the situation for himself.

But before she could say any more, her father was on the line. 'Chloe, what's going on? What's this about a man following you?'

She rubbed her forehead as she went to the machine and purchased a ticket. 'So you heard, then?'

'Yes, you know your mother has the phone speaker at full volume. It was hard not to, but it doesn't change the fact you're in danger and I don't think you should be doing this on your own.'

'I know,' she sighed. 'But I can't involve you.'

'Chloe, we have been around for a long time now. We've raised you to be an independent soul and we're extremely proud of you and all you've done, but we're still parents, whether you're two or twenty-seven. That will never change.'

'I know,' she whispered 'And I'm so lucky to have you both.'

'You remember the long conversation we had when you decided you wanted to leave for the bright lights of London? All the things we discussed to keep you safe?'

Of course she remembered. The conversation became a list of stipulations she had to address to their satisfaction before they would consider letting her go without them. Unsurprisingly, the issue of stalkers and how to deal with them never cropped up on this list.

'You'll speak to the police again?'

'Yes.'

'And you have sufficient locks on your doors?'

'Of course.'

'No walking alone at night?'

'Mostly.'

'Chloe.'

'I know, I'm sorry.'

'I know you're disciplined and like to be in charge of your life, Chloe. A trait you get from me, I'm afraid. But you need to know some things are outside of your control. This person sounds dangerous and not to be underestimated. You need to take care of yourself.'

'I am, Dad.' Chloe was like her dad in so many ways. There was no denying her meticulous planning was something she'd inherited from her father, but this was not the first time everything she'd planned for herself had been blown out of the water.

'Okay, well, I don't think you need any more of a lecture from me,' he said, finishing up. 'So I'll put you back to Mum.'

'Thanks, Dad.'

'I love you.'

Tears welled at his words of affection, and she wanted to run to him, right away. But there was no time for that. Not until this was over. 'I love you, too, Dad.'

Chloe caught the muffled sounds of the phone exchanging hands.

Her mum sighed. 'All right, as your father said, lecture over, but ring us later, yes? And if you don't, we'll be in the car and coming over quicker than you can say "over-protective parents". Agreed? We may be in the wilds of Dorset, but we can be in London in a couple of hours or so.'

A smirk covered her lips. 'Okay.'

***

SOMEWHERE BETWEEN WEST Kilburn and the stop for the three-two-eight bus, he found her. Travelling on the route that would take her to Westbourne Park, she felt him, closer than before. She felt his sickly warmth, the brush of his coat against her back as she stood with other commuters. She imagined his eyes on her, his face, the lingering gaze, and a shudder trickled down her spine. But this is what she wanted. At least if he was here, she wouldn't have to go to him. Now was the time to let Danny in.

She got off the bus at her stop, his footfalls intermingled

with the others. It was late now and the light was beginning to fade.

She turned into her road.

He's there, right behind me, she thought to herself. *I know it because I feel him. I feel his eyes, how they penetrate. That's good. He'll think I'm nervous, scared, and that's good, too. He'll think I don't want him here, but he's wrong. He thinks he knows where this is going, but he's wrong about that, too. He's wrong about everything, but I'll make him understand.*

26

W alking down the steps to her front door, she listened for him following behind. Still, she didn't turn around. Pushing the key into the lock, she opened the door. Pausing for one final moment before she would let this begin, she rested her hand on the door and closed her eyes. Now, with the door pushed open ajar, she turned.

'Chloe,' he said as he came closer, his eyes dark, windows to the chaos lurking within.

She made no attempt to push him away as he drew closer, or fight, even though she wore defiance like armour. She would allow him in. She wanted him to feel the power of this moment, so she could strip it all away.

She stepped inside and held the door for him, catching the flicker of bewilderment in his eyes.

'What's going on?' he asked, his head tilted in doubt.

'I'm letting you have what you want,' she replied. She started the game she was going to win. She'd break him down, make him wish he'd never met her. But she needed to be careful. The change from resistance to submission would be obvious, and it would make him suspicious. 'Isn't that what you've been waiting for?'

He chuckled as if caught out in a considerably less malicious escapade – a forgotten birthday or a thoughtless comment – and tucked threads of hair behind her ear. 'Yes, it is, Chloe. I'm so glad you've seen sense.'

Still, she could see his disbelief. She just needed a bit of time to convince him she meant it, and if it took a couple of hours in her home to do it, then so be it.

He followed, closing the door, hiding them from the outside world. She needed to keep calm. They stood in the hallway. Who would move first? But it didn't take long for him to take the lead. His eyes glinted with satisfaction. He'd got what he wanted. He believed he'd won.

Her emotions bounced from abject horror to vile repulsion at the risk she was taking by allowing someone so unstable in her home. But right now, she had to keep a smile plastered to her face. Her phone beeped inside her pocket. When she pulled it out, she noticed several missed calls from Tom.

He watched what she was doing and glanced down. Panic surged as he reached out and tried to take it from her grasp. She felt the horror manifest into something real and stick in her throat, suffocating her.

'What are you doing?' she asked, as lightly as possible.

'You don't need this now,' he said, pulling firmly and unrelentingly until the smooth glass and plastic slipped from her hold. 'I'll take care of you.' He tucked the phone into his back pocket. 'Which means I'll take care of everything. There's nothing you have to worry about.'

'But what if I need it when you're not around?'

'I'm not going anywhere, Chloe. I'll always be here.'

There was a terrifying glint in his eye that chilled her bones.

Loud banging against the front door halted the moment, cutting through the tension. They both glanced at the door.

'Chloe, are you in there?' Tom's voice rang through the hall.

She didn't want this. She'd tried to keep him away, told him not to come, but he wouldn't, not when he felt the way he did. And now he was walking straight into the danger she was trying to protect him from.

She thought quickly, meeting Danny's gaze. 'I have to answer that. I have to make him go away,' she said.

'Do you think I'm stupid?' Danny spat under his breath. 'You planned for him to come so you two can trap me.'

'No, really, I haven't.'

'Chloe, I expected better of you.' He shook his head. 'I think it's time I dealt with him, only on my terms this time.'

She placed her hands on his chest, stopping him from moving towards the door. 'No, please don't. Let me get rid of Tom. He will just keep on until I answer.'

'All these men, Chloe,' he replied with a sigh.

Another succession of bangs against the door. 'Chloe, answer me. I need to know you're okay.'

'Okay, Chloe, you can get rid of him. But do it quickly. I would hate for something to happen to him. Something he may not recover from.'

She looked at Danny pleadingly. 'I'll do it now. Please.'

She took a step, at which point he grabbed her elbow. 'But he needs to go now, Chloe.' He squeezed her arm tighter, his fingers digging into her skin. It would leave a bruise. 'Am I making myself clear?'

She nodded, gently removed her arm from his grasp, and hurried to the door. She turned the handle and opened it to see the man she really wanted in her life, more than anyone else. Her redemption, her salvation. The concern was written on his face, his eyes full of worry. She wanted to hold him, be held by him, and wipe Danny from her memory.

'Hi, Tom,' she began. 'Now's not a good time.'

'I was worried. I know what you said earlier, but when you didn't answer my calls I thought the worst. Did you get my messages?'

'My phone's dead.'

He stopped talking and looked at her. Really looked at her. 'Chloe, what's wrong? Is everything okay?'

'I can't do this right now. You need to go.'

'Has he contacted you again? Has he threatened you?'

Standing on the other side of the door, Danny applied more pressure to her arm.

She shook her head slightly, her eyes searching his. 'No, Tom. Leave me alone. I can't do this. I just need to be on my own.'

If she could take back the words that had caused his face to fall with disappointment, she would.

'But—'

She didn't let him continue and slowly closed the door, her eyes never leaving his. She watched his silhouette as it remained for a moment, then disappeared up the steps and away. Pain and relief tumbled inside. She'd hurt him, but she'd also saved him, and that was what mattered most.

Turning, she faced Danny, his face triumphant. 'Good girl. We don't need him. It's just you and me now.'

She nodded and didn't stop Danny from coming close to pull her into an embrace. Although connected physically, she was completely alone and felt the delusion radiate from him.

'We'll always be together. Even in death, Chloe. I'll never leave you.' He smiled again. 'But that's the joy. We've got the rest of our lives to discover all the things we love and all the things we hate.'

I hate you.

Her phone rang again, muffled in his pocket, a puncture in this artificial environment.

She bit her lip, fearing she'd break the delicate skin there as she prayed it would not be Tom. 'Should I answer that?'

He pulled the phone from his pocket and glanced at it. 'It's your policeman friend.'

The phone kept ringing.

He shook his head. 'No, I can't let you answer it. You understand?'

She nodded as her heart thundered and fingers itched to grab her phone from his hand.

He gave a little shrug and tucked the phone back into his pocket. It stopped ringing and Chloe knew it was time to buckle up and get on.

Her flat filled with a strange, surreal energy. 'I'm going to get a drink,' she said, putting a barrier of false serenity around herself. He wouldn't recognise what was authentic or fake anyway. He was so desperate for this to be real, so she could do what she liked.

She watched his confusion and smiled. He followed, disarmed, unsure, and she knew then she had begun to tip the balance of power. Now she was in control and had taken his away just by giving the illusion of consent. It felt good, after so long of being adrift.

'I could take you on a date. Somewhere nice,' he said quickly, while she filled a glass with water, and with a vulnerability she hadn't seen before.

She'd use it. If she had any good in her, she'd feel bad, but he didn't deserve that anyway, so she ploughed on. She remained where she was and leaned against the counter. 'Tell me,' she began. 'Why have you never found someone before now?'

'Karma, I suppose.'

She tilted her head, giving him the space to expand on that.

'I did some bad things before I met you,' he said. 'Things that I now regret.'

'What bad things, Danny? What have you done?'

He smiled and glanced down. 'You don't want to know. Not right now, anyway.'

'But I do want to know, Danny. I want to know everything about you.'

Her words snapped his gaze to her, an intense and frightening gaze that she fought to hold.

'You're right, of course,' he said. 'If we're to have a future together, we must be honest.' He inhaled, prepared. 'There was a woman. I was very into her. I may have made some mistakes.'

Chloe knew that 'very into her' meant manic and pathological obsession, but she remained silent, trying to hide the fact her knuckles had turned white from gripping the edge of the countertop so tightly.

'I wanted her so badly. I kind of lost it for a while, and even though I would change what happened, I know I can't go back. All I wanted was a normal life but it's always eluded me.'

'There is no normal in this life. Just people trying to do the best they can.'

'I know, but I never had any of it. None at all.' He sighed. 'It's a cliché, but I never had a family. Brought up in the care system.' He laughed bitterly. 'That's a joke because literally nobody cares in places like that. They just want their funding quota. Nothing else matters in between.'

'I thought you said it was okay?'

'No, I only tell people that so they don't feel sorry for me. I hate the...pity. Anyway, I can see now that my love was misplaced before.'

She understood the reference. Keeping her face neutral, she listened.

He looked at her, his eyes full of hope. 'But we can all change, can't we? We can redeem ourselves.'

'The only way to redeem yourself is to admit everything you've done, Danny.'

'What are you talking about?'

'Tell me what you did to Melissa. Admit it.'

There, she'd said it. Words that she'd been holding on to for so long.

She smiled at his confusion, enjoying it, as the sparks of empowerment fired her up and warmed her cheeks. Oh yes, she would enjoy this. All of it. She'd make sure he never did this again to anyone. It had been easy reeling him in. Someone as obsessive as him would soon bite, given enough temptation, and she'd given him just the right amount. Just the right amount of resistance, too, because someone like him lives for the chase. That's what it was all about, for someone like him. But for Chloe, when it came to chasing, it was the other way round.

After David's death, she'd tracked his movements for weeks, having followed him home one night after the court case – an action she wasn't really aware of until she was standing behind him on the train. He simply didn't realise he was her victim; she'd sought *him* out. She'd got to *him* first. The hunter had become the prey. She was coming for him.

'What?'

'I know you loved her in your own warped way and felt the huge betrayal when she chose to be with David.'

He shifted, his body rigid, and eyed her with suspicion. 'I don't understand.'

Not sure if he was about to lash out or leave, she kept her gaze on his as she approached him, keeping sight of her landline.

'You took things too far, didn't you?' The words were bitter in her mouth. 'You were blinded by anger, so much anger. And in that moment you decided you would punish her for defying you by choosing someone else. You couldn't have her, so no one else would. Is that right, Danny?'

Now, a wave of calm anger replaced the astonishment.

'You set that fire at the house on the night she died and now there's no more Melissa. Not after you'd finished with her. You made sure she would understand what you were capable of and the punishment you would inflict.'

'How do you know this?' he demanded angrily.

'David was my husband, Danny. I know everything.'

'Your husband?' Chloe saw fear in Danny's eyes.

She nodded, edged closer. 'Yes, that's right. I got the call about what had happened, how they were trapped, how they died. I went to the inquest. I watched from the gallery. I saw you in court with your clever lawyer. I knew who you were and what you did. I listened to every last detail. You got lucky with that Crown Court jury, didn't you? The "Not Guilty" verdict was another blow I had to bear.'

Sadness, disappointment, anger, all etched into his face. 'No, Chloe. No.'

'I thought about what I could do to stop the pain because I was in *so much* pain, Danny. Every day wishing for it to end.'

'Stop it, please.'

'And then it all came to me and I made a plan of my own. I would let you find me and I would let you feel like you had won.'

'No, Chloe,' he cried, shaking his head. 'You didn't do that.'

'Yes, Danny, I did. I let everyone believe I was vulnerable, but I'm not. I knew what I was doing. I found you in that club, the same club where you met Melissa. The one you go to when you need a new object of desire, where you scope out your new prey. Where we met. You think you found me, but it was the other way around. I let you create havoc in my life. All for this exact moment, to be here. To tell you that you've lost. You have no power over me. You never did.'

Surprise flipped to anger again. 'So you tricked me? You thought you could bring me here and get me to confess?'

'I just want to hear you say it,' she said through gritted teeth.

'Say what?'

'That you're a murderer.'

'I'm not a murderer. I needed them to see my anger, that's all. I needed them to know the devastation they'd caused. She chose him when she should have chosen me. I was her soulmate,' he said with a thump to his chest. 'I was.'

She shook her head, hoping not to dislodge the bitter tears that welled in her eyes. 'You wanted them to know what you were capable of, and you're glad they knew. Because they did know, didn't they? You wouldn't have left that unsaid. You wanted Melissa to suffer and know it was at your hands. You wanted to punish her.'

Shocked, he stuttered. 'Yes. No. I don't know! You're confusing me. She was my soulmate. At least I thought she was.'

'She rejected you. You were lonely, desperate for love and relationships but blind to the lack of interest women showed you, and that tipped into resentment and harassment when Melissa rejected you, didn't it? You wanted revenge.'

'No, not at first. She was lovely to me, really friendly, and I thought, "Any moment now, she's gonna realise who I am. We'll click, and it'll be perfect."' He sighed, and his jaw tensed. 'But it was not perfect. She backed away; thought I was coming on too heavy. Too intense. Just like you.' He put his head in his hands. 'I just wanted to see her one last time, but instead I saw David there, kissing her. They were laughing, touching each other. You know the way people do when they're in love. Like they need to be part of that other person, connected to each other.'

She swallowed the pain away as his description of their newfound relationship cut another scar into her heart.

'I couldn't take it. She needed to know she'd pissed me off. But I just wanted to scare them, to be able to save them, then she would realise it was me who loved her most. Me who saved her. But they'd changed the locks on the doors. I couldn't get in. The fire took hold so quickly. And then the fire crew arrived and I had to get out of there. I couldn't implicate myself.'

'But you did set the fire?'

'Yes.'

'Because of Melissa's relationship with my husband.'

'Yes.' He looked at her. 'But surely none of that matters now? Not now we've found each other.'

She glared back at him, as still as stone.

He reached for her and she flinched when he gripped her arms. Her reaction changed his expression in an instant. Suspicion filled his eyes. 'Chloe, why am I here?'

Everything rose to the surface. Her emotions, every painful scar that itched, every wound that throbbed, wanting to be noticed. And she let it happen. She breathed, her lips pursed tight in anger.

'Because I hate you. Because people like you are parasites that ruin lives. You have nothing. You're nothing but an empty shell of a human. You take what you want, you suck the love and joy out of others, and then you punish them if they want you out of their lives. And I want to make sure you never do any harm to another woman again.'

Anger shone brightly in his eyes. 'You bitch,' he said slowly. 'You set me up, just wanting some sort of confession from me.'

'No, what I want is for you to pay.'

'Don't push me, Chloe,' he warned.

Fury took over, directed at this man who was responsible for all her feelings of desperation. 'Do you think I'm scared of you?' she spat, before shoving him hard.

He stepped back to regain his balance, and then launched at her. 'I'm warning you.'

'Bring it on then, big man. Do your worst.' She thumped his chest, ready for the comeback. 'I hate you. I really, really hate you. I wish you were dead!'

'That's enough!' he bellowed, his grip tight on her arms.

She struggled, their eyes locked, and she didn't care that he might take this too far and hurt her – or worse. She just needed to rage, to let it all out.

Desperate with anger, he grabbed her hair, tugging her face up to meet his, and raised his fist in the air.

'Go on, then,' she panted. 'Hurt me. Give me something to go to the police with and show what you've done to me.'

He lowered his arm and released her, tried to cup her face with his hands, his emotion switching to sorrow and regret. 'No, no. This isn't how it was supposed to be,' he said, as he released his grip. 'What have you done, Chloe? What have you done?'

She took hold of his hand and placed it on her neck. 'I'm not finished yet. I haven't even started.' Grabbing his fingers under her own, she gouged her skin with his fingernails, creating long welts.

He snapped his hand away in horror. 'What the hell are you doing?' he yelled as he backed away.

'This is history repeating itself and I'm going to stop you from ever doing this to anyone else again.'

'Stop it,' he cried, and tried to protectively wrap his arms around her.

She moved to free herself from his hold, and they danced

a strange waltz as he fought her struggle. The doorframe was close, too close, and she knew this was her chance. She had to take it. Knowing it would hurt like hell, she reached out her hand to grasp the frame and forcefully jerked her head towards it, slamming her cheek against the painted wood.

'No!' he yelled. 'Chloe!'

She wailed and clutched her cheek as it throbbed and transmitted pulsing signals of scorching pain to her brain.

He panicked and released his hold, motionless, horror covering his face.

She let her hands fall and launched for him, reaching for her phone in his pocket. Grabbing it, she shoved him hard before running for the bathroom and locking the door.

Three loud thuds thundered against the door.

'Chloe?' he bellowed. 'Open the door.' Another three thuds. 'Chloe, open the fucking door!'

She stepped away from the door and hit 999 on the phone. 'Police!' she yelled. 'Please come quickly. He's here again! Danny is here, and he's trying to hurt me! I'm terrified!'

'What are you doing?' he bellowed. She heard him pace. 'Can't believe I've been *SO STUPID!*'

'I'm locked in the bathroom, but I think he'll break it down. I think he's going to kill me. Please, please hurry.'

27

The wailing sirens filled Chloe's ears. He'd been dangerously quiet since she'd called the police but he was still here, she knew it. She felt his insane energy filling the house, figuring out what to do.

Another three bangs, except these were at the front door and mixed with voices calling her name.

She heard the door opening and the muffled sounds of Danny talking.

Cautiously, she opened the door. She left the bathroom, listening closely, and moved silently through her bedroom to stand in the doorway, looking directly at the two police officers and Danny. The bruise on her face throbbed, and the tracks of bloody welts stung the skin on her neck.

They all turned and looked at her.

'Chloe Stark?' one of the officers asked, as he approached her.

Strange metallic voices echoed on his radio, followed by a series of beeps.

'Do you require medical assistance?' he asked, studying her face.

'She did this to herself,' Danny interrupted angrily.

The officer held out his hand, his palm facing Danny. 'Okay, sir. You'll have your chance. We just need to speak to Chloe first.' He turned to her. 'Are you okay?'

She shook her head. 'He was hurting me. I was so scared. This man has been harassing me for ages.'

A sound escaped Danny's lips, and he ran his fingers through his hair in frustration. 'She's fucking lying, for Christ's sake.'

'Sir.' The officer's tone was the authority needed to silence Danny.

'You psycho,' she spat. 'You'll soon be proved wrong when my skin is found under your nails.'

The policeman studied her, listening, taking it in. Her prompt had done its job. He moved to create a barrier between herself and him.

The other officer moved closer to Danny, his radio loud, too, with disjointed, far-off voices.

'I've filed a complaint,' she continued. 'He was here when I arrived home and wouldn't leave.'

The officer turned to face Danny. 'Is this true?'

The colour drained from Danny's face, although his smile was tight and rigid. 'Chloe and I have a complicated relationship, that's for sure, but this is not what you think.'

'We don't have a relationship at all. Look what you've done to me,' she said as she gently placed her fingers over the raised welts on her neck. 'I want you out of my life.'

'Now, Chloe,' he said. 'You know that's not true.'

'Okay, that's enough,' the officer interrupted, as he glanced over to his colleague. 'Take him outside.'

Danny raised his hands as the officer turned to him. 'Okay, okay. Fine. But this is insane. She did that to herself, for fuck's sake.'

He walked out the door, and the officer closed it behind him.

Now alone, the officer looked at her. 'It's all right. You're safe. You can talk freely now.'

She took a deep breath. 'I don't know what happened. He just turned on me.' She held her hand against her cheek. 'It was all so sudden and I...I was so frightened.'

'Do you need to go to the hospital? We can get someone to check you over. Your cheek is going to bruise, I think, and those are nasty scratches you've got there.'

'Yes, I'll go and get myself checked out. I'll call a friend if I need to. Thankfully, you came so quickly he didn't have the chance to do any real harm.' She gently touched the lump on her cheek, wincing as she did. 'But what now? He'll be back here again, I know it. This won't be the last of it.'

'We can take care of that; don't you worry. He'll be arrested and we'll be taking him down to the station. It should give you some time to think about what you'd like to do. Perhaps stay with a friend or family until you feel safe again.'

'And what then?'

'Someone will contact you once a decision is made either to charge or release him on further investigation.'

She nodded. 'Thank you.'

Raised voices came from outside, and Danny began thumping the door and calling her name.

The officer strode quickly to the door and opened it. Chloe followed behind.

'Right, I think we're done here,' he said as he grabbed hold of Danny's elbow, but Danny's anger made him difficult to restrain and the two officers had to work together to corral him out of the hallway he had managed to invade.

Danny made one final attempt to reach Chloe, but the

officers blocked him, pulling his arms behind his back to cuff him. They struggled as they read him his rights.

In the commotion, he fixed his eyes on Chloe. 'I get it, Chloe,' he murmured, with a cold menace that went unnoticed by the officers. 'You want to play. So we'll play.'

No words left her mouth as she watched the two officers remove him from her flat and up into the waiting car.

What had she done?

CHLOE HADN'T ASKED for any help in getting to the hospital. She knew what had to be done for her injuries to be recorded and added to her personal record, and she wanted to be alone for it. It was a process, simple as that, and she waited patiently to be seen, checked over, advised about support agencies that could help women like her, and then discharged. It was close to three in the morning when she turned the key into her lock and, exhausted, all she wanted was a hot bath and some painkillers for her face.

She should ring her parents, but it was the wrong side of dawn; the need to keep them in peaceful ignorance outweighed her need to speak to them. And, anyway, before anyone else was called, she needed to speak to Tom, hoping she could repair the damage of his earlier visit. She dialled his number. The first ring made her hesitate, the second caused doubt. The third never came because she hung up the call before he had the chance to answer. At least if he had been asleep he would have missed the early termination of the call. She could explain the missed call later.

Sitting on the side of the bath, she swirled her hand in the hot water, mixing her favourite jasmine bath crème with it. The room filled with scented steam, and for the first time in a long while she knew Danny could not reach her. She slipped her clothes off and placed them in the laundry bin, wanting to wash any trace of Danny from her life. Keeping her bathroom door open a little, something she could enjoy now she was free, she slipped under the water and let it soothe her. She lay back and closed her eyes, no longer listening out for any noise or creak inside the flat.

She'd got what she wanted, and that was for Danny to be arrested again for pursuing and harassing another woman. She'd wanted to make it stick this time; him implicated in an offence that would put him away and off the streets, especially given his past misdemeanours. She hoped she'd done enough.

Her bath and the painkillers did nothing to help her sleep. Her thoughts would not cease enough for her to slip away. She lay in her bed and stared at the ceiling. This battle was hers, for sure, but an uneasy creeping doubt left her anxious that she'd failed to win the war. She struggled to lose the image of his face in her mind. He had been so resolute, controlled, and that was not how she expected it to go. He wasn't scared. He wasn't worried the police had arrested him and had felt confident enough to leave her with those chilling words before being taken away. Feeling her emotions were running away with her, Chloe took a moment to calm. She was told by the officer to wait to hear from the station for a decision about what would be done with Danny and that's all she could do now.

Only after some sleep would she decide what to do next. She turned onto her side and hugged her phone close to her chest.

***

RINGING PIERCED the room and dragged Chloe from sleep. She clumsily reached out for her phone, pulling up the covers when she couldn't find it and saw it lying against her leg, halfway down the bed. She hurriedly accepted the call.

'Tom,' she murmured, relieved. 'I'm so glad you called.'

'I know you need space, but I saw you had called me,' he began.

'I know,' she said. 'Because I need to explain.'

He sighed. 'Chloe, there's no need. I know you have issues, and I shouldn't have come to yours last night.'

Her heart ached. She'd hurt and confused him and that was unforgivable. 'No, wait. You don't understand,' she interrupted. 'I didn't want to say those things to you. I didn't mean them. I still feel the same as when I left yours and I meant every word of what I'd said to you.'

'Then what's going on?'

'Danny was here. He made me say that. He stood on the other side of the door to make sure I did. I needed to keep him calm because he'd threatened to hurt you.'

'What?' Tom replied. 'Where is he now? Where are *you* now? Are you okay?'

'I'm fine,' she said. 'It's over. He's been arrested. I made sure of it.'

'How, Chloe?'

'It wasn't pretty, and I'm a little battle sore, but I got him.'

'You're hurt? Tell me where you are. I can be there in an instant.'

'I'm fine, really. I'm at home nursing a few superficial injuries, but nothing that won't heal. It was necessary to get what I wanted. I've got to wait for the officer to let me know what the next steps are, but I think he'll be detained for a while, given his history.'

'What history? Jesus, Chloe, what's going on?'

She cupped a hand over her eyes as she clutched her phone to her ear. 'Tom, I have a lot of explaining to do. I want you to know everything. Can I see you? Can we talk?'

'That's all I want. I've been waiting.'

'I know you do. Can I come over? I'd really like to see you.'

'Me, too,' he replied. 'You have no idea how much. But I'll come to you and I want you to stay put and not open the door until I get there. Okay?'

She smiled. It felt good to have people who cared enough to stick around. 'Promise. I'll see you after work?'

'Forget that,' he replied. 'I'm not going into the office today. I'll leave here in a little while and come over.'

'Sounds great,' she said, not able to stop the smile.

'And maybe pack a bag?' he said, 'I'm bringing you back to mine, where I can take care of you properly.'

She laughed. 'I'd love that. I wouldn't want to be anywhere else. And thank you.'

'For what?'

'For understanding and giving me the chance to explain.'

Her heart fluttered with hope. He would hear her out, listen to her explanation and, hopefully, he would understand and know she was a grieving person when she planned this, her mind in a bad place. A dark, dark place.

Her mother had cried when Chloe called, relieved that Danny had been arrested. Her father had to take the phone from her while she composed herself, and Chloe feared she'd be met with rationality and instructions on what she should do next, but instead he spoke only kind words of love. It was the first time she had allowed herself to cry, too. Properly. To really let out the pent-up grief and anguish. She didn't know what lay ahead, but she felt something leave her, an emotion, a grief, that could remain in the past. Gabby and Laura were thrilled in equal measure and wanted all the details, despite being horrified at the injuries Chloe described. They didn't hold back with their opinions but, more importantly, their love and support. They even managed to make her laugh, and she was truly grateful for them being in her life and caring for her as they did.

Tiredness still held onto her after she'd made all her calls, and she would need plenty of coffee to rid herself of the grogginess. But she was seeing Tom, and she wanted that more than anything.

She wasted no time packing an overnight bag and placed it by the door. She tucked her keys into her coat pocket and put her phone on the table in the hallway before heading to the kitchen to chuck some coffee into a mug, flooding it with boiling water, and threw back another couple of painkillers to dull the ache in her face. Keen to see him, she rushed to the door when she heard the knock and hurriedly pulled it open.

It took a moment to register his form and recognise the features of his face because he was the last person she expected to see. But there was no denying Danny was very much here, looming over her, his arms outstretched and clutching the door frame. His body menacingly filled the space as his wild eyes drilled into her.

28

'Hello, my love,' Danny murmured as he leaned in closer, the heat of anger etched into his fatigued features. A shadow of stubble had formed on his cheeks and his eyes were enshrouded with dark circles.

Chloe was speechless. He'd made bail. The bastard had managed to wriggle out of this, too. Like Teflon, nothing stuck to him. But this was something she'd overlooked, and the terrifying reality of what could happen next froze her to the spot. He was dressed in yesterday's clothes, and Chloe realised he'd come straight from the station. No planning, no manipulation. This was Danny stripped back to the bone – angry, embittered, and desperate. And desperate people were dangerously volatile.

'Why did you do it, Chloe? Why did you betray me like that?' he asked, as he took hold of her wrists and marched over the threshold, kicking the door shut with his foot.

She struggled in his unyielding hold, truly afraid. 'You shouldn't be here,' she stammered. 'I was told that you'd have to stay away.'

'You think I care what the police say?' Still gripping her,

he smiled down at her and roughly cupped her face so that she caught the salty tang of his unwashed hand. 'It could have been so easy, but now you've made an enemy of me.' He sighed, seeming genuinely upset. 'And you shouldn't have done that. You really shouldn't. I loved you so much, and now there's no point to anything.'

She twisted her hands in his hold, trying to break free. 'What are you talking about?' she demanded. 'I'll call the police again.'

'This is it for me,' he said, walking her backwards into the living room. 'I'm done with love and the hurt it causes. I wish you hadn't done it, Chloe. I wish you hadn't thrown me out like rubbish. Just like Melissa and all the others.'

'Wait, stop,' she cried, panicked and her mind racing. 'What are you doing?'

From a distance, she heard her phone buzzing on the hall table where she'd left it and she desperately wanted to answer it, to call for help.

'Where else would I be, other than with the one I love? Because I do love you, Chloe, despite everything you've done. I always will.'

'You don't love me,' she spat. 'You're not capable of it!'

He shook his head, calm, and with a terrifying glint in his eye. 'You need to stop fighting me, Chloe, and accept what has been gifted to you – a love that will never die.'

She worked her way out of his grip and rushed for the kitchen and the back door. She released the catch as he wrapped his arms around her and swung her to walk back into the room. They fought in their separate ways – her to be free and him to restrain – and he won the battle as he manhandled her towards her dining table and pulled out a chair.

'Sit down,' he barked, as he plonked her down unsteadily. 'This is what you've driven me to.' He crouched down to her level, keeping both her hands firmly in his grasp. 'And now it has to be this way. But it's okay because I will be by your side until the very end.'

'What do you mean?' she cried, still struggling. 'I'm expecting people. They'll be here any minute. You need to leave.'

A look of pity flashed across his face. 'Oh, Chloe, we both know that's not going to stop me. This will all be over before anyone can get here.' He shifted. 'I'm sorry. I didn't want it to come to this, but you leave me no choice.'

'No, Danny. Whatever you're thinking of doing, this is not the answer.'

'Don't you want to know?'

She didn't. The knowledge might send her mad.

'Fire,' he said, his smile long and wide. 'Because, like love, fire can dance and flicker, but it can also burn and hurt you.' Although crouched down, he leaned forward and rested his head against her leg. 'But I don't like it when that happens. I don't like the burn of love.' He looked up, the smile back. A smile of the deranged. 'And what's the best way to fight fire?' He stared. 'Well?' he demanded.

Startled, she shook her head, her breath fast.

'With fire, silly. I can remember the day my care home burnt to the ground. I still remember the smell. It travelled for miles – the smoke and fumes choking the air. People complained, but I loved it. I've always loved the smell of smoke, and the way flames sway and climb, all differing colours of orange and red as they devour everything in their path. It's hypnotising. But however much you watch it, it's still not enough. It'll never be enough. Only when you can touch it, let it surround you, that's when it will be enough.'

'The fire at Melissa's—' she whispered. 'That's why you set her house on fire.'

'Of course. It wasn't just anger. It was so much more than that. It was the glory of the flame.'

'What happened?' she whispered. 'To the home? Did people...'

He shook his head. 'Everyone was out of the building when it went up.'

'And did you know that?'

He didn't answer. Instead, he pulled the lighter from his pocket and flipped the lid, watching as a small orange flame appeared and danced.

'Danny,' she said, her voice quivering, 'please let me go. I don't want any trouble. I just want my life back.'

'And what about mine, hmm? What do I get? An empty flat and a lonely life where no one cares. Is that what I get?'

Tears fell from her eyes as she struggled to speak.

'Well?' he demanded. 'Answer me.'

'I-I don't know.'

'But this,' he murmured, as he stared at the flame, transfixed, 'this is the answer. The salvation.' He moved his gaze to her. 'And we're going to do it together.'

A loud sob escaped her lips. 'No, Danny, please.' The weight of him against her and the closeness of the flame rendered her incapacitated.

He smiled, his eyes bright, like a child. 'No, no, you don't get it. There's no need to be afraid. The flames will heal us and they will represent our love. We will be together, now and forever.'

'I don't want this,' she sobbed, huge tears tumbling down her cheeks. 'I don't want to die.'

He looked touched by her distress, a crazy kind of sympathy. 'Ah, it's okay,' he said, as he gently caressed her cheek. 'I'll be with you. I'll hold you in my arms. I'll keep you safe. It will be beautiful.'

She tried to free herself from his hold. 'No!'

The door in the kitchen creaked, then light, quick footsteps pattered over the floor.

They both turned, both desperate to know the identity of the visitor.

The woman who had warned Chloe away from Danny and had been following her since appeared in the doorway. She was calm but serious, and it only added to Chloe's terror.

'Hello, Danny.'

Danny faced her. 'Hannah?'

She walked further into the room as Danny stood, closing the lid of the lighter to extinguish the flame.

Chloe stared at them both, confused, desperate and trapped without any physical restraints. Her phone buzzed and she clung to the idea that whoever it was – Tom, PC Allan, anyone – would act on their instincts quickly because she was running out of time.

'What the fuck do you want, Hannah?' Danny said, irritated.

'I wanted to see what you were capable of, despite everything that's happened.'

Danny rubbed his forehead with the back of his hand. 'This doesn't concern you. This is about me and Chloe.'

'That's where you're wrong,' the woman replied. 'It was my business when you killed my sister, and it's my business with Chloe. You don't get to disappear from the mess you made. I told you I'd come looking. I warned you. You knew I'd find you eventually, and now here I am.'

He shrugged, the lighter loose in his hand. 'So what? I don't care that you're here. It's too late for your revenge now.'

Hannah glanced at Chloe, then returned her focus to Danny. 'What are you going to do?'

'Go away, Hannah. Why don't you skip along to your family? I'm sure they'd have plenty to say about this.'

'Don't bring them into this. Haven't you tortured them enough?'

'Me?' he bellowed, thumping his hand to his chest. 'Me? What about them and what they told Melissa about me? All the poisonous lies to turn her against me.'

Chloe stared and found the family resemblance immediately in Hannah's features. Melissa had been more strikingly beautiful, but Hannah had the same eyes and a softer attractiveness about her, a warmth. Chloe couldn't believe she hadn't seen it before. This woman had tried to warn her about the danger of associating with Danny, unaware of what Chloe already knew. Regardless, Hannah had watched over her, wanting to protect her, and now she was here, risking her life for a stranger.

Chloe's phone fell silent, no more calls. She admonished herself. She was the only one to blame for the tragedy about to unfurl.

'They did nothing but tell the truth,' Hannah said.

'No, no,' he spat, pointing his finger at Hannah. 'We were so close to being happy. I almost had it and then nothing. She vanished. Didn't want to know me.'

'You abused her trust, and you wore her down until she didn't know what to think.' Hannah's voice trembled. 'You pursued her. You hunted her down until she was frightened of her own shadow. My parents wanted to help, that's all. They wanted to protect Melissa from you.'

'Don't say her name!' Danny bellowed, both hands against his temples as if he was trying to contain all the jumbled thoughts and memories from breaking out. 'She's not here. She's not here.'

'No, she isn't!' Hannah cried. 'And whose fault is that?'

'Shut up! Shut up! I need to think.'

'Danny,' Chloe said. 'You don't have to do this. You can turn this around, if you really want to.'

'But you followed me,' he said. 'You started this. You tricked me and I fell for it. I thought you could care about me, but you just wanted revenge. I've been so stupid.' He strode towards Chloe.

She turned her head, not wanting to look him directly in the eye, for fear of being sucked into his madness.

'But it's okay,' he said desperately. 'Because I will forgive you. I love you, and that's what people in love do, isn't it? Forgive each other?'

'But when does it end, Danny?' Hannah demanded. 'When will you stop?'

'I thought I told you to shut up!' Danny bellowed, turning to face Hannah, then pacing back and forth, shaking his head as if fighting an internal battle.

Chloe's eyes darted between the two of them, fear jumping in her chest. This woman was pushing him too far. He'd lose it in a minute and send them all up in smoke.

'Danny, please,' Chloe said. 'Please take a moment to think about what you're doing.'

He flipped the lighter and a small yellow flame appeared again.

'Wait,' Chloe snapped, holding out her hand. She cast her eyes to the left, past Hannah and the kitchen beyond. The door was temptingly open, so close and yet so frustratingly out of reach. She thought of the communal garden and the builders who would arrive soon. 'There will be other people here in a minute. Do you want to hurt them, too? Innocent people?'

'Will there be, Chloe?' he asked. 'Are you sure about that?'

Her stomach sank. 'What have you done?'

'Nothing,' he said, confused. 'Do you think I go around killing everyone off?'

She wanted to scream that, yes, of course she thought that, because that's exactly what he did.

'I happen to know that John and Louise have paused the works while they wait for materials. As for the other residents, they all left for work early this morning, long before you were up and about, anyway. Lazy bones.'

The terrible realisation he'd never be out of her life hit Chloe hard. He'd always come back for her and she'd forever be looking over her shoulder, if she survived this.

In a blur, Chloe rushed from her chair and shoved Danny hard, grabbing Hannah's hand as she hurried towards the kitchen.

But Danny's reaction was just as quick, and he grabbed Hannah's other arm and yanked with such force she catapulted back towards him. The strength of it pulled Chloe, too, back into the living room.

Danny kept a tight hold of Chloe while deflecting Hannah's fists, and when Chloe began to fight him, too, he shoved her out of the way, as his anger intensified into a primal rage. Chloe could only watch as he landed a full blow to Hannah's face, knocking her to the floor, her body crumpling like a rag doll. Unconscious. Chloe cried out at the sight of her.

'What have you done?' she cried, as she tried to approach her. 'Oh God. What have you done?'

'She's of no concern to us now,' Danny said, pulling her back to clutch her close to him. 'This is about us and our love.' He rocked her gently, his arms wrapped tightly around her. 'Now, it's time. Our love will transcend this world so we can be together in the next.'

'No, Danny,' she sobbed. 'No!'

He held her in a tight embrace as he flipped the lid of the lighter and watched the flame dance one last time. She began to scream as he moved, but he calmly placed a hand over her mouth. She could only stare in horror at the flame that licked against the fabric of the curtains. Once it had caught, it elongated and the fire swiftly travelled upwards. Danny tossed the lighter onto the dining chair, igniting that too.

She struggled hard, but he held her still as he watched the flames come alive, sweeping across the ceiling, where swirls of black smoke drifted.

'No, Danny!' she screamed. 'Let me go!'

He brought his lips to her ear. 'No, my love, be still. It can't hurt you,' he said in a trance-like state. 'My love will protect you.'

Seconds felt like hours as he encased her in his arms, ready to let the flames take them, but Chloe fought to be free. He whispered to her again, something she couldn't hear, the flames high and roaring. The fire found a new path and ignited the shelving against the wall, consuming photo frames and ornaments that popped and shattered as the flames destroyed everything they touched. The swirls of smoke had become thick, toxic clouds that hovered above them, and the piercing intermittent bell of the smoke alarm began to sound. She coughed, and the heat seared her skin.

Struggling hard, she found an inner strength that boosted her, and with this newfound energy, and probably her only chance of survival, she used her arms to burst free from his hold and stagger away.

She turned. 'I hate you, do you hear? I hate you. You think I'm frightened of you? I'm not. You don't control me and we'll never be together! I'll see you in hell first!'

'No,' he wailed, a wounded cry. 'You don't mean that. You can't.'

'I do,' she cried, and she pushed him hard enough that he stumbled and fell. 'I never want to set eyes on you again.'

With another desperate cry, he crawled towards her and reached out. She used a foot to push him away and he sobbed, stumbling into the foetal position and rocking himself gently. He had given up.

He might lie there and do nothing, but that was something Chloe would never do.

The room glowed orange, the heat intensifying, and she coughed again as smoke began to claim the room and catch in her throat. She hurried to Hannah, burying her mouth in the crook of her arm to protect herself, needing to act fast. She would not let her down now.

'Hey, come on,' Chloe said, her hands on Hannah's shoulders, gently shaking her awake as the smoke filled her lungs. 'Wake up!' She patted Hannah's cheek hard. 'Come on, wake up!'

Hannah slowly stirred and began to cough, the smoke in her lungs.

With all Chloe's might, she dragged Hannah into a sitting position and willed her to stand. 'We need to get out of here. Now!'

Hannah nodded and dragged herself upright, leaning heavily on Chloe as she did.

Chloe glanced behind at Danny, who had not moved, waiting silently for the flames to take him. 'Danny, come on!' she shouted, holding out a hand to him, an instinct to help him as well. 'Now!'

He did nothing but stare at the flames around him.

She shouted to him again but couldn't wait any longer, feeling as if the smoke would choke the life out of her. They hobbled out towards the smoke-filled kitchen and through the back door into the garden. On the grass a few feet from the door, they both collapsed onto the ground, dragging in the fresh air as smoke billowed skywards from the doorway.

'Chloe!'

The voice was unmistakable, and she turned her head towards the sound, her sore eyes blurry. 'Tom?'

He dropped to his knees and tugged her into a tight embrace. 'Jesus, what the hell has happened?'

'Danny,' she croaked. 'He came over...started the fire.'

He looked her over urgently. 'Are you hurt?'

'No, I don't think so.'

'What about her?' he asked, looking at Hannah with confusion.

Hannah sat with her knees drawn up, her arms resting against them and her head bowed down. 'I'm fine,' she mumbled.

Tom turned his attention back to Chloe. 'And where is he now, Chloe?'

Her head swam, everything a thick haze.

'Chloe,' Tom repeated. 'Where is he?'

Chloe looked to the door. 'He's still in there. I tried to get him out, but he wouldn't listen. I couldn't move him.'

Tom stood and rushed towards the door.

'*No!*' she screamed, as she reached out for him, the fabric of his T-shirt slipping through her fingers. She launched towards him. 'Don't go in there!'

The sound of sirens grew louder, and Chloe knew they were close. She grabbed Tom's arm. 'Please, Tom. Wait, the fire crew is almost here.'

He was breathing fast, his eyes wide. 'I have to help. There may not be time to wait.'

'No,' she said, as something popped and crackled inside her flat. 'But I can't lose you. I've lost so much because of fire. Please, I'm begging you, don't go in there.'

He held her shoulders. 'It'll take seconds, a minute, but I have to get him out of there. And I have to do it right now.' He didn't wait for her reply, just turned and raced towards the door that billowed thick, black smoke.

She followed him to the door but couldn't go any further when smoke caught in her irritated throat. She willed the sirens closer as she watched him disappear, coughing to clear her airway.

'Come on, Tom,' she whispered, as she wrung her hands together and stared at the door. 'Please,' she begged, a silent prayer, a promise. 'Please bring him back to me.'

And as if someone had listened, her wish was granted. Tom emerged through the smoke-filled doorway, Danny's arm slung over his shoulder, dragging him outside to safety. He dropped him down onto the grass with little care and fell to his knees as he coughed out the putrid smoke.

Danny remained still, no longer the threat he had been, the ability to fight for anything – Tom, Chloe, or his life – all but abandoned. He sat cross-legged, staring into the distance, his mouth moving, whispering into nothingness.

Chloe saw the blue lights flashing and then the crew appearing from around the corner of the building and cried tears of relief. After briefly checking no one was hurt, they organised themselves and got to work. Rolls of hoses surrounded them, and the crew shouted their instructions as they swarmed the area, guiding jets of water against the smoke and flames ravaging her home.

29

W ith a sigh, Chloe pushed the key into the lock and let herself into Laura's flat, dropping her bag on the floor. The trip to her home to assess the damage and oversee the repairs had pretty much exhausted her.

Today was the first time Chloe had been given the go-ahead to return there and she didn't want to put it off, feeling she might never go back if she delayed. She met the builders to talk repairs, timescales, and costs, and also to collect some more of her clothes. The builders had rallied when they found out what had happened, and John and Louise didn't hesitate in offering their services to assess what needed to be done. But that was no surprise. They had a vested interest in knowing the structure of the building hadn't been compromised, so Chloe didn't waste too much time wallowing in guilt about the disruption to their schedule.

The damage to her bedroom had been minimal. With her clothes tucked away in a wardrobe, they were saved, but getting the aroma of smoke out of them was proving difficult. Laura had been an angel and had taken everything in her stride, arranging dry-cleaning trips or doing multiple wash loads for Chloe.

Laura had rushed to the hospital on that fateful day and refused to leave her side until Chloe had been checked over and discharged. Once home, she took up the mantle of nurse until Chloe's mother arrived. It was everything Chloe needed, and so much more than she deserved, after what she'd done.

They had talked, long late-night discussions over hot chocolate or tea when Chloe couldn't sleep – her chest yet to clear, making lying down uncomfortable. They discussed what Chloe had done and why, and when Chloe buckled up for a lecture, justifiably so, instead she was given understanding and compassion. Laura absolved her of any blame in the circumstances, which was more than Chloe allowed for herself. Laura also understood that Chloe needed a quiet space to process all that had happened to her, even giving her the privacy to visit Hannah in the hospital alone. When she did visit Hannah, she was relieved to be told that a little concussion and smoke inhalation were the only effects of Danny's little game, and she would soon be out once the doctors were happy with their tests.

Chloe was less thrilled that Tom had also given her some space. In the melee after the fire, she'd tried desperately to explain her part in all of this, but she couldn't put coherent sentences together and the words she did say were fractured and made very little sense. He'd held her gently, kissed her, told her to rest, and said that they would talk about it later, when she was better. The ambulance had whisked her away, but she'd wanted him to join her, and she spent the entire stay at the hospital checking her phone, waiting for his call. But her phone was silent, and had been since she returned home.

It had been three days since the fire, and there had been nothing. No contact at all. She'd had plenty of well-wishers, either texting or posting on Facebook, but nothing from him, the person she wanted to hear from most. It began to eat into her conscience that he would not want anything more to do with her. She had already warned him she had secrets to share, and perhaps this horrible mess was too much for him. She couldn't blame him.

'Why don't you give him a call?' her mother asked, as she placed a cup of tea on the table in front of Laura's sofa, where Chloe was sitting, legs up under a blanket. Her face ached in unison with her heart, and while she could take painkillers for the bruises, there was nothing that would help her sorry heart.

'No,' she said. 'I want him to do what he feels is right for him, not out of a sense of obligation.'

'But you could just talk. It might help both of you.'

Chloe shrugged. 'Maybe, but if I've lost him, I'd rather keep it like this. I'm not sure I could face him if he didn't want to see me again. And I don't blame him.'

Her mother sat down next to Chloe and hugged her close. 'Come on, love. Don't be so hard on yourself. You seemed to be holding it all together so well that none of us knew just how much you were hurting. You were all alone, trying to figure it out, and I'm sorry that I didn't see the signs. None of us did. If you want to blame, every one of us has something to be sorry for.'

Chloe snuggled closer. 'But it's not the same. I knowingly misled all of you. I thought I was in control when that couldn't have been further from the truth.'

'You were grieving.'

'I was in an abyss of grief, and I realise now how irrational I'd become. Luring Danny in to get him locked up was my chance at retribution for David, but, Jesus...at what cost? By the time I came to my senses – and Laura and Tom had a lot to do with that – I was out of my depth completely. He was too dangerous, too unbalanced. I wasn't prepared for that. I was so, so stupid, and I'm so ashamed.'

Another squeeze. 'Sweetheart, do not go down that route,' her mum said. 'You took on more than you realised. You were in a bad place and made some bad decisions, but you shouldn't be ashamed. We've all done things we regret. You helped Hannah and tried with Danny, and he got out. You turned it around, so I'd say you need to be kinder to yourself. It's about time you gave yourself a break.' She hugged Chloe hard, prompting the river of tears that fell from Chloe's eyes.

Her mum smoothed Chloe's hair and whispered words of comfort, letting Chloe release all that she'd been holding in.

'Do you feel okay now?' she asked when Chloe calmed, spent of emotion.

She nodded.

'And David?' her mum asked hesitantly. 'How do you feel about him now?'

'I'm ready to move on. It's time. A part of me will always miss him and the whirlwind he created in my life. I realise now we were over a long time before he left to be with Melissa, and that's just how it is.' Chloe wiped her eyes, feeling hopeful for the first time in a long while. 'He was never coming back to me. I just couldn't face up to that fact. And then the fire happened, and everything got a little skewed after that.'

'Maybe some counselling will help,' her mum said. 'There might be things to unpack there, and you deserve happiness. You deserve the ability to let it go.'

'Yeah,' Chloe agreed. 'You're right. Some counselling sounds like a really good idea.'

'Leave it with me. I've got a couple of people at work that can recommend some good therapists. You can take it from there, if you like.'

What Chloe would like was to never leave her mother's

arms. For now, she just wanted to bask in the love, warmth, and safety her mother gave; she never wanted those feelings to end. 'Thanks, Mum. I love you.'

'And I love you,' her mum replied, with a soft kiss on Chloe's forehead. 'Always have, always will.'

CHLOE STEPPED ONTO THE TRAIN, having discussed with Laura and her mother the need to make this visit one last time. The journey was inconsequential, and she enjoyed the feeling of being entirely alone, knowing she had no need to check over her shoulder any more. Danny was no longer a threat. For now, anyway. He had been taken to the hospital under police escort and was arrested once discharged by the doctors. Despite giving up and waiting for the flames to claim him, he'd suffered no injury except a little smoke inhalation.

PC Allan had visited her while she was in the hospital and had explained why Danny was released so soon after his arrest. Danny had countered her allegations with claims of his own, and despite the police having access to all of Melissa's previous complaints lodged against him, they were not satisfied they had enough evidence to charge him. So they had to release him, pending further investigation. PC Allan shared his own frustrations at Danny's disregard for the law and all the loopholes he successfully manipulated, and so he had stipulated multiple times there was to be no contact with Chloe during the investigation. He'd tried to call her on that fateful day with an update so she could take the necessary steps to protect herself, but by that time Danny was already with her. This was proved correct when she finally was in possession of her phone and saw the countless missed calls from PC Allan and Tom.

It was clear to everyone that Danny had planned to leave

this world behind, to not have to worry about facing the consequences of his actions, and that's what spurred him on. The information made Chloe shudder. He'd planned to die all along. And to take her with him.

The early morning springtime sun warmed her back, and for the first time in a long while she felt good about her future. She'd been very lucky, and she knew it. She'd survived, unharmed, and so had all the people she loved. Guilt would haunt her for a while yet, but happiness was something she'd work towards and she would make time to ensure she got it.

Weaving through the headstones, she searched the names. She didn't remember exactly where the plot was situated, so it took a few minutes to find Melissa's grave. When she did, the immaculately maintained grave demonstrated the love Hannah had for her sister. There were fresh flowers in a sunken vase in front of the shiny black marble headstone with words of love written in gold. An oval picture of Melissa was inset at the top of the headstone, in a formal style, as if part of a family shot. Chloe had brought with her two yellow roses tied together with a hessian bow and placed them down on the lush, neatly tended grass. The grave was settling in, becoming established, the same as David's. Melissa's grave was in a quiet corner, but there were no trees here, only bushes that marked the boundary line.

She sat, tucking her skirt beneath her, and tilted her head up towards the sun. It was such a beautiful day. She glanced down at the earth and felt the need to place her hand there. Any bitterness towards this woman blew away on the breeze. What had she done but fall in love with the wrong man and collide with Danny? She paid for his obsession with her life, as did David, and that was where the injustice lay. Yes, David hurt Chloe, but he didn't deserve what Danny had done in his fit of rage. Neither of them did.

She thought of how frightened Melissa would have been. How desperately she would have tried to rid herself of Danny, but how resilient he had been in pursuing her, and how she turned to David for help. How could any of them have known the consequences of that? She just wanted to live her life, to be happy, and Danny took that from her. Chloe had invited him into her world knowingly. With a purpose. And now, despite the remorse, Chloe realised that she had much to be grateful for. She got the chance to live again. He'd been caught and would now face a more robust judgement for his crimes, if she believed all that PC Allan had told her.

A little part of her felt for Danny, too. All he wanted was happiness. He'd suffered abandonment all his life and he just wanted to love and be loved, but he didn't know how. Delusion and an imbalance of mind prevented it. She hoped he'd get the help he needed, but after today she decided she would give him no more of her time. He'd had far too much of that already.

Aware of someone here, Chloe instinctively glanced over her shoulder.

Hannah stood above her, a bunch of fresh flowers in her hand. 'Hi, Chloe.'

Chloe stood, faced her, and saw all the residual hurt and grief sitting behind her eyes. 'Hi, Hannah. I'm sorry. I wanted to come and pay my respects to Melissa. I should have called to let you know. I hope you don't mind.'

'Of course not. That's a lovely thing to do,' Hannah said, as she placed the bunch of flowers down next to Chloe's roses.

'How are you?'

Hannah smiled, but it betrayed a sadness that seemed ever-present in her soul. 'I'm fine. My lungs are finally clear now. I'm just left with a little cough and a bit of a bruise still. Other than that, I'm all good. Physically, anyway. And you?'

'Same,' Chloe said. 'I was very lucky, and I wanted to thank you again for what you did. You helped me, and I only ever showed anger towards you.'

Hannah glanced sadly towards her sister's gravestone. Tears welled in her eyes. 'I should have explained what I was doing. I should have tried to talk to you more, but I didn't know if that would make it worse. I was frightened of what Danny would do if he saw us together.'

'Hindsight, eh?' Chloe said, as she reached out and took Hannah's hand in hers. 'You did a wonderful thing, though. You helped me in a moment when I had no one, and I'm so thankful. That's another reason why I wanted to come here to pay my respects to Melissa. I've had a lot to think about. She must have been terrified, not knowing who to turn to, and was punished for simply falling in love.' A breeze surrounded them, fluttering their clothes, and Chloe liked to imagine that Melissa and David were with them, too. 'I'm so sorry you lost a sister through all of this.'

'I couldn't save her. I wished I could, but instead I decided to do something for her memory. So I resolved to stop him in any way I could.'

'And is that why you went to that woman in Whitechapel? His ex?'

'You know about that?'

'Yes, the day I confronted you...well, I followed you, once you thought I'd gone. All the way to her flat.'

Hannah smirked and rolled her eyes. 'Well, I guess that proves why I'll never have a job at MI5. I didn't have a clue. But yes, after Melissa's death, I found out about Natalie.'

'That's her name?'

'Yes. I'm not proud to say I had my own obsession with Danny and a need for justice after what he'd done. So I went to see her. I wanted to help her in some way, too. I used to check in every now and then. Make sure she was all right. Eating and stuff. Just be a friend, I guess.'

Chloe nodded, understanding her own obsession with Danny. 'I managed to speak to her, too, even though she wasn't happy about it. But I managed to stop Danny from ever finding out. He never knew that I'd met her. I'm thankful for that.'

'And so is Natalie.'

'I visited her yesterday, told her about Danny and what you'd done. She needed to hear it. I watched as an invisible weight lifted from her, making her at ease. It's helped her so much; she can finally move on and I'm thrilled for her. But it's not my sister. She's still gone.'

'You need to be kind to yourself. You did everything you could for Melissa. She knows that. And I truly believe that she's with you. Here, and in your heart.'

Hannah gasped a sob and smiled as tears spilled down her cheeks. She squeezed Chloe's hand hard. 'Thank you.'

Chloe nodded. 'She'll always watch over you, and you have memories that you can keep alive, but it's time for you to live now. That's what she would want you to do.'

'I know. I've been a ghost, following him around, waiting to protect the next victim he latched on to.' She looked at Chloe, frowned. 'It never occurred to me to do what you were doing. Why was that?'

'Because you were more rational than I was,' Chloe replied. 'My grief left me isolated and alone, so I plotted and planned and kept it a secret from everyone. I had no regard for my safety until it was too late, and I couldn't escape him. It was wrong. I put people in danger, and I have a lot of making up to do, but I'm going to put it right.'

'I think you have been to hell and back, and you're very brave.'

'Maybe. And perhaps a bit stupid, too. Wouldn't recommend it.'

Their gentle chuckles carried on the breeze.

Hannah sighed. 'I miss her.'

'Of course you do, but maybe it's time for us both to lay our ghosts to rest. To move on.'

They hugged, and Chloe found peace in this unexpected moment.

'What are you going to do now?' Hannah asked, as she sniffed and wiped her nose.

'I'm staying at Laura's while my flat is repaired and redecorated. From there, who knows.'

'But Tom figures in, surely?'

Chloe shrugged. 'Maybe. I haven't heard from him properly since the day of the fire. I might have totally frightened him off. I don't know.'

She smiled. 'Can't imagine that. From what you've shared with me when I was in hospital, it's obvious that he really cares about you. And you deserve happiness, too. Remember that. Listen to your own advice and let the past remain in the past.'

'I hear you,' Chloe said with a laugh.

'Well, I guess this is it,' Hannah said with a smile. 'If you ever need a chat, you have my number.'

Chloe nodded. 'I do, and I'd like that very much.'

'I'll be in touch.'

Chloe walked away as Hannah crouched down, busying herself with the flowers, bunching them together to place in the vase of her sister's grave.

Chloe hoped they would remain friends. Something lovely had flourished from something so terrible and so life-changing that she wasn't about to let it dwindle into something as distant as a yearly text at Christmas. It was something to be treasured, like so many other things in her life.

With each step she made through the serene gardens of remembrance, the huge weight that had pushed against her shoulders for months now lifted, dispersing into the temperate air. She was free. Perhaps not yet happy, but content and ready to move on.

30

The intercom for Laura's front door startled Chloe, and her heart thumped as she jumped up from her chair. It would be a while before she would fully relax. Laura and her mum had reluctantly agreed to leave her while they popped to the shops, and she regretted badgering them about it.

She walked to the door and held the receiver, as she calmed her breathing. It wouldn't be Danny. He would be locked away for a while now, having been refused bail. She took a breath and picked up the phone. 'Hello.'

'Hi, Chloe.'

Her breath caught in her throat at the sound of Tom's voice. It was both lovely and terrifying. Why was he here? To end them before they'd begun? 'Tom?'

'I know you need space, and I've tried, but I really need to see you,' he said. 'To check you're all right.'

'Come up,' she said, as she pressed the button for the main entrance.

She waited, and when she heard the tap of his fingers on the other side of her door she pulled it open and saw him there, for the first time in days, and realised how much he meant to her. How much she'd missed him.

He held a small bunch of flowers and wore a smile that made her heart flutter. 'How are you?'

'Better,' she said, as she stepped back to let him in. 'Thanks for coming to see me.'

He handed her the flowers. 'I have been trying to be patient, but I couldn't do it any more. I'm sorry. I guess the last thing you need is another guy calling and calling.'

'Depends on the guy,' she said, admiring the colourful bunch of spring blooms. 'These are lovely, and I'm so glad you've come. I've been wondering and...worrying, if I'm honest.'

'Believe me, I've been doing the same.'

She smiled at him. 'Would you like some tea?'

'Sounds perfect,' he said, with a gorgeous smile on his handsome face.

She walked to the kitchen. 'Please, sit,' she said, gesturing to the grey padded chairs that surrounded a glass-topped dining table. 'I'll just find a vase,' she said, as she hunted through Laura's cupboards, her nerves getting the better of her.

Tom walked to her, gently took the flowers from her grasp and laid them down beside the sink. 'Actually, I'd really like to talk.'

She nodded, silently went to the table and pulled out a chair to sit.

Tom did the same, and chose to sit next to her, positioning his chair to face her. 'How are you? Really?' he asked again. 'Laura's brought me up to speed with everything that's happened. Are you okay?'

Butterflies danced in her stomach as she pinned all her hopes on the fact he was here for anything except a 'goodbye' speech. 'I think so. Full of guilt for what I've put you through. I can suffer the minor injuries from the fire.' She glanced down. 'But you, well…that's a little harder to bear. I always worried you'd hate me, once you knew what I'd done.'

He reached out and touched her, and she found she wanted more.

'I could never hate you,' he said warmly. 'Although I wish you had confided in me. I don't know if I could have helped, but maybe I could have persuaded you to take a different route. But, more than that, I feel sorry that you were so alone.'

'I was totally lost. I thought I had it all planned out, but really I was just falling apart.'

His hand moved from her arm to smooth her hair. 'You were doing your best in nightmare circumstances.'

'That's what my mum said, too. That I should go easy on myself.'

'Sounds like good advice. You should take it. I don't blame you, and you shouldn't either.'

She inhaled as her stomach flipped at his touch. 'Thank you. Might take a little longer for me to catch up with that, but I'll try.'

'So, what's happened to him now?' he asked.

'He's been discharged from hospital and arrested again,' she replied. 'He breached his bail conditions the minute he turned up at my door.'

'How did he get bail, for Christ's sake, especially when he did what he did to Melissa and David?'

'Well, that's the joy of being found not guilty of that particular little crime. Brand new case, brand new procedure, as far as the police were concerned.'

Tom shook his head in disbelief.

'He knew exactly what he was doing – he was never worried by my threat to go to the police. So he turned up that day with a lighter, ready to start another fire, wanting us to be united in death. Something about the sanctity of fire being the same as love.'

'He'd certainly given it some thought,' Tom replied.

'He had. Only this time he was ready to die, too, making breaching his bail irrelevant.'

'Jesus, Chloe. You must have been terrified. I know I was, when you didn't answer your phone.'

'PC Allan said that when I hadn't returned his calls, he was just about to send a car over, but then the fire call came through. That's when he figured out what Danny had done.'

Tom shuffled a little closer and took hold of Chloe's hand. 'I wish I could have been there.'

It didn't matter if this was to be the end of them, she wanted to be honest, finally. To share everything. 'I know I had choices,' she said as she held on to him. 'I know I was in a bad place, but it's like in my heart I wanted it, too. I wanted revenge, desperately. It gave me a purpose, gave me life, in a way, and that made me capable of anything, I think.'

'Chloe,' he whispered sadly.

She looked in his eyes, wanting to see his true feelings. 'Am I just as bad as him for wanting revenge? To manipulate him like I did?'

'No, you're nothing like him,' he said without hesitation. 'Nothing at all. I think you're someone good. Someone lovely, actually, but someone who got lost in her own grief and need for justice.'

'But, as it turns out, I couldn't get that right, either. I didn't want him to die. I tried to get him out of that fire but I couldn't manage them both. Hannah was so unsteady on her feet, and Danny had just given up. I couldn't lift him. Time was running out. And you,' she said, 'you risked everything to help him, and me. And I let you.'

'No, I did what I did because I wanted to.'

'But anything could have happened.'

'It was a few feet into the building. I knew I could do it quickly.'

She nodded. 'I just want you to know that I'm sorry. I was careless, with everything.'

He gently moved a wisp of hair from her face. 'You are not that person. It was a shadow of you before. One who was hurt and needed revenge. I get it.'

'I think I need some time to process what I've done. It scared me how easy it was to step over the line. And I understand this will probably change how you feel about me. I won't hold you back. You can leave, but I hope...I really hope we can still be friends.'

'What are you talking about?'

'Us, or rather the end of us. I understand.'

'No, that's not what's going on here. I wanted to give you some space, that's all. You've been through so much, and I thought the last thing you'd need is me hanging around, bothering you.'

'So we're not over?'

'No way,' he said. 'I've been counting the hours until I could see you. I thought you'd back off if you thought I was too keen. I've been going out of my mind worrying about you. All I wanted to do was hold you and, I don't know, take you away or something. Anything to put that smile back on your face.'

'Really?' she said, her mood lifting.

'Really,' he said, cupping her cheek with his hand. 'I wouldn't be here if I didn't want you. Or doing this.' He placed a finger under her chin and tilted her face up to his, brushing his lips against hers.

The room swam, and she felt it might swallow her whole as she succumbed to the feelings that flooded her body, so grateful to have Tom in her life and a second chance at happiness. But fear tugged at the tender seedlings of happiness that prepared to root in her weary heart. 'Can we take it slowly? After all that's happened...'

He ran his thumb across her cheek. 'We can take it as slowly as you like. I'm not going to rush you into anything. I want this to work, really work, and I'm prepared to take this at your pace,' he said, as a smile crept across his lips. 'But... maybe dinner sometime would be nice?'

An image of what waited for her in her newfound freedom sprang into her mind, along with the instruction she'd given Hannah at Melissa's grave. *It's time to live.* Now was the time to begin.

'Dinner sounds great,' she agreed.

An overwhelming desire to kiss him again made Chloe lean forward to press her lips to his. The kiss was soft, gentle and full of hope, something she desperately craved.

'Tell me when and where, and I'll be there,' he said.

'Well, there's always tomorrow,' she murmured with a smile.

'Of course,' he agreed. 'The perfect time.'

THANK YOU FOR READING

Did you enjoy reading *You're Not Alone*? Please consider leaving a review on Amazon. Your review will help other readers to discover the novel.

ACKNOWLEDGMENTS

So many people have helped me bring this book to life and I'm so grateful. I'd like to thank Sarah Wood for her extensive knowledge of police procedures and the law. I couldn't have plotted the story without you. To A. Morrison for the vast knowledge of the behaviours and psychological characteristics of stalkers. I hope I did it justice.

Huge thanks to everyone at Inkubator Books, particularly Lorie, Brian and Garret for their continued guidance and encouragement. To Connal for his advice and for helping me see the wood for the trees. To the creative team who produced my amazing book cover. I love it. And to Claire for her all her help and support. Thank you all.

To my readers, thank you. You guys are the best. To my friends and family for their unending support, thank you. I couldn't have done it without you.

And lastly, but never least, thank you to Paul and Emily for their love and encouragement. You make every day perfect and I love you both with all my heart.

If you have been affected by any of the themes in this book, please head to one of the many charities that can offer support and guidance in relation to stalking: www.suzylam

plugh.org, www.protectionagainststalking.org or www.paladinservice.co.uk to name a few.

ABOUT THE AUTHOR

G. M. Lawrence writes psychological suspense novels that have sizzling suspense, plenty of heart and a thrilling twist or two. She decided to start writing as a hobby in 2015 and after a few half-hearted attempts at a novel, she decided to commit to it. Now, with a creative writing course under her belt, she loves nothing more than to open her laptop and let the words flow.

She lives in Hampshire in the UK with her husband, daughter, and two cats who love to bring as much chaos into their lives as possible.

Visit G.M. online at:

https://gm-lawrence-q8c5x4.mailerpage.com/

Made in the USA
Middletown, DE
21 March 2023

27293796R00201